BITTER BUSINESS

GINI HARTZMARK

FAWCETT COLUMBINE

NEW YORK

A Fawcett Columbine Book
Published by Ballantine Books
Copyright © 1995 by Gini Hartzmark

Library of Congress Cataloging-in-Publication Data
Hartzmark, Gini.
    Bitter business / Gini Hartzmark. — 1st ed.
        p.   cm.
    ISBN 0-449-90989-1
    I. Title.
    PS3558.A7157B58   1995
    813'.54—dc20   95-22801
                                                                        CIP

Text design by Mary Wirth

Manufactured in the United States of America
First Edition: November 1995
10   9   8   7   6   5   4   3   2   1

TO ANN ROCCO

ACKNOWLEDGMENTS

I WOULD LIKE TO THANK Leon Danco for sharing his insight into the special alchemy of family businesses and Heather Raaf, M.D., for her encouragement and willingness to answer my questions about forensic pathology, no matter how ridiculous. My apologies to them both if I've twisted their facts to fit my fiction. Many thanks to Jerry Stovall and Chip Humes of Arizona Plating and Anodizing Co. I'd also like to thank Linda Unger, Esther Goldenberg, and Elizabeth Gardner for their assistance. And, as always, Michael.

Sometimes an author encounters a name so difficult to resist that she must use it in a book. Thanks to the real Joe Blades for graciously allowing me to borrow his.

BITTER
BUSINESS

1

If Daniel Babbage hadn't been dying of cancer, I would never have met the Cavanaughs. Looking back, that much at least seems certain, even if there are other things—important things—that I will never know and never understand. Babbage was notoriously secretive about his clients, and I have no doubt that under other circumstances he would have chosen to deal with the Cavanaugh family alone. For close to thirty years Daniel's job had been as much about keeping secrets as providing counsel, and if nothing else, the years had taught him that there will always be some things that are best kept locked away.

But now the cells in Babbage's pancreas had betrayed him and the touchstones of his faith had become the radiation and chemotherapy treatments that took him from the office for long stretches and left him weak and exhausted. Finding themselves in his situation, other men, no doubt, would have abandoned the practice of law and used whatever time they had left to pursue their long-deferred dreams. But Babbage was a quirky and reclusive bachelor, and for whatever reason, he had decided to play out the last dramas of his life within the mahogany-paneled confines of Callahan, Ross, Peterman and Seidel.

And so, after the initial shock of diagnosis, Daniel had begun to make arrangements. He ordered the famous octagonal conference table removed from his office and replaced it with a deep sofa of tobacco-colored leather. Gradually, he relinquished his administrative duties at the firm, including his seat on the powerful compensation committee, which sets salaries and allocates profits among the partners. Finally, and with the greatest reluctance—like a stripper working a very cold hall—he'd begun to assign his files, one by one, to other attorneys at the firm.

I made the trip down the hall to Daniel's office in answer to his summons and found him lying on the couch, propped up on pillows. Madeline, his longtime secretary—a stern woman who wore her glasses on a chain—hovered nearby. Daniel was reading a case file, holding the manila folder in front of his face like a choirboy. When he heard me enter he peered over the top of it, tilting his chin down to see me better above the half frames of his reading glasses. He was a small man, just this side of sixty, with a head of candy-tuft white hair and an affably jowly grin. His eyebrows were thick and licked up into pointy tufts above his eyes, which were moist like a baby's.

"Kate!" he exclaimed, laying down the file and making a token effort to sit up. "Thanks for making yourself available on such short notice. I understand that the services of our youngest partner are very much in demand these days. Skip Tillman was crowing about you over lunch just the other day. He said it was you who rammed the Norwich Industries deal through. You should have heard him."

Skip Tillman was the firm's managing partner, and from the first day I'd come to work at Callahan Ross he'd never expected me to do anything but fall on my face—an opinion that he'd also taken no pains to conceal. It was strange, but I felt no flutter of victory to hear that he was now singing my praises.

"So who's doing what to whom?" I inquired, settling comfortably into the chair Daniel reserved for visitors. Babbage's specialty was representing family-owned businesses, and as he was fond of pointing out, in his work the same themes were always playing themselves out—love and hate, money and power, trust and betrayal, fear . . .

"You did some work for me two years ago on the Superior Plating file," he said. "What do you remember about the company? Anything?"

I took a deep breath and ratcheted back through my mental inventory of cases.

"Superior Plating and Specialty Chemicals," I recited easily. "The company is a large metal plating and anodizing operation located on the near south side. It was founded in 1936 by James Cavanaugh, who died young and turned it over to his only child, Jack, who built it into one of the biggest operations of its kind in the country. Their main business is applying metal coatings like chrome, gold, and brass to manufactured metal products—everything from shower doors to streetlights." I closed my eyes and cast my mind back. "If memory serves, they also have an unusual sideline for a plating company— a division that makes proprietary compounds for niche industries like film processing and embalming, hence the name Superior Plating and Specialty Chemicals. Unless things have changed, it is wholly owned and operated by the Cavanaugh family—Jack Cavanaugh is the company's CEO and there are a bunch of middle-aged children in management."

"That's very good"—Babbage chuckled—"especially for someone who only billed six hours to the file."

"I think you had me looking into the possibility of a two-for-one stock split," I replied. "I can't remember why they didn't pursue it."

"They figured that whatever they were going to save in taxes they were going to end up paying in legal fees. They decided to give the money to Uncle Sam."

"Is the father still around?" I inquired. "I only met him once, but I remember him being tough as nails."

"If you think that Jack's tough, you should have met his father. Now, *he* was quite a character. I think that's how we politely refer to bastards once they're safely dead. They say that in his day James Cavanaugh drank more whiskey, screwed more women, and smoked more cheap cigars than any other son of a bitch in Chicago."

"Charming," I observed dryly.

"I wouldn't be so quick to turn up my nose if I were you, Ms. Millholland," Babbage admonished. "You'd probably have to go back a few generations, but you'd find a couple of your ancestors who were no better than James Cavanaugh and one or two who were a damned sight worse."

"Point taken," I replied.

Daniel was right about my family, of course, but he was wrong in thinking I was looking down on the Cavanaughs. It seemed, however, pointless to go into it. Sometimes I forgot how protective Babbage could be of his clients.

"Hasn't Jack Cavanaugh retired by now?" I asked. "I remember he seemed to be getting to that age. . . ."

"He'll be seventy this summer, but believe me, the only way he'll be leaving Superior Plating is feetfirst."

"Come on, Daniel," I protested. "I thought that frog-marching these old guys into retirement was one of your specialties."

"This one I'm leaving for you, Kate. Jack Cavanaugh and I go too far back—he was my first client. He hired me when I was straight out of law school. Now I realize he picked me because I was the cheapest lawyer he could find, but at the time landing him as a client was quite a coup. In my mind Jack was a bona fide industrialist. It didn't matter that he'd just inherited a run-down factory, a payroll full of his father's drunken cronies, and a balance sheet that was bleeding red. To me, he was a captain of industry. Since those days Jack and I have been through a lot of things together—baptisms and funerals, foreclosures and Christmas dinner. I'm even his son Eugene's godfather. . . ."

"I'd think that would make talking to him about stepping down easier."

"You might think so, but it doesn't. You have to understand that for a man like Jack Cavanaugh retirement is just another word for euthanasia."

"Do any of his children have what it takes to succeed him?"

"Yes. But not the one who Jack's been grooming to take over."

"I see," I replied, pulling out a legal pad to take notes.

"Philip's the oldest and the heir apparent. When Jack turned sixty-five he made Philip president of the company and gave him the day-to-day running of the business—on paper anyway."

"And in practice?"

"In practice, Philip has the title but no authority. Everyone knows that Jack is still calling the shots. He lets Philip build his card houses and whenever it suits him he strolls over and knocks them down."

"So what does Philip do about it?"

"Nothing. That's the problem. Now, Philip's sister Dagny is another story. She doesn't take one ounce of shit from her father, and as a result he doesn't give her any."

"What does Dagny do at Superior Plating?"

"She's the company's chief financial officer."

"And you think she's the one who should take over for Jack."

"It's completely obvious to everyone but Jack. But even if he did figure it out, he'd never do it."

"Why not?"

"Because feminist progress and just plain common sense aside, men of Jack's generation don't pass over a son in favor of a daughter."

I thought that one over for a minute.

"Do any of the other children fulfill the anatomical requirements for top management?" I inquired.

"Eugene's the only other son," Daniel replied, choosing to ignore my sarcasm. "But he's not in the running."

"Why not?"

"He's just not front-office material," Daniel answered a shade too quickly.

"So who does that leave us with? Anybody else in the picture?"

"Lydia." Babbage sighed. "She was Jack and Eleanor's surprise package—back then we called them bonus babies. Eleanor died three days after she was born."

"So Philip's the oldest and Lydia's the baby of the family," I said, trying to keep them straight in my mind.

"She's more of an *enfant terrible*. In my line of work you can always tell which kid had the bad luck to grow up after the company's cash flow turned positive. Lydia's thirty-three going on thirteen. She's had four kids, three husbands, and it's a safe bet she spends all her money on shrinks."

"Does she work for the company?"

"She draws a salary, but believe me, they pay Lydia to shut up, not show up."

I looked over the notes I'd made.

"Let me see if I've got this straight. Jack Cavanaugh is the CEO of a large and highly profitable plating and specialty chemical company. His oldest son, Philip, has the title of company president, but no real authority. His sister Dagny has the brains to be CEO, but no balls, while brother Eugene has balls, but no brains. In the meantime baby Lydia gets herself psychoanalyzed and presumably makes trouble. Jack, who is pushing seventy, plans on living forever, while Philip, I presume, can't wait to give him the shove."

"Correct on all counts," replied Babbage.

"Jesus, Daniel!" I exclaimed. "Is this a corporate file you're handing me or a soap-opera plot?"

"It gets worse. Read this. Jack received it by messenger at his home first thing this morning." He handed me a faxed copy of a single sheet of letterhead stationery. I scanned it quickly. It was from Lydia's attorneys, announcing her decision to sell her shares of Superior Plating and Specialty Chemical stock.

"I bet this made Jack's day," I observed. "How many shares does she own?"

"Twelve percent of the company. Jack owns fifty-two percent and the rest is divided equally among the four adult children."

"Can I see a copy of the buyback agreement?" I asked. Family-owned companies invariably had some sort of agreement that said that if one family member wanted to sell their shares, the rest of the family got first dibs on the stock.

"Jack had me draw one up when Lydia turned twenty-one and got control of her shares."

"Good, then it should be straightforward. We'll bring in the investment bankers to do a valuation. Then we'll start haggling over the share price."

"Unfortunately, with Lydia, nothing is straightforward."

"What do you mean?"

"We prepared a buyback agreement, but Lydia refused to sign it."

"You're kidding!" I exclaimed. "Why wouldn't she sign?"

"Because Lydia is a little girl in a woman's body," Daniel Babbage answered with surprising venom. "A spoiled, wealthy little girl who likes trouble the way that a vampire likes blood."

IT WAS SPRING IN Chicago, but you wouldn't have known it. The sky was the color of cold slate and it seemed to bleed into the drab hues of the concrete until the entire city seemed washed in muted shades of gray. It was snowing again and the March wind, blowing in unpredictable gusts, flung wet flakes into the faces of the miserable lunchtime crowds.

Huddled in the back of a cab on my way to meet Jack Cavanaugh, I couldn't help thinking about Daniel Babbage. At the office we all worked hard to maintain the fiction that his illness was a temporary inconvenience, tiresome but best ignored. But I knew that pancreatic cancer is painful, difficult to treat, and invariably fatal. Daniel, no weakling when it came to facing facts, undoubtedly knew it, too.

Up until now I'd done very little work for Babbage, but that didn't prevent me from liking him enormously. Daniel's uncanny ability to put people at ease had served him well over the years and I for one was not immune to his avuncular charm. But more importantly, Daniel was one of the few people at the firm who seemed completely unimpressed by my family. For that alone I would be undyingly grateful.

There's no getting around the fact that the Millhollands are famous in this town. There is even a statue of my great-great-grandfather, Theodore Millholland, in the park on East Lake Shore Drive across the street from the Mayfair Regent Hotel. Every morning before the guests get up, the doorman goes over and chases off the homeless men who sleep at his marble feet.

Theodore's father made his money running guns and selling opium to the Chinese, but nobody built him any statues for it. Theodore proved his genius by giving some of that money away, thereby securing for himself and all the Millhollands to follow a level of respectability and influence that is beyond price.

Unfortunately, from my point of view, it is also beyond escape. The Art Institute, the Lyric Opera, Pres.–St. Luke's Hospital, the Chicago Symphony, the University of Chicago—go into any temple of healing, education, or culture in the Windy City and you're sure to find the name Millholland carved somewhere into the hard, gray stone. It doesn't help that my parents enthusiastically embrace their role as scions of philanthropy or that my mother, Astrid, and her coven of well-bred friends rule north-shore society with a grip so absolute that they are referred to as "the syndicate" only partially in jest.

It's no secret that I went to law school in order to escape them and the gauntlet of parties and shopping that in my parents' world fills the gap between debutante and bride. But once I got there, I fell in love with the elegant rationalism of the law. By the end of my first year I'd concluded that I'd rather work hard at something I'm good at than to blindly do what was expected of me just because I was Astrid Millholland's daughter. Daniel, with his long experience of dynastic families and difficult children, seemed to understand completely.

No matter what I do, there will always be people who will not be able to look at me without seeing my entire family tree spread out behind me. There will always be rumblings that my success is not really my own—that it's been bought and paid for with generations of Millholland money. Over the last few years, as I've grown more sure of myself and my talents as an attorney, I've become less hysterical about that stuff. Recently I'd been too busy to give it much thought at all. I was taking on new clients and new cases at a frightening rate. I'd begun to feel like a juggler who suddenly finds herself in the spotlight with one too many chain saws in the air. And that was before Daniel Babbage and his Cavanaughs.

I was flattered that Daniel had asked me to take over the Superior Plating file. But I confess that I was puzzled, too. I am a deal lawyer, a specialist. Someone you call in to orchestrate a complex transaction or craft the terms of a tricky acquisition. My strengths are my technical knowledge of securities law and my tenacity as a negotiator. I'm the person you call in when you need your lawyer to play hardball with their lawyer, not when you need your client's hand held.

On my way to my first meeting with Jack Cavanaugh, as the bitter wind tossed snowflakes like confetti into the air, I realized that try as I might, I could not think of one good reason why Daniel Babbage would choose me to take over the Superior Plating and Specialty Chemicals file.

2

J ack Cavanaugh's house was one of those mansions that are all the more remarkable for being in the center of the city. On the corner of Schiller and Astor, just a few blocks from the thrumming commerce of Michigan Avenue, it was a turn-of-the-century brick pile with a deep porch, tall windows, and massive pillars of red granite that had been polished to the color of dark blood.

I paid the cabdriver, climbed the wide stone steps, and rang the bell. From deep inside the house I heard the high-pitched barking of a small dog. The yapping grew louder and more hysterical until the door was finally opened by a very pretty woman, not much older than me. She had classic features, long blond hair swept straight back from a high forehead, and skin that had no pores that anyone had ever noticed. She wore a red-and-black suit that I recognized from Escada's spring line. Whenever she moved there was the faint jingle of expensive jewelry.

"You must be Kate Millholland," she practically purred, stooping to pick up the silly powder puff of a dog in time to prevent it from sinking its teeth into my ankle. "I'm Peaches," she said, holding the shih tzu up next to her face. "I'm Jack's wife."

Daniel hadn't said anything about a current Mrs. Cavanaugh and I certainly hadn't anticipated the elegant confection before me. But even in the half-light of the entryway, I realized that I'd seen her somewhere before. It took me a couple of seconds to figure it out. Once I did, I felt stupid. After all, during my first year at Callahan Ross, I'd driven past a sixty-foot billboard of her face every night on my way home from work. She had been Peaches Parkenhurst back then, the anchor of the six o'clock news.

"Let me take your coat," she offered. "I'm so glad you're here. Ever since Jack got that hateful letter from Lydia, he's been in an ab-solute state—just storming around the house. I'm just thankful that he wasn't planning on going into the office today. He and Philip are flying to Dallas to visit a customer. It's a good thing, too. In the mood Jack's in there's no telling what he might do. I almost feel sorry for Philip." Her voice was wonderful, silky and melodious with a subtle undercurrent of the south. She played with it as she spoke, pitching it at different levels to keep it interesting. "But I don't know what I must be thinking, chattering away like this," she declared as if the thought had suddenly occurred to her. "We don't want to keep Jack waiting."

I followed in the wake of her expensive perfume. She led me through the heart of the house into a high-ceilinged room that was decorated like a department-store version of a drawing room at Versailles.

Jack Cavanaugh was forty years older than his wife and a full head shorter. A muscular bulldog of a man, his gray hair was brushed straight back from his face. He seemed every bit as tough as I remem-bered, wearing his dark suit like a mantle and carrying himself with the quiet authority of a man who knows that other men fear him. He did not smile, but shook my hand with a fierce grip while his black eyes fixed on me with the disconcerting intensity of a shark circling its dinner.

"What can I get you to drink, Kate?" he asked once Peaches had withdrawn, leaving us to perch on her bandy-legged furniture and discuss business. His voice was gruff, flat, and stripped of pretense.

"I'll have a diet Coke if you have one," I replied. "If not, water is fine."

Jack Cavanaugh got up, crossed the room to an ornately carved armoire, which, when opened, revealed a fully stocked bar. He took two glasses down from the shelf, dropped a handful of ice cubes into each one, and proceeded to drown them in bourbon. He handed me a drink, sat down in his chair, and drained half his glass in one long swallow. It was one o'clock in the afternoon and I hadn't yet had anything to eat. I took a sip and suppressed a shudder.

"I don't know what Daniel's told you about me," he said, "but if you're going to be my lawyer, there's something you and I had better get straight from the start. Superior Plating is my company and at my company things get done my way. That applies to all of my employees from the guy who sweeps the floor to my lawyer. And it applies double to my children. I don't give a rat's ass about anything Lydia or her lawyers have to say. There is no way that I'm going to let a pantywaist little schemer like Arthur Wallace hoodwink my daughter and cheat my grandchildren out of their birthright."

I took a swallow of bourbon and looked Jack Cavanaugh in the eye.

"Who," I demanded, "is Arthur Wallace?"

JACK CAVANAUGH POURED HIMSELF another bourbon and walked over to the window.

"My daughter Lydia has rotten luck and piss-poor taste in men," he explained. "She's been married three times and every time's been a bigger mistake than the one before. Arthur Wallace is mistake number three."

"So you think that Lydia's husband is behind her decision to sell her shares?" I ventured.

"Lydia doesn't really want to sell her shares. What could she gain from it? She already has everything she could possibly want. Believe me, this is all Arthur's doing. He's been trying to figure out a way to get his hands on Lydia's money from the minute he first laid eyes on her. I've told her so a hundred times, but she won't listen."

"How long have they been married?"

"It'll be two years in October. The twins were born six months after the wedding. What a mess."

"So you don't think Lydia herself is interested in the money? She doesn't have any liquidity issues or big expenses. . . ."

"Oh, Lydia always has big expenses. I've never seen anyone spend money like she does, but she knows that she can always come to me for money."

"What does Arthur do for a living?"

"He's some kind of stockbroker. That's why this whole thing doesn't surprise me. He thinks that I don't see it, but he's been snooping around for months, asking questions, trying to figure out what Lydia's shares are worth."

"What are they worth?" I asked.

"I have no idea and I don't care. Why put a price on something that's not for sale?"

"That may be, but when Daniel and I discussed Lydia's letter this morning, we agreed that our first step should be to bring in a team of investment bankers to do a valuation of the company's assets. I know that Lydia has never signed any kind of buyback agreement, but I assume that she'd still be willing to entertain an offer from the family, especially if the price was right."

"You must not have heard me," Cavanaugh growled. "I told you, Lydia's not going to sell her shares."

"I understand that as her father you know much better than I do what's going on in her mind. But look at it another way. She hasn't signed the buyback. She's hired a lawyer. I'd say it's just prudent to be prepared."

"And I'm telling you that there is no way that Lydia is ever going to sell those shares."

"How can you be so sure?" I demanded.

"Because," Jack Cavanaugh announced grimly, "I'll burn the whole damn company to the ground before I let that happen."

WHEN I GOT BACK to my office I found my secretary, Cheryl, waiting for me with a stack of messages and a pained expression on her face.

"Who are these Cavanaughs who keep calling?" she demanded, waving a wad of pink message slips at me as I passed her desk. "The phone has been ringing off the hook since you left. You've got messages from Dagny, Eugene, and someone named Philip, who is in need of some serious sphincter relaxation exercises. Are these people all related or something?"

"It's a file I've picked up from Daniel Babbage," I replied somewhat incoherently as I plunked myself down onto the familiar worn leather of my desk chair.

"Oh gee, just what we need around here, more work." My secretary sighed, taking her customary seat and casting a weary glance at the files that lay in ramparts across my desk. "So what's the deal with the Cavanaughs?"

"They own the Superior Plating and Specialty Chemicals Company. This morning one of the CEO's children, his youngest daughter, Lydia, sent everyone a letter saying that she's planning on selling her shares. I just came from a meeting with him."

"How did it go?"

"I suggest you buckle up. This one's going to be a royal pain in the ass."

"Speaking of pains, your mother called while you were out."

"What did she want?"

"You know she'd never tell me. She doesn't believe in fraternizing with the help. She did say that she wants you to call her—it's very, very, important." Cheryl rolled her eyes. "Ten to one they just got a new shipment of shoes at Neiman Marcus."

Cheryl was a smart kid from Bridgeport who went to Loyola Law School at night. She'd been my secretary since I came to Callahan, and over the years had managed to develop her own brand of mother-daughter relationship with my mother, that is to say, Mother drove her crazy, too.

"What makes you think the Cavanaughs are going to be a pain?" demanded Cheryl. "I mean, besides the fact that they keep calling all the time."

"So far I've only met Jack, but if he's any indication, I'd rather wait awhile before I meet the rest of the family. Let's say a year or two. . . ."

"I hate to break it to you, but it's going to be more like an hour or two."

"What do you mean?"

"You've got a meeting with Dagny Cavanaugh at three-thirty. Madeline, Mr. Babbage's secretary, set it up."

"Are we doing it here?"

"No, at Superior Plating."

"I guess you haven't lived until you've seen a plating plant," I groaned. "Wait a minute, don't I already have something at three?"

"You had a meeting at three with Skip Tillman and the lawyers for Meteor Software, but it's been moved up."

"To when?"

Cheryl looked at her watch. "Forty-second-floor conference room in three minutes."

"But I haven't even had a chance to look at the file," I protested. "I was going to do it this morning, but then this damn Cavanaugh thing came up."

"I guess you'll just have to fake it," Cheryl advised. "You know how crazy Tillman gets if you're late. Have you had anything to eat yet today?"

"Does bourbon count?"

"You've got to be kidding. I have half a corned beef sandwich in my desk. You can eat it in the elevator on the way up to the forty-second floor."

"What would I ever do without you?"

"Miss your appointments, get lost, and starve to death," was my secretary's forthright reply.

I MANAGED TO LEAVE the Meteor Software meeting in time for my meeting with Dagny Cavanaugh and with my reputation intact. Unfortunately, I also took away with me four pages of things that Skip Tillman had, with a nod of his patrician head, managed to dump in my lap.

I took State Street south from my office and followed Cheryl's directions through the low-rent end of the loop into the working-class neighborhood that's produced five of the city's last six mayors. Bridgeport is an uneven enclave where tidy bungalows and corner taverns fill in the spaces between factories and vacant lots. I passed a meatpacking plant, a cardboard box company, and a lot filled with rusting scrap, including a couple of trucks and a city bus in various stages of disintegration.

I missed the plant the first time around. I was expecting to see a sign but there wasn't one, so I ended up driving past it—a squat, windowless brick building set back from the street behind a ten-foot chain-link fence topped with barbed wire. Bits of newspaper had caught in the barbs and the shreds of newsprint undulated in the wind like seaweed rocked by an ocean current.

Inside, it wasn't much better. A slack-jawed receptionist presided over a scarred Formica desk and a couple of chairs that looked like they'd been salvaged from the waiting room at the bus terminal. It was a wonder that Jack Cavanaugh didn't get the bends every day going from the opulence of his house on Astor to the industrial shabbiness of his plant. I also thought it was a pretty safe bet that Peaches didn't drop in on her husband at the office very often.

"Kate Millholland to see Dagny Cavanaugh," I said.

The receptionist dragged her eyes from her copy of *Cosmopolitan.* "I'll let them know you're here," she replied in a weary voice.

I wandered the perimeter of the waiting area, an expanse of brown linoleum surrounded by cinderblock walls that had been painted a depressing shade of yellow and hung with grainy photos of industrial goods. Family-owned companies, I knew, were less likely to squander money on nonessentials, and in a company like Superior Plating, where customers didn't come around to call, the only place they'd give a damn about appearances would be the bottom line.

"You must be the lawyer who's taking over for Daniel Babbage," boomed a curt male voice as I examined a photograph of what I took to be a lamppost.

I turned to see a broad, battering ram of a man in his late thirties with a shock of black hair, a military bearing, and the imprint of Jack Cavanaugh on his face. He wore navy-blue work clothes, immaculately pressed. The hand he extended was clean, but so callused that when I shook, it did not feel warm, only dry and hard.

"I'm Kate Millholland," I said.

"Eugene Cavanaugh," he replied. "Around here they call me Gene. Dagny's still with the auditors. She asked me to show you around." He cast a disapproving eye over my clothes. "Are those the only shoes you've got?"

"I don't mind if they get dirty."

"Good. They're going to." He handed me a pair of safety goggles and reached around the back of the reception desk and pulled out a scuffed white hard hat. "Put these on," he instructed sternly. "Visitors have to wear them in the plant."

I did as I was told and immediately felt ridiculous. My expensive suit of plum-colored wool and my Ferragamo pumps—things that conveyed authority in my world—seemed frivolous and ridiculously out of place here. I followed Eugene down a narrow corridor and through a set of double doors.

"I don't know if you know anything about our business," he said, his tone implying a certainty that I did not, "but we're a metal plating operation—mostly chrome and bronze. Occasionally we do some gold, but generally there's not much call for it."

"What about specialty chemicals?" I asked. "How much of your business is done by that division?"

"Like I said, we're a plating operation. Specialty chemicals are just a sideline."

I followed him into a large area that reminded me of the work bays in an auto garage. There was the same rock music playing too loud on an unseen transistor radio, the same concrete floor stained with motor oil. In one corner a first-aid kit was bolted to the wall between a fire extinguisher and a greasy, dog-eared safety poster. Wooden pallets loaded with cardboard boxes ringed the walls. Men in dark blue coveralls were slitting open the boxes, pulling out what looked like car wheels. Catching sight of Eugene, the workers sharpened up perceptibly—casual conversation evaporated and everything moved a half step faster.

"You see how dull the finish is on those?" asked Eugene, pointing to the wheels that, once out of their boxes, were being loaded onto a conveyor belt. "They're made of aluminum. We polish them and plate them so that they're shiny like you see on cars in the street. That belt takes them into the polishing room."

I followed him into another area separated by a large, overhead garage door. In it, workers muffled to the eyes bent over powerful polishing lathes. The noise was deafening. Sparks flew. Despite the fact that the machinery gave off a lot of heat, the men all wore heavy hooded sweatshirts under their coveralls, which they topped with baseball caps, protective goggles, and bandannas tied around the lower half of their faces. On their hands they wore thick work gloves. In the entire room there was not one inch of exposed skin. The walls, the ceiling, the floor, even the men were all covered with a gray metallic dust.

"That's aluminum dust," bellowed Eugene, looking down at my shoes, which, along with my stockings, were completely covered with gray film. "They're removing all the irregularities from the metal surface. The plated finish is only as good as the polish job."

I picked my way carefully across the work floor and followed Eugene through a doorway hung with long strips of clear plastic that kept the aluminum dust from escaping the polishing area. We walked down a short hall in which someone had dumped the bench seat from an old truck. It was obviously used as a couch by workers on break. Above it hung a hand-lettered sign: THIS CORNER IS NOT A GARBAGE DUMP. PICK UP YOUR TRASH OR GET SHOT!

Eugene pulled open a heavy sliding door at the other end. The smell was like a slap in the face, pungent and corrosive. In the uneven light from hanging strips of neon tubing and whatever feeble sunlight made its way through the grimy skylights were a series of rectangular tanks each about six feet wide, eight feet deep, and twenty feet long. They looked old. The outsides were scaled with corroded metal and the green traces of acid. Around the perimeter ran a rickety wooden platform under which fluid, an unhealthy shade of green, stood in brackish pools.

"This is one of our four chrome plating lines. The unfinished goods are put on racks, which are moved from tank to tank by a hoist-and-crane system," said Eugene, pointing toward the ceiling. "It's basically a four-step process with a rinse in between each step. The first tank is a heavy-duty industrial cleaner that's heated to one hundred and sixty degrees. Whatever is being plated goes from the polishing room into there first so that we can be sure that it's free from any grease or dust that'll interfere with the process. From there it goes into the second tank that's filled with water and then into the etching tank—that's this one here, which contains caustic soda that's also heated. The idea is to take away the first layer of aluminum or steel—again, to make sure you have a very clean, smooth surface to plate. Once it's been etched, it's rinsed again and then it goes into that fifth tank over there, which is the tri-acid oxidizer. That's the desmutting step. It gets rid of any smut or trace elements that are still on the metal surface. Then it's rinsed again and goes into the chrome bath. Come up here and take a look."

I followed him up the pitted wooden steps onto the walkway, weakened over time by dripping acid, that ran along the side of the tanks. Overhead, rusted metal fans spat and clanked while the heat from the chemical tanks pushed up past my face like a fetid desert wind. Eugene stopped in front of the last tank and rested both hands casually on the edge. One of his sleeves was pushed back, exposing a tattoo of a snake. It circled his wrist and slithered up the inside of his arm. I looked down into the tank. It was filled with hot, bubbling liquid a brilliant shade of yellow—chrome yellow, in fact. It looked like the kind of thing you'd show pictures of to children in order to frighten them about hell.

"What's your safety record like?" I asked, stepping back from the edge.

"We have guys from OSHA and EPA through here every day. In the last twenty-five years we've only had one serious accident, and there was no question of it being our fault."

"What happened?"

"One of our workers forgot his paycheck at the plant one Friday a few years back. That night, after about a dozen beers, he decided he couldn't wait until Monday to come get it. He and a couple of his buddies came by here, broke a window, and climbed in to retrieve it. Nobody knows exactly how it happened—they were all so drunk—but one of them tripped and fell into this very vat."

"Did he die?"

"Dying was the easy part of what happened to him."

"What do you mean?"

"Let's just say," said Eugene Cavanaugh, his face impassive, "that they decided not to have an open-casket funeral."

3

Dagny Cavanaugh's secretary came to tell me that her boss was ready to see me. She was a young woman, pretty under too much makeup, with a short black skirt pulled tight across hard haunches and the kind of hairdo that looked like it was the product of a small explosion. For some reason, the very sight of her seemed to send Eugene into a cold fury.

"Cecilia! What are you doing down here?" he demanded sharply.

"I'm doing my job," she snapped, planting her hands firmly on her hips. "You got a problem with that?"

"You know that you're not supposed to come into the plant."

"Dagny told me to go to your office and get the new lawyer. Loretta said you were giving her the tour. What was I *supposed* to do?" She shot him a look like a sulky teenager.

"You should have had me paged."

"It's not *my* fault if Tammy at the switchboard was busy," she sassed back.

They glared each other to a stalemate. Neither of them seemed interested in ending their awkward little scene for my sake, so I decided to rescue myself. I thanked Eugene for showing me around and Eugene, looking murderous, managed a civil reply.

"Come on," said Cecilia, with a dramatic flip of her hair. "I'll take you to Dagny." After we'd gone a few yards but were still within earshot, she added, "Eugene is so uptight. I guess when you leave the marines they give you a rod up your ass as a going-away present."

There being absolutely no appropriate response to that kind of remark, I elected to follow her in silence. We went down the stairs and through a set of fire doors into a large work area where shiny cylinders were moving down a conveyor belt and then being carefully shrink-wrapped and packed into boxes.

At the sight of Cecilia, all work on the line ground to a halt. The men stopped what they were doing and leered. As we passed I heard catcalls and the sound of lips being smacked. Cecilia made an elaborate show of ignoring them, but I noticed that she turned the swivel up in her hips and every couple of seconds she gave her hair a provocative toss.

As we left the factory floor a wave of fervent gratitude washed over me. My hardworking and intelligent secretary made my life easier in a thousand ways every day, while I had no doubt that this one was nothing but trouble.

DAGNY CAVANAUGH RECEIVED ME in a sparsely furnished meeting room where mismatched chairs ringed a conference table that was littered with computer printouts and half-filled Styrofoam cups—no doubt the detritus of her earlier meeting.

"Thank you so much for coming," she said, springing to her feet to greet me. "I'm sorry to have kept you waiting. I had my end-of-the-quarter session with our outside accountants, and today, for some reason, everything took longer than I expected." She waved me into a seat. "My father told me that you're going to be taking over for Daniel. How's he doing?"

"He still comes in to work every day. His secretary told me that he's finished with chemotherapy and in remission, but no one knows how long it will last."

"I'll have to call him and let him know he's in our prayers."

Dagny was an attractive woman in her early forties who looked thirty and carried herself with a relaxed self-confidence that isn't taught in any MBA program. More handsome than pretty, she wore a luxuriously simple navy-blue suit over a peach-colored silk blouse and somehow managed to make the combination seem both elegant and appropriate for a metal finishing plant. She had a fringe of shiny dark hair, intelligent eyes, and a wide smile. I liked her immediately. It was hard to imagine that anyone wouldn't.

"Daniel's told me so many nice things about you," she continued. "I know that we'll enjoy working together. But I confess it's going to take me a while to get used to not calling Daniel every time there's a problem. I've known him my entire life. I know it sounds like a cliché, but I really do think of him more as a member of the family than as our lawyer." She laughed. "I guess that's an occupational hazard when everyone in the company is related. Business feels like family and family feels like business. Did Eugene show you around the place?"

"We'd gotten as far as chrome plating when your secretary came to get me. I was sort of hoping to get a chance to see some of your specialty chemical operation—"

"Cecilia went into the plant?" Dagny cut in, genuinely horrified.

"Eugene didn't seem too pleased about it."

"Eugene hates her," Dagny replied shortly. "My little brother has very definite views about what is and isn't appropriate behavior for women, and frankly Cecilia gets a kick out of goading him. But it isn't Eugene I'm worried about, it's the guys on the plant floor. When she goes down there they act like they've never seen a woman before.

She's going to cause an accident one of these days. You've seen that polishing equipment—you take your eyes off of what you're doing for one minute and you can lose your hand. Cecilia knows she has no business in the plant, but she always finds some excuse. I honestly think she has some sick need for attention." Dagny sighed. "We have such a hard time finding and keeping good clerical help. They all want to work downtown in some fancy place like Callahan Ross."

"I don't think Cecilia would have much luck at Callahan Ross," I replied. "Not dressed the way she was today."

"I know it seems hard to believe, but Cecilia came to her job interview with no makeup, her hair in a bun, and wearing a flowered dress with a lace collar. For the first three months she came to work looking like she'd just left church. Then boom, as soon as her three-month probationary period was up, she let her hair down and switched over to her hooker wardrobe."

"Why don't you say something to her about it?"

"It's obvious you're not an employment attorney. Technically Cecilia should be able to walk from one end of the plant to the other stark naked without anyone raising their eyes from their work. From what I've been told, her attire is irrelevant unless it interferes with job performance—and she's a surprisingly good secretary. If I mention her wardrobe to her, I'm afraid I'll just be opening myself up to a lawsuit."

"You're right. I hadn't thought about it that way."

"Welcome to employee relations in the nineties. Dad can't understand it at all. He tells stories about when he first took over the company from my grandfather—who knows if they're true—but back then he says that if he caught one of his employees stealing, he'd grab him by the scruff of the neck, beat the living daylights out of him, and literally kick him out onto the street as a lesson to the other workers."

"I haven't spent that much time with your father, but I can believe it."

"Dad called me this morning and said he had a meeting with you at the house. Did he tell you what he wants to do about Lydia and her shares?"

"I think he wants to beat up her husband and kick him out onto the street as a lesson to the other family members," I replied.

"So he's blaming Arthur? I should have guessed."

"Why do you say that?"

"Whenever Lydia pulls a stunt like this, Dad always finds some reason why it's all somebody else's fault. And believe me, she's been pulling stunts like this ever since she could talk."

"He really believes she could have no valid reason for wanting to sell her shares."

"Maybe she doesn't. Maybe she's trying to get attention, or express anger, or work through some unresolved crisis from a past life—you'd have to ask her therapist. I don't know and I don't care. All I know is we have a golden opportunity to get rid of Lydia as a shareholder once and for all. I think we've got to grab it and run with it."

"I take it you're in favor of buying her out."

"Are you kidding? I'd buy her out in a minute and I'd mortgage the company to the eyes to do it. Don't get me wrong; Lydia is my sister and I love her, but that doesn't make me blind to the fact that she has never been anything but a drain on this company. While she's sitting on her rear end getting in touch with her inner child and thinking up ways to make trouble, the rest of us have a business to run. Have you ever read Karl Marx?"

"In college," I replied, surprised at the question.

"Marx said that what a man doesn't work for has no value to him. I'd say that pretty much sums up Lydia's relationship to Superior Plating. To her it's just a dirty factory in a part of town she doesn't like to visit. But this dirty factory is what pays for her trips to the shrink and that awful collection of modern art of hers. Besides, we have a responsibility to our employees—the people who put food on their tables and braces on their kids' teeth with the money they earn at Superior Plating. She has no interest in what we do, no understanding of what goes into making the money in the check she so casually cashes every month. Every day is a struggle around here. We're being squeezed by foreign competition, we have OSHA and the EPA breathing down our necks—" Suddenly Dagny broke off and burst out laughing. "Oh my God, I can't believe it! I'm starting to sound just like my father."

"Your father says that Lydia has no financial reason for wanting to sell—that if she needed money she knows she can always come to him."

"Sure, if she needed money—and a lecture—she could go to my dad. And no matter what Dad told you about Arthur, he's no fool. I'm sure Arthur's explained to Lydia how much money she will make if she sells her shares. There's a difference between needing money and wanting financial freedom."

"Do you think your father's right? Is this whole thing her husband Arthur's idea?"

"Lydia obviously got the idea from somewhere. She didn't come up with this all by herself, but it doesn't matter where it came from. I just think we should do everything in our power to make it as easy as possible for her to sell us her shares."

"I have to tell you that when I spoke to your father this morning he did not share your point of view. He says that if Lydia sells her shares, she'd be cheating her children out of their birthright."

Dagny leaned back in her chair.

"Dad has this fantasy about all four of us working together and then passing the company on to our children. The trouble is, that's all it is—a fantasy. It's hard enough for the four of us to get along day to day. Who knows what our children will be like? Believe me, a lot is going to happen between now and our children's generation and not all of it is going to be pretty."

"How do your brothers feel about Lydia selling out? I didn't have a chance to ask Eugene—"

"I have no idea what Eugene thinks—if anything. He usually doesn't get involved in issues like this."

"But he has a seat on the board," I protested.

"We all do. But Eugene prefers to deal with the day-to-day problems on the plant floor. Everything else he leaves to Dad. Though who knows? Recently he's been showing signs of independence. Dad's turning seventy next month and I think it's making all of us think about the fact that he's not going to be around forever."

"And Philip?"

"As far as Philip is concerned, the sooner Lydia is out of the picture the better—and good riddance to her. The two of them have never gotten along, not even when they were kids. She just sticks in his craw and he sticks in her craw. . . . So I don't blame him for wanting to get rid of her. Can you imagine anything worse than having the person who's been driving you crazy since the third grade sitting on the board of directors of the company you're trying to run?"

"So you're pretty sure that Philip would vote with you to buy her out at any price?"

"I'm sure he wants to buy her out, but the price is where it's bound to get sticky. Philip is an incredible skinflint. He'll want to buy Lydia out all right, just as soon as he's sure that he's not paying her one penny more than he has to."

"When I met with your father this morning I tried to convince him to let me bring in an investment banking group to do a valuation of the company. That way, if it turns out that Lydia really is serious about selling her shares, we'd at least have the information to make her a realistic offer. My guess is that Lydia's already got her own investment bankers trying to work out what her shares are worth."

"She does. I got a letter from Mark Hoffenberg at First Chicago this morning asking for information about the company."

Inwardly I cursed Jack Cavanaugh for his stubbornness. He might think that his little girl couldn't be serious about selling her shares, but once he crossed paths with Hoffenberg he'd know how medieval villagers must have felt when Viking ships appeared.

"If Lydia's using First Chicago, who would you recommend for us?" asked Dagny.

"I've worked with them all," I said. "Personally I liked Bob Halloran at Goodman Peabody, but I've got to be straight with you. I couldn't even get your father to discuss the idea of a valuation. No matter how I approached the subject, he just stonewalled me. According to him, Lydia isn't going to sell. Period. End of story. He's chairman of the board, CEO, and the largest shareholder. Until he changes his mind, my hands are tied."

"Go ahead and call your friend at Goodman Peabody and see if you can set something up for Friday. Dad will have changed his mind by then."

"What makes you so sure?"

"I've invited him and Peaches for dinner Wednesday night."

"You must be one hell of a cook."

"Now that you mention it, I *am* cooking his favorite dinner. I'm also planning on telling him that if he doesn't agree to buy out Lydia, I'm resigning from the company."

"Do you really think it'll work? Aren't you afraid he'll call your bluff?"

"It's not a bluff. I get job offers all the time. This last one's a good one—I'd be heading the metal coatings division at Monarch Metals."

"I thought they were in Boston."

"They are," she replied matter-of-factly. I remembered what Daniel had said about Dagny not taking shit from her father. Suddenly the situation with Superior Plating seemed less hopeless.

Dagny glanced quickly at her watch. "I have a conference call in a few minutes with one of our vendors," she apologized. "Why don't we take a walk over to my office and I'll get you a copy of the letter from

Lydia's investment bankers. They've asked for a ridiculous amount of information. You're going to have to tell me how much of this stuff I really have to provide. If I give them everything they're asking for, it'll take weeks to get it together. I've also had Cecilia run off a copy of our most recent financials." She stood up and stretched. "That feels so good. I think I've been in that chair since ten o'clock this morning."

I followed her through a series of narrow passageways that were all paneled in the same imitation woodgrained stuff that seemed to have been indiscriminately applied to every surface in the fifties. She led me into a small suite of offices. I have a terrible sense of direction, but I guessed we were adjacent to the reception area where I'd come in.

Dagny's office was off by itself at the end of the hall. At the threshold she stopped so suddenly that I literally ran into her. My automatic apology dried up in my throat as I saw what it was that had stopped her dead.

"Oh my God," said Dagny, the rising note of alarm in her voice turning my stomach to lead.

Facedown on the blue carpet in front of Dagny's desk, her hair splayed around her head and her short skirt hitched up to reveal red satin panties, lay the inert form of her secretary, Cecilia.

CHAPTER

4

"Cecilia?" called Dagny, her voice hovering somewhere between bewilderment and alarm. "Are you okay?"

There was no response from the motionless figure on the floor. For a minute we just stood there, two women in business suits caught completely off guard. Then Dagny ran to her desk and picked up the phone. Silently praying that Cecilia had just fainted or, better yet, had passed out drunk, I dove and knelt beside the prone figure on the blue carpet.

Shaking her gently, I called out her name. Nothing. I shook harder. Her body was inert, eerily unresponsive. I felt a tightening in my chest and knew that it was fear.

"Call nine-one-one," I commanded Dagny, who by then was already on the line with the police dispatcher.

I checked Cecilia's wrist for a pulse and found none. Pushing aside her long hair, I searched frantically for the carotid artery. I found the spot but there was no pulse.

I took hold of her shoulders. She was surprisingly heavy, and as I turned her over onto her back, her head lolled sickeningly to one side. I bent my face over hers but felt no whisper of breath. Her skin was pink and felt warm against my hand. But there was something about her eyes, open yet unfocused, that chilled me.

Trying not to think, I checked her mouth for foreign objects. Then I pinched her nose closed with one hand, placed my lips over hers, and exhaled. I moved both my hands over her breastbone, wondering desperately if I was even close to the right spot, and began the series of compressions I'd learned in CPR.

When they brought in the Red Cross to teach classes in cardiopulmonary resuscitation at Callahan Ross, everyone joked that it was a clear case of self-interest. The older partners just wanted to make sure that when they had their big heart attacks everyone would know exactly what to do. I swear that when I signed up for the course I never dreamed that I'd ever use what I'd learned.

"One and two and three and four and five," I counted out loud. "Go to the front of the building and wait for the paramedics," I ordered Dagny. She hesitated. Then, nodding tensely, she disappeared out the door as I began the next set of compressions.

I do not know how long it took. At some point, like a distance runner in "the zone," the world just went away. I was aware of nothing, not the passing of time or the accumulating ranks of Superior Plating employees who began crowding into the doorway. Five compressions and a breath, five compressions and a breath, that was what my world had narrowed down to—my face pressed against the face of a woman I'd barely met. Now I felt the thin fabric of her blouse under my hands, felt the resilient softness of her skin, smelled the lush flowers of her perfume. . . .

I did not hear the paramedics come. At some point strong hands grasped my shoulders and pulled me away. A man's voice spoke, but at first I didn't register the meaning of his words. Gradually the adrenaline released me from its grip and I saw the room as if for the first time.

On the floor in front of Dagny's desk a half-dozen blue-uniformed emergency medical technicians swarmed around the still-motionless body of her secretary. One of the paramedics, a woman who wore her glossy hair in a French braid that made me suddenly think of horses, began asking me questions: What was her name? When did I find her? How was she lying? Did I move her? How long did it take me before I started CPR? Did I know whether she had any history of heart disease? Diabetes? Drug use?

As I stammered out my replies another paramedic, a black man with a bald head, slid some sort of tube down the unconscious woman's throat. Another EMT took a thick needle and started an IV drip.

"Pupils dilated and unresponsive," said one voice. "Blood pressure is zero."

"Defib?" demanded another.

"We're so close to the hospital, let's just keep her ventilated and get her in," replied the black paramedic, who seemed to be in charge.

The woman with the French braid turned to me. "You can ride with her in the ambulance. Let's see if somebody can find her purse."

I sputtered an incoherent protest, but no one paid any attention. They were already bent over the stretcher. I looked around the room desperately for Dagny, but she was nowhere to be seen. As we were walking out the door someone shoved Cecilia's battered black shoulder bag into my hands.

THE SIREN WAILED AND throbbed above us as we navigated the narrow city streets. I wondered which hospital was nearest and decided it was probably Michael Reese. Cecilia, still unconscious, lay strapped to the stretcher while the black paramedic kept up his ministrations—shining a penlight into her eyes, taking her blood pressure, checking the IV line.

I sat on a narrow bench, crouching thigh to thigh with a second paramedic, one I hadn't noticed back in Dagny's office. He was good-looking in a beefy sort of way, with a lantern jaw and what I knew instinctively must be a quick eye for the ladies.

"Nice work in there," he said.

"Thanks."

"Did she do drugs, do you know?"

"I have no idea. I've never seen her before."

"So you don't work with her or nothin'."

"No. I just had an appointment with her boss."

"What kind of place is that back there where she works? It's some sort of factory, isn't it?"

"They do metal plating."

"So you don't work there?"

"I have an office downtown."

"Whadya do?"

"I'm an attorney," I replied uncomfortably. The circumstances, I felt, were not ideal for small talk.

"You're kidding. I would never've taken you for a lawyer, on account of you being so young and good-looking and all."

We hit the bump of the curb and made a sharp turn into what I prayed was the entrance to the emergency room.

"Save it, Frank," snapped the black paramedic. "It's show time."

I HATE EVERYTHING ABOUT hospitals—the smell of suffering mingled with disinfectant, the constant drone of unwatched TVs and babies crying, the way that tiny acts of compassion are overshadowed by the monumental cruelty of bureaucratic indifference. It is the same in every hospital I have ever been in. And I have been in my share.

My husband died of brain cancer the year we both graduated from law school. The months that preceded his death were filled with painful tests and poisonous medications. They were months of bitterness, stoicism, and despair. By the time I came through them, I had used up a lifetime's allotment of patience with hospitals.

The paramedics wheeled Cecilia into the emergency room at a dead run and disappeared behind double doors marked NO ADMITTANCE, leaving me to battle a wearily indifferent admitting clerk through two inches of Plexiglas. I looked through the purse in my hands, not my own, but the one I'd been numbly clutching since we left Superior Plating. I turned it upside down on the Formica counter in front of me and scrabbled through the mess: bus transfers and used tissues, two condoms still sealed in their foil packets, a hairbrush grotesquely clotted with blond hairs, and a half-eaten candy bar.

From the front of a tattered romance novel a bare-chested man stared up at me with unbridled lust. Thrust between its pages I found what I was looking for. Attached to an Illinois driver's license with a paper clip were four soiled dollar bills, a disconnection notice for an apartment in Uptown, and finally, a dog-eared insurance card, all in the name of Cecilia Dobson.

Relieved, I passed the identification to the clerk, who disappeared to make copies. Behind me a toddler with a runny nose played with the knobs of the candy machine while an old woman in bedroom slippers and a greasy raincoat sat in a chair by the door and sobbed.

After the clerk returned I set out in search of the pay phones. I found them cleverly positioned between a blaring television set and the speaker of the public address system. Three of the four were not working and a girl who looked as though she was about fourteen was using the fourth. In one hand she cradled a very new baby and in the other the receiver.

"But I don't have no money for no bus," she was insisting to whoever was on the other end.

Back in the cramped waiting room I found a row of vinyl chairs that were bolted to the floor and sat down to wait. I tried hard to worry about Cecilia Dobson, but felt instead an unreasonable pang of longing for the quiet order of Callahan Ross, where clients wait among the brass lamps and the Chippendale. After a while my beefy paramedic returned, emerging from behind the steel doors of the emergency room with a Styrofoam cup of coffee in each hand. On his face was a broad smile that I suspected of having been practiced in the bathroom mirror. My heart sank.

"I've got cream and sugar in my pocket if you want," he said, sitting down beside me and nodding in the direction of his chest. It was obvious that he spent his off-hours lifting weights. He wanted to be sure that I noticed.

"Black is fine, thank you," I replied. "Do you know if she's going to be okay?"

"They're still working on her. They'll come out and get you when they know anything. I just wanted to see how you're doing."

"Fine," I replied primly.

"You did a great job back there." He moved a little closer. "Not many people woulda kept their heads the way you did."

"Thank you," I said, pressing my knees together and wishing he'd go away.

"I know how upsetting something like this can be. You know, I see a lot of stressful things on my job. I handle life-and-death situations every day." He leaned so close to me I could smell what he'd had for lunch. "I know how to handle it. I can help you deal with the stress. . . ."

I gritted my teeth and grimly evaluated my options. I was debating whether to declare myself HIV positive, a lesbian, or both when the doors to the emergency room swung open and a tired-looking nurse in pink scrubs motioned to us.

"They want to see you now," he said, giving my hand a squeeze. "You want me to come with you?"

"No," I replied hastily, scrambling to my feet.

"If I'm not here when you get finished, I want you to call me. All you have to do is dial nine-one-one and tell them you need Frank." His last line had the polished delivery of a professional.

THE DOCTOR'S NAME WAS Kravitz, and despite the camouflage of her white coat, I could see that she was pregnant. She saw me in a cramped supply room with a folding chair in one corner. Through the open door I could see doctors in their shirtsleeves and tennis shoes doing their weary dance from treatment room to treatment room while a metallic voice from the PA system urged Dr. Patel to report to the oncology service.

"Are you a relative?" Dr. Kravitz asked.

"No, I'm not. I'm just one of the people who found her."

"Can you tell me what happened?"

I described how Dagny and I had found her as best as I could.

"They said she worked in some sort of factory. What kind was it?"

"It's a plating plant."

"Did she work near any chemicals?"

"No. She worked in the office."

"And after you found her you immediately called nine-one-one?"

"Her boss made the call. I turned her over and started CPR."

"Had she vomited?"

"I don't think so."

"Was there any sign of injury or violence?"

"No."

"To your knowledge, did she ever regain consciousness?"

"Not while I was with her."

"And as far as you can tell, she never resumed breathing on her own?"

"No. Is she going to be okay?"

Dr. Kravitz looked at me for a moment. "I'm afraid she's dead," she said softly. "We pronounced her a few minutes ago."

I was quiet for a minute. I wondered how many times the doctor had to break this sort of news. I wondered if it got easier with practice.

"How did she die?" I asked finally.

"We don't know yet. We probably won't know until we get the autopsy results. I can send a social worker in to talk to you if you feel that would be helpful."

"No. I don't want to talk to anyone."

"Are you sure?"

"I never laid eyes on her before today," I answered woodenly. "She really was a stranger."

WHEN I RETURNED TO the waiting room Dagny was there.

"I'm sorry it took me so long to get here. We were trying to reach her family," she explained breathlessly.

"And did you get a hold of them?"

"No, not yet. We checked her personnel file. She listed a sister as next of kin, but when we called the number it had been disconnected. We're still working on it. Do they know what's wrong with her yet? Is she going to be all right?"

"She's dead," I said, wishing I could think of a less naked way to say it.

"Dead?" demanded Dagny, staggering backward at the news as if from a blow. "How can that be? She was fine an hour ago. You saw her yourself. How could something like this happen?"

"They don't know. They'll have to do an autopsy."

"Oh my God," Dagny whispered, sinking into a chair. "She was so young, just a kid. I think she was only twenty-two. What could have killed her so fast like that?"

"They wanted to know if there were any chemicals where she worked."

"There are chemicals in the plant, but we're tremendously conscious of safety. Besides, she worked in the office. She'd never come into contact with any of them."

"They also wanted to know whether she used drugs."

"I suppose it's possible," Dagny replied, obviously still struggling to digest what had just happened. It was hard enough for me, but for Dagny, who had worked side by side with the dead woman, it must have been even worse.

"I feel so terrible," Dagny continued. "I don't know anything about her. I don't know where she lived or if she had a boyfriend. I was so concerned with the superficial things that annoyed me about her that I never took the time to find out the big things."

"You cannot start blaming yourself," I said firmly. "Whatever happened, it isn't your fault."

Dagny looked up sharply. "That doesn't matter. Philip is still going to blame me."

"That's nonsense," I replied. "They don't even know how she died. How can he be worried about whose fault it is?"

"You don't understand my brother. Placing blame is how he reacts to a crisis." She cast her eyes vaguely around the waiting area. "Do you think we need to stay here for anything? I should get back to the office and see if they've been able to reach her family. I've got to tell everyone what's happened."

"I don't know."

As we discussed what to do, a tall, thin man in his late thirties approached us. He had thinning hair and a reddish-gold beard that gave him a vaguely professorial air. From the pocket of his tweed jacket he produced a gold detective's shield. Leading us to a relatively quiet corner of the waiting room, he explained that the police are called in to investigate any case of death that cannot readily be explained by the person's age or medical condition.

Drawing a small notebook from his pocket, he asked us questions that took us efficiently through the events of the last two hours. We answered as best as we could, though I was surprised at the extent to which the crisis had fogged my memory. I had been so focused on Cecilia that there were a hundred things I seemingly hadn't noticed—the time, whether anyone had been in the next room when we found her, whether she'd had anything in her hand. Still, for a man whose job it was to question the newly bereaved, sobbing mothers and fresh widows, Dagny and I must have made for a pleasant, if unproductive change.

In the end, his questions hadn't taken very long, and when we were finished, I gave him Cecilia Dobson's purse, for which he laboriously wrote out an evidence receipt. He also gave me one of his cards. I turned it over in my hand. It read: DETECTIVE JOE BLADES—HOMICIDE.

CHAPTER

5

When I got back to the office, Cheryl had already gone for the day. On Monday nights she had civil procedure and left at five o'clock on the dot. Shrugging off my coat, I dialed Daniel Babbage's extension only to be told by the switchboard operator that he'd already left the office. I tried his home number but got no answer. I felt too restless to do anything but flip blindly through the message slips that Cheryl had left for me. From every available surface the stacks of files rebuked me for work undone, but I was powerless to begin. Cecilia Dobson might have been a stranger, but her death had dealt me a sucker punch nonetheless. Sitting impotently in my own office, I realized that I simply had no idea how to pick up the routine of my life after someone died.

When the phone rang I nearly jumped out of my skin.

"Please, God," I whispered as I picked up the receiver, "let it not be my mother."

"Hey, Kate. It's Stephen," came a familiar voice, hollow from his speakerphone. "I just called to see what you were up to tonight."

"I'm going out to get drunk," I replied. "You're more than welcome to join me if you'd like."

IN THE WOOD PANELED bar of the University Club I put as many scotches as I could between myself and the death of Cecilia Dobson. Stephen, who is six-foot-five and weighs two hundred and thirty pounds, can, as a rule, carry a bigger load of Chivas than I can, but tonight he didn't even try to keep up.

Stephen Azorini is a client—the one I sleep with—which is, of course, against the rules. But then Stephen has been breaking rules from the first day I met him, when we were both in prep school and he walked off the lacrosse field in the middle of a game against Culver Academy to ask me out. Since then we have been many things to each other, not all of them easy to explain. In high school our relationship was fueled by a combination of lust and rebellion; in college, with Stephen at MIT and me at Bryn Mawr, we passed naturally into a casual albeit intermittent friendship. When we both found ourselves at the University of Chicago for graduate school—Stephen picked up a Ph.D. in chemistry during medical school the way another man might acquire a second pair of pants—we saw each other seldom despite the fact that we were separated by no more than a city block.

Stephen came to my wedding. There is a photograph of him dancing with my little sister, Beth, in a silver frame in the music room of my parents' house, though I honestly don't remember seeing him there. So much of what happened that day is a blur. What is clearer in my memory is the first night, just after Russell was admitted to the hospital after being diagnosed with cancer, when Stephen appeared unbidden at his bedside to offer whatever help he could.

And now? Stephen is the CEO of Azor Pharmaceuticals, the company he founded straight out of medical school and which has been streaking across the high-tech heavens ever since. I am his lover and his lawyer. Beyond that I can't be sure of anything.

After Russell died I was horrified by how quickly well-meaning colleagues began circulating word of my "availability." I reacted by asking Stephen to be my escort whenever I had an unavoidable social obligation. It worked. There is something about Stephen that tends to discourage competition.

Stephen Azorini is handsome the way that professional basketball players are tall. Women actually stop to stare at him in the street. They want to run their fingers through the luxuriant waves of his dark hair, to stare deeply into the smoky blue of his eyes, and, I suppose, to have his babies—or at the very least have the fun of trying. When he's in my office Cheryl is visited by a steady stream of secretaries with invented excuses who come in the hopes of catching a glimpse of him. I honestly have no idea how he stands it.

Tonight Stephen was looking tired, but it suited him. He had spent the last several months trying to organize a joint venture between Azor Pharmaceuticals and Gordimer A.G., the Swiss pharmaceutical giant, in order to speed development of a new immunosupressant drug. Stephen's scientists had laid the groundwork for the creation of a new compound that could potentially prevent organ transplant rejections.

While their scientific achievement was nothing short of dazzling, Azor lacked the financial muscle to make the arduous journey from discovery to drug development. Stephen, who was relentlessly pushing the deal toward closure, had entered what he referred to as his "full-sell mode": flying between Chicago and Geneva alternately begging, threatening, and cajoling; granting the concessions and making the promises that would sustain a project that he believed in with a fervor approaching mania.

Stephen knew that something was bothering me. I didn't often feel the need to hide out at the bottom of a bottle. But I was grateful that he didn't ask.

All the time that Russell was dying we never talked about it. We had endless discussions about tests and treatments, of course, drug choices and surgical options, issues of morbidity and mortality. Stephen even helped me choose the clothes that Russell would be buried in. He stood beside me at the funeral, filling in for my absent older brother and a father who did not share my sorrow. But we never talked about feelings, what it was like to walk with full knowledge into a pit of unspeakable grief.

Since then we seem unable to grasp the vocabulary of emotions. Perhaps we never had it in the first place. Tonight I was just grateful for the scotch and the companionship, the familiar rumble of Stephen's baritone as he filled me in on the progress he'd been making with the Swiss.

I didn't tell him about Cecilia Dobson until I was ready and then I barely touched on the desperate scene on the floor of Dagny's office.

"It's just an accident that I was there when she was found. We didn't say ten words to each other and now I feel like I'm going to be carrying her around with me for the rest of my life."

"You will," Stephen answered simply. "It happens to doctors and nurses. Ask anyone who routinely deals with death. They all have one that stays with them."

"The worst part is not that it happened but that no one seems to have any idea why."

"She probably overdosed on something."

"That's what the paramedics think. But when will they know?"

"They'll probably do the autopsy in the next day or so, but if it was drugs it'll take longer—a week to ten days to get the toxicology results back."

"Ten days?" I wailed, surprised at how much the thought of waiting bothered me. I wanted it all to be over, her death explained, her body buried.

"I think I'm going to have to start shopping around for another lawyer," Stephen chided. "You can't be as tough as they say you are if you let a little thing like this rattle you."

"It's easy for you to joke," I protested. "You weren't there. My arms are sore from doing CPR on somebody who was probably dead already. I can still smell her perfume in my hair. . . ." I picked up my glass and drained it in order to keep from crying.

"You're right," he said. "I wasn't there. And you didn't spend four years in medical school learning to pretend that suffering doesn't bother you."

"I don't know if she suffered," I answered, searching the depths of my glass for who knows what.

"It wasn't her I was talking about," he said. "It's you."

I GOT TO THE office later than I expected, but with less of a hangover than I deserved. Cheryl stopped me as I passed her desk.

"Don't go in there," she warned, pointing at the closed door to my office.

"Why not? What's going on?"

"Philip Cavanaugh is in there. He was already here when I got in to work this morning."

"Why isn't he in the reception room? What's he doing in my office?"

"He was making Lillian crazy, pacing back and forth and asking her every five minutes when you'd be here, so I said he could wait in your office. Between you and me," Cheryl confided, "he seems like a real prick."

"Could you bring us some coffee, please?" I asked, taking a deep breath and squaring my shoulders to face Philip Cavanaugh.

"Oh, and your mother called," she added as I prepared to open the door. "Twice."

*   *   *

PHILIP CAVANAUGH LOOKED LIKE a watered-down version of his father. I knew that he was only forty-six, but nature had already imprinted him with the crueler marks of middle age. Short and almost completely bald, he held himself very straight, as though straining for every extra inch of height. Instead of making him look taller, it merely made him seem pompous, a puffed-up little Napoleon stretching to look down on the world. When he spoke he affected a dry little cough, as if something worrisome had gotten caught in his throat and he was constantly trying to dislodge it.

"I understand you were at the plant yesterday for that unfortunate business with Cecilia Dobson," he said after a frosty exchange of introductions.

"How's Dagny holding up?" I asked, and made a mental note to call her later in the day and ask her myself.

"This whole thing has upset everybody. It's been a terrible inconvenience. I didn't get back from Dallas until late last night, but I understand the police kept the office staff late turning the place upside down and asking everybody questions."

"What were they looking for?"

"A suicide note, apparently."

"Did they find one?"

"Not that I know of."

"Were they able to locate her family?"

"I have no idea. I've instructed Dagny to turn her entire personnel file over to the police." He gave one of his dry little coughs. "As far as I'm concerned, the entire episode is closed. I won't have our office routine disrupted and I won't tolerate time wasted on gossip."

Cheryl came in with coffee in a silver carafe and cups and saucers on a tray. Philip primly accepted a cup and I gratefully poured one for myself.

"I understand that we're going to be dealing with you over this mess with Lydia," he began once Cheryl had withdrawn. "Why isn't

Daniel handling it? It would be so much simpler. He knows everyone. He's dealt with Lydia before."

I explained about Daniel's illness. But surely he could make an exception and take care of just this one case? protested Philip.

I couldn't believe that he had the audacity to make the suggestion, but refrained from saying so. Working in a large law firm, I had no shortage of experience in dealing with pompous, difficult, anal-retentive men, but Philip Cavanaugh seemed an especially extreme case. I wondered what had happened to turn him into such an uptight jerk and wondered how Dagny, who had grown up in the same family and worked in the same business, managed to seem so intelligent and straightforward.

"I understand you saw my father and my sister yesterday," he said in an aggrieved voice. I couldn't help but wonder if it was fear of being left out that had propelled him to my office. "What did you and Dagny talk about?"

"Lydia's letter," I answered, taken aback by the question. His sister's office couldn't be more than ten feet from his own. Why didn't he ask her himself? Why drag all the way downtown and waste an hour in order to ask me? "We discussed the possibility of the family buying back Lydia's shares."

"Lydia will never sell those shares," Philip announced, shaking his head in a gesture of disapproval that bordered on disgust. "This is just another case of Lydia standing up and saying 'look at me.' She wants to make us jump through hoops. She'll keep us negotiating until we're blue in the face, but I guarantee we'll never reach an agreement. Believe me, this stunt is no different from any of the others."

"What others?"

"Lydia pulls crap like this all the time. For example, last year she announced that she was going to take her job as director of community relations more seriously. More seriously, what a joke. You've been to the plant—what do we need a director of community relations for? It's just a title my father made up so that we can justify Lydia's phony salary to the IRS. But Lydia went ahead with it. She pushed our sales manager out of his office and ordered ten thousand dollars' worth of new furniture. Her first week on the job all three secretaries gave notice."

"Why?"

"They refused to work with her. Dad had to give them raises. By the end of the second week they were all calling her Princess Lydia. By the third week they were saying it to her face."

"And by the fourth week?"

"She stopped coming in. She told Dad that her doctor didn't want her near all the toxic chemicals in the plant. She was pregnant with the twins at the time."

"And was that the real reason?"

"There are no toxic chemicals in the office," snapped Philip. "She'd gotten bored, that's all. She thought it would be glamorous getting dressed up and coming to work every day. She's always envied Dagny . . . but it's all a game to her. At first she got a kick out of pretending to be the big important businesswoman, but when she got down to the nitty-gritty—the grind of getting up and going to work and actually doing a job—then she lost interest."

"Dagny seemed to think that you'd be happier with Lydia off the board."

"Happier? I'd be ecstatic. But as I said before, I think the possibility of that actually occurring is remote."

"Because you think she doesn't really want to sell?"

"Why would she want to sell? If she didn't own any shares in the company, then she wouldn't be able to use them to torture us whenever she felt like it. If you knew Lydia you'd realize how ludicrous it is to take her seriously."

I thought about my conversation with Dagny and the letter that she'd received from Lydia's investment bankers. I was getting whiplash bouncing from one family member to another's prediction of what was going to happen.

"Have any of you talked to her about this since receiving her letter?" I demanded in frustration. "If it's attention she's after, maybe that's all she wants."

"When I want to speak to Lydia about anything, you'll be the first one to know," Philip announced, with a dry cough.

"Why's that?"

"Because I have absolutely no intention of speaking to my little sister without an attorney present."

AFTER PHILIP HAD GONE I buzzed Cheryl and asked her to set up a meeting for me with Lydia Cavanaugh.

"Sure thing," she said. "Your mother's on hold for you on line two."

"I'll give you fifty dollars if you tell her I'm not here," I pleaded.

"I bet she'd give me a hundred just to put her through. Would you please stop being a baby and just pick up the phone?"

I took a deep breath and punched the button.

"Hello, Mother," I said sweetly. "Welcome home. How was your trip?"

My mother had just returned from her semiannual swing through Europe with her friend Sonny Welborn to shop the couture shows.

"The clothes were awful and the French get ruder every year. The models were all emaciated and very unattractively made up. I don't think I saw one item of clothing that one could actually wear in public. I did order some things at St. Laurent, so at least the trip wasn't a complete waste of time. But that's not why I called. I wanted to remind you of your obligations."

"Saturday night at eight o'clock," I cut in quickly. "It's been on my calendar for six weeks. Dinner for Grandma Prescott at the Whitehall Club."

"I assume you've already invited Stephen?"

"Of course," I lied, scribbling a note to have Cheryl call Cindy, his secretary, and arrange it.

"I'm glad that's all taken care of. But that's not why I called."

"Oh?"

"I wanted to let you know that we had to change the Children's Memorial Hospital committee meeting to this afternoon at four, but I was able to have it moved to our house so that it would be more convenient."

"Convenient for whom?" I demanded.

The committee had become yet another source of grievance between us. Fed up with my mother's constant harping about my lack of community-mindedness, I'd allowed her to browbeat me into working on a committee to raise money for a sorely needed new wing for Children's Memorial Hospital. Unfortunately, while the goal of the committee was admirable, our inability to successfully schedule our first meeting had proved to be something of an obstacle. Bridge games, trips to Palm Springs, golf tournaments all sprang up and had to be accommodated.

"You'll have to go ahead without me," I said. "I have a new case and there's no way that I can be in Lake Forest at four o'clock."

"But this is the only time that was clear for everyone. Surely you can rearrange your schedule." If Philip Cavanaugh hadn't descended on me unannounced, I might have been able to swing it, but now I was so far behind it was out of the question.

"Mother, you can't call me at one o'clock and expect me to shuffle things around and be able to drive out to the suburbs the same afternoon," I protested.

"I called you twice yesterday and again this morning," my mother countered archly. "Or didn't that secretary of yours bother to give you my messages? Perhaps if you'd had the courtesy to return my calls, you'd find yourself with rather more notice."

"I'll see what I can do," I replied, recognizing that once again I'd been outmaneuvered.

"Don't make us all wait for you," instructed my mother. I could hear the satisfaction in her voice long after I'd replaced the receiver.

6

"Nothing surprises me anymore," Daniel Babbage announced across the white linen of his usual table at the Chicago League Club. "I've seen marital favors withheld, board meetings that ended in fistfights, and sons who cleaned out their father's offices when the old man was out of town. But I have to tell you, Kate, a dead secretary is a first, even for me."

"How did you hear about it?" I asked, giving my dinner roll a surreptitious squeeze.

The Chicago League Club was an institution, a hundred-year-old bastion of political incorrectness whose unofficial motto had until recently been "No Democrats, no reporters, and no women." Two years ago the rules were finally changed to allow the great-granddaughter of one of the founding members and a black U.S. Circuit Court judge to become members. Unfortunately, less progress has been made in the quality of the food.

"Jack called me at home last night," replied Babbage. "He told me that you were there with Dagny when she found her."

I explained briefly how Dagny and I had discovered Cecilia Dobson's body. I felt vaguely uncomfortable talking about death in Babbage's company, but he did not seem in the least bit disconcerted. Cecilia Dobson's passing was nothing to any of us—an unsettling episode, a gruesome lunchtime anecdote, nothing more.

"So tell me, what did you think of Dagny?" he asked when I'd finished.

"I really like her. She's very impressive."

"I'm sure you realize that no matter what it says on the organizational chart, Dagny's the one who'll be running Superior Plating after Jack steps down."

"That's not what she says."

"Why do you say that?"

"Yesterday she told me that she's had an offer from Monarch Metals to head their coatings division in Boston. She says that if her father doesn't agree to buy out Lydia, she's going to take it."

Daniel's face was lit up by an enormous grin. "I told you she's as tough as her old man."

"Philip came to see me this morning."

"And?"

"I don't think he likes me."

"Don't take it personally. Philip doesn't like anybody. You impressed the hell out of Jack, though. He said that you drank bourbon with him in the middle of the day. He said it showed that you had balls."

"Just what I've always wanted."

"So what did you make of Peaches?"

"I'm not sure. I only spoke to her for a minute. But I guess I expected Jack to be married to someone closer to his own age. What do his children think of her?"

"They hate her, naturally."

"Why naturally?"

"Don't be naive, Kate. Second wives are like dynamite—an inherently explosive commodity. None of the Cavanaugh children can stand her. Philip thinks that she's a gold digger and is terrified that Jack's going to die and leave her all his money."

"Is he?"

"No. Peaches comes from a very wealthy family herself. I don't think Jack feels any pressure to provide for her after he's gone. Besides, he's obsessed with the idea of his children running the company together after he dies. I can't imagine him not leaving them at least the Superior Plating shares."

"Doesn't Philip realize that?"

"He should. It's obvious to a boob. But not to be too hard on Philip, I don't think that Jack's ever been explicit about his testamentary plans. Every couple of years Philip manages to get up the nerve to ask his father about it and Jack always tells him the same thing: 'Don't worry, I'll take care of everything.' "

"What about Dagny? Does she hate Peaches, too?"

"Not exactly. She just dismisses her as a frivolous twit—which really is not the case."

"And Eugene? What does he think of his stepmother?"

"First of all, he'd be furious to hear you call Peaches his stepmother. All the Cavanaugh children are very careful to refer to her as their father's wife. And to answer your question, Eugene in particular doesn't approve of Peaches. He and his wife are part of a very conservative, almost fundamentalist movement in the Catholic church. Eugene believes that the Bible is explicit in spelling out women's proper role in the world. Suffice it to say, Peaches doesn't exactly fit in with that."

"He and the dead secretary didn't get along, I'll tell you that," I said, describing the scene between them by the plating tanks. "In the back of my mind I guess I thought there might have been something extracurricular going on between them."

"Not likely," Babbage replied with a shake of his head. "Believe me, Eugene is as straight as they come."

"And Lydia?" I asked, steering the conversation back on track. "How does she feel about her father's wife?"

"You can imagine that Lydia isn't thrilled about having a step-mother who's three years younger than she is and twice as good-looking."

"There aren't many daughters that would be," I countered. Having not yet met Lydia, I was probably more likely to give her the benefit of the doubt.

"True. But in this case it's more complicated than that. Lydia feels very threatened by Peaches, sure, but she's also fascinated by her."

"What do you mean, fascinated?"

"Fascinated, filled with an unhealthy interest, obsessed. . . . About a month after Jack and Peaches were married, they started getting crank calls. Someone was calling in the middle of the night and then hanging up the phone. Jack was rattled, but Peaches knew exactly what to do. She'd had trouble of this nature before, you see. Back when she worked for Channel Seven she was stalked by some weirdo who'd seen her on TV and become obsessed with her. You might have heard about it. It caused quite a stir at the time and Peaches was instrumental in getting the state to pass anti-stalking legislation. So when she started getting these hang-up calls, Peaches wasted no time in calling the police. Normally these kinds of cases are a nightmare, but Jack has some pull downtown and Peaches is still considered something of a celebrity, so they were able to cut through all the bureaucratic red tape and get the calls traced. You'll never guess who was making them."

"Who?"

"Lydia."

"I bet Sunday dinners were a little awkward after that."

"You could say that."

"The whole situation just strikes me as creepy."

"I'll tell you what's creepy. Lydia's been gradually changing her appearance."

"Changing her appearance? In what way?"

"Slowly, over the course of the last year, she's been doing things—growing her hair long like Peaches, having it lightened to the same color. Peaches buys a dress and a week later Lydia shows up at a family function wearing the same one. When you meet Lydia I guarantee you'll be struck by the resemblance."

"I look forward to it," I said as Davis, Babbage's favorite waiter, arrived with our entrées. I eyed my veal cutlet suspiciously. I ventured a cautious bite—tasteless but otherwise unobjectionable.

"Peaches has actually shown a lot of backbone through all of this," continued Daniel, cutting into his steak, "but about a month ago she reached the point where even she'd had enough."

"Why? What happened?"

"Like so many family crises, the whole thing started out as what should have been a happy occasion. When Jack and Peaches got married they did it very quietly—just the family down at Tall Pines—that's their place down in Georgia. So this past February, when their first anniversary rolled around, Dagny decided to throw them a party. She invited everybody—friends, customers, Peaches's family even came in from Atlanta. There were well in excess of a hundred guests.

"Dagny is the sort of person who does everything well and that night was no exception. It should have been a wonderful evening—especially for Jack. His favorite daughter had gone out of her way to do something special for him and his beautiful wife. Despite what happened, you could tell he was really touched."

"So what happened?"

"For their anniversary Jack gave Peaches a diamond necklace that he'd given to Eleanor, his first wife, on their first anniversary. Naturally, Peaches wore it to the party."

"And when Lydia saw it she went ballistic."

"You could say that. I honestly thought there would be murder done. Lydia arrived late to the party, as usual. Arthur was out of town and I gather there was some sort of problem with the twins— with Lydia there's always something. Anyway, the party was in full swing by the time she got there and the first thing she did was go off in search of her father to give him her best wishes. I'll tell you, Kate, when she laid eyes on that necklace around her stepmother's neck, her hostility was like an electrical current running across the room."

"What did she do?"

"She made the biggest, loudest, ugliest scene I have ever witnessed, and I have witnessed some doozies. Fortunately, Dagny had the presence of mind to collar her brothers, and between the three of them they managed to get Lydia out of there before the evening was totally ruined. As it was, everyone was shaken up. Lydia's behavior was frightening. She was so completely out of control it was almost like she was having a seizure. She was literally foaming at the mouth as Philip and Eugene bundled her out the door."

"Wow."

"So now you understand why Jack thinks that Lydia's started this business about selling her shares in order to get attention."

"More like revenge, I'd say."

Daniel sighed and laid down his knife and fork, shaking his head slowly in some unshared recollection.

"None of this would have happened if Jimmy had lived," he whispered.

"Who's Jimmy?" I asked.

"Jack and Eleanor's oldest son."

"I thought Philip was the oldest. You mean there was another brother? What happened to him?"

"He died. Afterward it changed everything for the Cavanaughs." Daniel touched his napkin to his lips and then replaced it in his lap, smoothing it carefully before picking up the story.

"Jack has a plantation down in Georgia—the story is that his father won the land in a poker game, but who knows? It doesn't matter. When Superior started making a little bit of money, Jack built a house on it for Eleanor. She was a Georgia girl who missed the South, and besides, he loves to hunt. They named it Tall Pines."

"What was she like? Eleanor, I mean."

"She was a beautiful, old-fashioned woman and Jack just worshiped her. She ran the house, raised the children, gave her time to the church, and instead of complaining that he was never there, counted herself lucky to have a husband who worked hard to make a success of his business. When he came home she treated him like a king. He was obviously devastated when she died. I think he stayed drunk for an entire year."

"And Jimmy was their oldest?" I prompted.

"Yes. He had just turned thirteen when his mother died. Philip was twelve, Dagny ten, and Eugene nine. Lydia, of course, was just a few days old. A nice, big, Catholic family. Eleanor is buried down at Tall Pines. So is Jimmy."

"How old was he when he died?"

"Seventeen. It is such a shame. He was a wonderful young man. Smart, athletic, a natural leader . . ."

"How did he die?"

"He drowned." Daniel paused, his eyes clouded over by remembrance. "Jack and the children were down at Tall Pines for Christmas—they went down every year. Jimmy and Philip decided to do some hunting, so they built a blind on the edge of the big pond that sits in the middle of the property and settled down to wait for something to come by to shoot. They hadn't been there very long when they noticed a local girl walking by herself down toward the water. She caught their eye. It's private property, after all, and quite an out-of-the-way spot, but at first they didn't do anything. Truth be told, they'd probably brought a couple of six-packs along to ward off the chill, and as long as she didn't scare off the birds, they were happy to mind their own business. It wasn't until she'd walked quite a way out into the water that they realized what she was trying to do.

"Both boys dove in after her, but Jimmy, being older and a stronger swimmer, got to her first. By the time Philip reached them, both young people had gone under. The pond is very deep. It's fed by a spring; so it's almost as if there's a current. Later, of course, they found out that she'd filled her pockets with stones. Nobody knows exactly what happened—whether Jimmy got tangled up in her dress while he was trying to save her or whether in her panic she just dragged him down. Philip dove for them until he had to give up from exhaustion. Finally he dragged himself out of the water and trudged the six miles back to the house to tell his father what had happened."

"And after that, like you said, everything changed."

"Everything. For seventeen years Jack had been talking about the day when he would retire and Jimmy would take his place running the company. Philip, who to this day blames himself for not having been able to save his brother, felt he had to step up and try to fill Jimmy's shoes. The other children were crushed.

"In a motherless family, the oldest child becomes a sort of surrogate parent and they had all relied on Jimmy, especially with Jack working all the time. Eugene, especially, was just devastated. He'd worshiped his eldest brother, followed him everywhere. After Jimmy died, Eugene started acting out—running wild and getting into trouble. It took the Marine Corps to straighten him out. While I'll grant you that neither of Jack Cavanaugh's boys is perfect, both Philip and Eugene have spent their entire adult lives feeling as though they don't measure up to their father's expectations. That's not an exactly unique scenario in my experience—hard-driving, successful fathers are often disappointed by the real or imagined shortcomings of their sons. But the Cavanaugh boys are stuck in an especially insidious situation: they don't stand a chance against the ghost of their sainted brother."

"For crying out loud, Daniel," I exclaimed. "These people don't need a lawyer, they need a therapist."

Daniel gave a dry lawyer's laugh.

"I've always worried that one of these days the AMA was going to come after me for practicing psychiatry without a license. That's what makes working with family businesses different. When you get right down to it, business is always about people, but in a family business those people are all related. They share a history. They don't just work together. They eat Thanksgiving dinner together and remember that you used to wet the bed. In a family business, when you get down to the bone in any business crisis, it's almost never about business. It's about the interpersonal relationships in the family."

"Well," I said after the waiter had cleared our plates, "what I want to know is, while the family is working through their interpersonal relationships by fighting over the business, how does the business survive? I mean, when you come right down to it, it's not Jack Cavanaugh who's the client, but Superior Plating and Specialty Chemicals."

"That's right," Babbage replied. "And it's your job to safeguard the company, from Jack Cavanaugh himself, if necessary."

BACK AT THE OFFICE I phoned Dagny Cavanaugh while my work beckoned, unheeded. Since the first morning that Babbage had called me into his office, I'd felt tragedy gathering around me like a fog. Though I knew they were unrelated, Cecilia's death, Daniel's illness, even the story about what had happened to Jimmy Cavanaugh seemed to cast a sort of pall.

Dagny Cavanaugh, with no secretary to answer her phone, picked up herself after a half-dozen rings.

"I just wanted to see how things are going," I said after we'd exchanged pleasantries. "I saw your brother Philip this morning, and he said you were still pretty upset."

"It's not just me. It's everybody. The police were back again this morning. They finally managed to track down Cecilia's family. It turns out she had a son. A little boy who's four years old and lives with her mother."

"How awful. And she never talked about him?"

"She never saw him," replied Dagny, her voice trembling with indignation. "I just got off the phone with her mother. She belongs to some sort of fundamentalist Christian church. She told me that when Cecilia became pregnant the family gave her the choice of accepting Jesus as her savior or giving up all rights to the baby. I guess Cecilia refused to be saved. Now the little boy is being raised in this cult."

"So how did they take it when they found out what happened?" I asked.

"Her mother just kept on telling me over and over again that she wasn't going to pay for the funeral."

"Maybe they really can't afford it?"

"No. That's not it. I got her to give me the name of her minister. I wanted to call him and see if he would reason with her. He explained to me, as cold as ice, that in their church, when a child refuses to be saved, that child is declared dead to the family and the congregation. They buy a casket, hold a funeral, the whole thing. The Dobsons won't pay for a funeral for their daughter because in their minds they've already buried her."

*   *   *

I HATED LEAVING THE office in the middle of the afternoon to drive to my parents' house. Even before I'd picked up the Superior Plating file, I was in danger of being dragged down by the undertow of too much work. The absolute last thing I needed was to burn a couple of hours dragging myself to Lake Forest for some pointless meeting. I was so aggravated at my errand that I completely forgot that they were doing construction on the Kennedy Expressway, which gave me an extra half an hour to contemplate the sorry state of road construction and family dynamics in the city of Chicago.

By the time I arrived at my mother's door, I was twenty minutes late and in an evil mood. A maid I'd never laid eyes on answered the door, but that didn't surprise me; in domestic-employment circles, having once worked for my mother is akin to having been wounded in combat. Rocket, our ancient and arthritic black Lab, skittered across the polished marble of the foyer to greet me. He was an old, fat dog that wheezed like a freight train and hobbled like an old man. I dropped down on one knee and scratched his head.

I introduced myself to the maid, who, unimpressed, took my coat and disappeared with it. I stood beneath the graceful curve of the staircase and checked my reflection in the large gold mirror that has always hung there. Growing up in that house, I distinctly recall catching glimpses of myself in that mirror and for a fraction of a second seeing my mother's face looking back at me. But when I'd stop and really look, I would see what was actually there reflected in the glass.

My mother is a great beauty. Even closing in on sixty, she possesses the miraculous alchemy of skin and bone that is a magnet to the eye. I have her eyes, her skin, her hair, the same expression of irritated petulance when someone crosses me, but somehow when it was all put together and passed along to me, the magic got left out. Today the face I saw in the mirror was tired. My hair was working itself loose from its customary French twist. I pushed the hairpins back into place; then I walked the hallways of my childhood home to find my mother.

CHAPTER

7

I followed the sound of voices into the music room, so named because Vladimir Horowitz had once played there for Richard Nixon and his wife, Pat. I vaguely remember meeting them—a dark little man who I told my nanny looked like a monkey and his sour-faced wife, so sad and thin. The room, like all of the places in my mother's house, was beautiful. The walls were covered in yellow silk the color of dull gold and the cabbage-rose chintz of the sofas was offset by the blue-and-white-striped damask of the side chairs. There was an antique Steinway baby grand piano at one end of the room, and beyond that, French doors that opened out onto the lawn, rolling out into a bluff that dropped precipitously at the edge of Lake Michigan.

We had moved into this house from an apartment downtown when I was five years old. My older brother, Teddy, was nine. Up until then our building on Lake Shore Drive had been my entire world. Gladys, the elevator operator, would take me on rides, and Winston, the doorman, would slip me lemon drops and tell me stories about growing up the eleventh child of an Arkansas sharecropper.

The move to Lake Forest seemed to me an exile to the end of the earth, and all the years I lived there it never really felt like home. When I was twelve my little sister, Beth, was born—a bonus baby, as Daniel had called Lydia. After that a steady stream of mademoiselles entered our life, sweet French girls who came to nanny in America in order to improve their English, and left once they were fluent enough to give notice to my mother.

And still the house held memories that would not pass. My brother Teddy killed himself when he was fifteen. He hanged himself in the garage on a Saturday night so that he could be sure, at least once, of commanding my parents' attention when they rolled in drunk after a party. And it was in this very room that my mother and I had the most vitriolic of all our arguments. It was an hour before my wedding and all the regular furniture had been taken away, save the piano, and replaced with tables for the reception. They were covered in white linen, decorated with white roses, and set with antique silver and Spode. I'd fled there from my mother, trailing twenty feet of satin and tulle, after the stress of the day had led her to pick fights with the caterer, the minister, the photographer, and finally with me. In front of a handful of terrified waiters, Mother accused me of deliberately marrying into a family of overweight Poles who spoke no English for the express purpose of humiliating her in front of her friends. When I ventured to protest, she grabbed a fistful of silverware from a nearby table and threw it, grazing the bodice of my dress with a butter knife, so that a half-dozen pearls were cut loose from their moorings and clattered noisily to the floor.

But today the music room was free of ghosts and filled with people—more than a dozen, all women. They were all dressed like the businesswomen you see in the movies, their daring little suits much more fashionable than anything I could wear without comment to work. Their hand-sewn Italian pumps showed no signs of having climbed in and out of taxicabs. I was secretly amused.

My mother made a great show of happiness at my arrival in order to make me feel my tardiness all the more. She saved her look of disappointment at my dowdy work clothes for when none of her friends could see her face. I knew that I had met all of the committee members on countless other occasions but found that except for Sonny Welborn, I could recall none of their names. I always had that problem with my mother's friends. Their elegant clothes, their expensively understated jewelry, their perfect hair all lent them a homogeneous quality in my mind. Kissing the air next to their powdered cheeks, I made the circuit of the room. Then, taking a seat, I waited expectantly for the meeting to begin.

It rapidly became clear that the business of the Children's Hospital Building Committee would be conducted on Lake Forest rather than Chicago time. Sonny Welborn gave a report, designer by designer, on the clothes she and my mother had seen on the runways of Paris. Two uniformed maids appeared to serve tea and sandwiches. Someone else launched into a bitter complaint about the number of foreigners who were buying houses in Palm Beach.

When, after repeated pleas on my part about moving things along, we finally got down to business, I was horrified to learn that everyone in the room felt an overwhelming need to restate the obvious. After an hour I felt like I'd been nailed to my chair for an eternity. I was seized by a distinctly unladylike desire to scream.

When one of the maids came to tell me that I had a phone call from the office, I made my excuses gratefully and realized that truly, any business crisis was better than this. I ducked into the library and picked up the phone. It was Cheryl.

"I thought you might need rescuing," she announced.

"Bless you," I replied fervently.

"Besides, I had a question."

"What?"

"Does Daniel Babbage like you very much?"

"What do you mean?"

"I mean, did you ever do something terrible to him? You know, something for which he might want to exact revenge?"

"Not that I know of. Why?"

"I just got off the phone with Jack Cavanaugh. What a jerk. I can't imagine why Babbage would dump him on you unless he was trying to punish you for something."

"What did Cavanaugh want?"

"He wanted to talk to you. *Now!* When I told him that you were out of the office and unavailable, he threw a blue fit and started screaming at me. I hate guys who do that. The asshole would never raise his voice to you, his attorney. But I'm just a secretary, so he thinks it's okay to treat me like dirt."

"Does he want me to call him back?"

"No. You don't have to. He didn't really need to talk to you in the first place. It turns out he just wanted to set up a meeting between you and his daughter Lydia. I'd already set it up for nine o'clock tomorrow morning, just like you asked."

"Is he going to be there?"

"I don't know. He said he'd fax you instructions. I've got to leave for class in about half an hour, so I'll just put them on your desk."

"Anything else?"

"Anything else? There are so many elses I wouldn't even know where to start. I'm running out of excuses. People are starting to notice how behind you're getting."

My stomach churned.

"I'll be leaving here in ten minutes," I said, looking at my watch. "Have Daniel's secretary bring me the three most recent binders in the Superior Plating file and leave them on my desk—also all of their incorporation documents. I'm planning on working until midnight so that I can get caught up on some of this stuff."

"No you're not. You're meeting Stephen for dinner at L'Auberge at seven o'clock."

"Tell me you're making this up," I said. I had a sick feeling in the pit of my stomach. "I could have sworn that dinner with Stephen was Tuesday night."

"Today is Tuesday."

"Shit. You'll have to call him and tell him I can't make it."

"Last week when you told me to put this on your calendar, you made me swear a blood oath that I wouldn't let you cancel. Those Swiss guys flew in especially for this."

"You're right. I have to go."

"I guess it's safe to assume that you forgot to bring clothes to change into. L'Auberge is very dressy and the Swiss are very formal."

I swore.

"I guess you'll just have to borrow something of your mother's," said Cheryl. There was no mistaking the amusement in her voice.

I WAS STANDING IN my mother's dressing room in my underwear. Of the two of us, she was the one who was having a good time.

"I can't believe you wear that cheap-looking brassiere," she lectured. "Wherever did you get it? Victoria's Secret?"

"It's beige, for God's sake, Mother," I protested. "How can you look cheap in beige underwear?"

"I didn't mean that kind of cheap. I mean that it's of poor quality. I don't know what it's made out of, but it's probably some sort of synthetic. I believe they make it out of old panty hose. I don't know how you expect your clothes to fit correctly when you don't have the proper foundation garments."

I looked at her hard to see if I could detect even a hint of self-mockery, but for my mother the business of getting dressed was deadly serious. She turned to reach for a bare slip of a fuchsia cocktail dress with spaghetti straps.

"Where's the rest of it?" I demanded. "I can't wear that to a business dinner with a bunch of pharmaceutical executives."

"Tonight, for once, you're going to wear what I tell you to wear," declared my mother, her eyes flashing with pleasure. "And after we've picked a dress, I'm doing something about your hair!"

A CAT ON HOT bricks is nothing compared to what I felt like by the time my mother had finished her ministrations with the hot rollers and her makeup bag. When at last she had declared herself satisfied, I practically flew out of the house, desperate to be free of her and anxious to get to the restaurant on time. The Swiss may be formal, but they are punctual as well.

From the minute the parking attendant swung open the door of my car I knew that something strange was going on. The doorman practically clicked his heels as he greeted me. The maître d' sprang to my side and gallantly swept my mother's coat from my shoulders—a full-length Russian sable that she'd pressed upon me at the last moment. As he escorted me to the table where Stephen and the two executives from Gordimer A.G. were waiting, heads turned. But I hadn't completely realized the full extent of what Mother had done until I saw Stephen rising to his feet, a look of undisguised wonder in his eyes.

In Stephen's face I saw what, in my hurry, I hadn't noticed in the mirror of my mother's dressing table. In the slinky dress and skyscraper heels, with Mother's dark red lipstick and my hair now all soft curls cascading in torrents over my bare shoulders—I looked sexy. It was a completely new experience for me.

Dinner was very odd. We were meeting to discuss financing options for the proposed joint venture between Azor and Gordimer. But while I outlined the international tax implications for various capitalization structures the two businessmen from Switzerland took turns looking down my dress.

Men, I reflected, are really very simple, obvious creatures.

AFTER STEPHEN HAD HANDED the gentlemen from Gordimer into their taxi, we stood beneath the striped awning of the restaurant and waited for our cars to be brought around.

"I don't have to tell you that the big pharmaceutical houses have seen their profits go soft in the last couple of years," I advised him. "Gordimer's no exception. They've all been gobbling up small, research-oriented companies with good product in their pipeline. Companies like Azor. I think you should keep that firmly in mind while you're deciding whether or not to jump into bed with them."

"I love your hair like this," Stephen said, marveling. "Why don't you follow me home for a drink?"

"Have you been listening to what I've been saying?" I demanded.

"You told me I should be careful before I jump into bed. Would you rather we dropped your car at your office?"

"I have to go back to the office and work. I have a meeting with Lydia Cavanaugh tomorrow morning. I have to review the file."

Stephen bent his head and kissed my neck. I was flabbergasted. I had never known Stephen to be affectionate in public.

"You can pick up the file when we drop the car. I'll wake you up early—when I get up. That way you'll be able to read the file when you're fresh."

"I am never fresh in the morning."

"Please?" Stephen whispered, sliding his hand down my spine to the small of my back.

Out of the corner of my eye I noticed one of the red-jacketed parking attendants watching us with great attention. He was licking his lips.

"Okay, okay," I relented.

The whole way back to my office I kept shaking my head. I parked my car in the empty garage. Stephen pulled in beside me. Fred, the night security guard, did a double take while I signed in. In the elevator, to my utter astonishment, Stephen stood behind me and played with my hair.

The reception room was dark, softly lit by a few brass lamps that the janitorial staff allowed to burn all night. I checked the alcove where we had pigeonholes for messages and picked up mine. Out of habit, I flipped the switch that illuminated my name on the night call-board. All the other names were dark.

Stephen trailed me into my office, whistling a complicated passage from Bach. I didn't turn on the overhead light. I didn't want to see all the files piled up and waiting for me in the morning. Instead, I switched on the small reading light on my desk. I slipped off the heavy sable of my mother's coat, feeling it rub agreeably against my bare skin. I laid it carefully over the end of the couch. Stephen shifted some files to make room for himself next to it. Then he stretched his long legs out in front of him and watched me from the darkest corner of the room.

Cheryl had left the files I'd asked for on my chair. I leaned over carefully in the tight dress, throwing the unfamiliar tangle of my hair over my shoulder. The fax from Jack Cavanaugh was on top. I scanned it quickly. While he acknowledged that Lydia was attending our meeting in the hopes of beginning negotiations for the sale of her shares, he announced that no other family members would attend in order that I might have a better chance of gaining his daughter's confidence and dissuading her from selling. I groaned.

I flipped through the folders that Cheryl had pulled for me, checking to make sure that I had everything I would need in the morning. As I clipped Jack's fax onto one of the files, I felt Stephen's eyes on me like a cat watching a careless bird.

"Is that all you need?" he asked softly. I was surprised, when I turned, to find him standing over me.

He took my hands and pulled me to him in one long, smooth motion. Sometimes, when he is close, the sheer size of him overwhelms me. I am tall enough that I spend my days looking most men in the eye. With Stephen, even when I stand on tiptoe he must bend himself to me.

As I heard the quiet growl of the zipper of my dress being lowered inch by inch, I cast a cautious glance toward the door. The hallway was dark. We were alone in the churchlike confines of Callahan Ross and Stephen had made a bed for us of Russian sable on my office floor.

I DID NOT EXPECT Lydia to come to our nine o'clock meeting alone and she did not disappoint me. A phalanx of lawyers preceded her into the conference room. Her husband was at her side.

Arthur Wallace was a small man, slim and dark, with a manicured black beard and the narrow waist and slim hips of a dancer. It was easy to see why Jack Cavanaugh must have hated him on sight. My own impression was that he was an oily little man, obviously on the make, whose birdlike eyes seemed to display an almost infinite capacity for calculation.

The resemblance between Lydia and Peaches was startling. There was the same blond hair, swept straight back from the face, the same carefully applied makeup, the same kind of expensive designer suit I was confident that Peaches would have chosen for the occasion. But while Jack's wife radiated warmth and telegenic charm, unhappiness was telegraphed by Lydia's every gesture. Her face was set in a discontented frown calcified by habit.

As I introduced myself her eyes darted around the room, as if looking for someone else, and the hand she gave to be shaken was stiff with rings.

"Where's Babbage?" she demanded as she claimed the seat at the head of the table. "I told Daddy specifically that I wanted to meet with the company's head lawyer and not be pushed off on some young flunky. No offense."

"Why ever would I be offended at being called a flunky?" I inquired coldly. For years people had been bowing and scraping before Lydia, giving her exactly what she wanted. So far it didn't seem to be doing anybody any good. I decided on a different approach. "The first time I went to court after I graduated from law school, the judge looked right at me and asked where the lawyer was. Women lawyers learn early not to take offense. To answer your question, Daniel Babbage is dying of cancer. I am replacing him as corporate counsel."

Lydia looked at me and chewed her gum. If I'd offended her, she didn't show it, and if I had, I didn't care. I'd been up since five o'clock in the morning reading the Superior Plating file and I was in no mood to take shit from anybody, especially anybody named Cavanaugh.

"Well, he couldn't have picked a worse time to be sick," she said finally. "It would have been easier to deal with someone who knows our family."

"Your family is wondering why you've chosen to sell your shares," I cut in.

"It's a purely business decision," replied Lydia, her tone of voice implying the exact opposite.

"I see." My internal bullshit meter was already edging toward the red zone. "Would you mind being more specific? What exactly are your concerns with the way in which the company is being managed?"

"If you can call what's going on at Superior Plating management." Lydia sniffed. From the looks she was getting from her lawyers I could tell that she'd been coached not to get into a discussion of her motives. But Lydia, I guessed, had never been one to take direction. Besides, it was obvious that she couldn't resist an audience.

"My father runs the company like he runs the family. It's all just an extension of his own ego. He reaches into the company's coffers like he's putting his hand into his own pocket. Who do you think pays for his plane? His horses? His houses? Now that he's married that bimbo, he's been looting the company to keep her in style. Who do you think's paying for all those shopping trips to New York? It's disgusting."

"Have you discussed this with the other board members?"

"What do you mean?"

"Have you talked this over with your brothers and sister?"

"Why? I know exactly what they'll say. This family has always been divided. There's an inside group and an outside group. Philip and Dagny are the insiders because they go to the office every day and suck up to my dad. Eugene and I are left out in the cold. The three of them pay themselves whatever they feel like. Whatever's left over they pay out in dividends like throwing scraps to a dog. Well, I for one am fed up."

"I've read through the minutes of the board meetings for the last five years," I reported. "I saw no mention of you ever having raised any of these concerns. I'm interested in why you seem to have suddenly developed such strong feelings about the manner in which the company has been run."

"That's immaterial," interjected one of Lydia's lawyers, a man named Cliff Schaeffer, who was married to a woman I went to law school with. "We came here to discuss the terms of a possible buyout—"

"I told you. It would be pointless to even try and discuss it with Daddy on the board," Lydia continued, completely ignoring him. "He just pats me on the head and tells me to go out and play. Daddy's behavior is all very preconscious. He has difficulty dealing with the conflict between his image of me as an idealized child and the reality of my being a grown woman capable of making decisions on her own. He's blocked because he doesn't want to face his own fears about aging and declining sexual potency. It's obvious from his decision to marry Peaches. If he's not wiling to listen to his inner child, it's futile to expect that he'll be able to listen to his actual child."

"You still haven't told me why you want to sell your shares," I prodded.

"I have a new therapist who has been helping me fight back against my father's domination for the first time in my life. Finally I'm beginning to understand the systematic financial oppression that men like my father perpetrate. She's made me realize the importance of severing the connection between financial and emotional control so that I can deal with each of them separately."

I stifled a giggle, but Lydia didn't seem to notice. She just droned on about her inner child in a tone of great gravity. I looked at the other people in the room. Arthur Wallace watched his wife with the same rapt attention made famous by Nancy Reagan whenever she appeared at her husband's side. In the meantime Lydia's attorneys shifted restlessly in their seats.

As she spewed out a steady stream of psychobabble about how her shares in Superior Plating represented the bonds of emotional slavery to her father, I began to make a mental list of other attorneys at the firm whom I might be able to convince to take on the company's file. Any affection I might feel for Daniel Babbage aside, it should have been clear to everyone in that room that Lydia Cavanaugh Wallace was a very disturbed woman. This was clearly turning into the kind of case I'd gone into corporate work specifically to avoid—messy, personal, and offering no satisfactory conclusions.

I looked across the conference table at Lydia, still engrossed in her rambling monologue about her inner self. Cecilia Dobson's death was an omen, I decided. One that I was not about to ignore.

CHAPTER

8

Once Lydia had run through her reasons for feeling oppressed, she signaled the end of the meeting and swept out of the room. Cliff Schaeffer, her lead lawyer, hung back for a quiet word with me. Besides having been at school with his wife, I'd been across the table from him on a couple of deals. In general I'd found him a snarling pit bull of an advocate, not to mention something of a jerk.

"Since when did you start representing mental cases?" I asked with more truth than tact.

"The shares belong to her," he replied. "She has the right to sell them if she wants."

"I'm not disputing that. I'm just curious about how you bill her— is it only for a forty-five-minute hour?"

"What's your point?"

"My point is, how can you know whether she's even really going to sell? She's sat on the board of Superior Plating for the last seven years. She's drawn a salary from them for the last fourteen and not once has she voiced a single concern about her shares or how the company is being run. Don't you think that if she's capable of making a snap decision to sell her shares, she's just as likely to change her mind and decide to keep them? I understand that you're going to get paid either way, but how can you expect me to negotiate in good faith with a nutcase?"

"*I'm* not a nutcase," Lydia's attorney protested, "and neither is Mark Hoffenberg and the bankers at First Chicago. Now that I think of it, Lydia's husband Arthur's no slouch either. I'll grant you that my client is a little . . . well, shall we say, emotional. But that doesn't mean she's not capable of making a good business decision."

"You mean, with you pushing and Hoffenberg pulling?"

"Let me give you a little bit of advice, Kate. If you don't want to see a big chunk of your client's stock being sold to an outsider, I'd get busy and come back with a respectable offer—and pronto."

ONCE I MAKE UP my mind about something, I stick to it, and since I had definitely decided to end my brief tenure as counsel for Superior Plating and Specialty Chemicals I wasted no time in going to Daniel Babbage's office to tell him of my decision. I didn't intend to go into my feelings about the Cavanaughs but would merely explain that my caseload was too heavy for me to give the file the attention and the hours that it was obviously going to require. I wanted, in all fairness, to tell him immediately, before events moved ahead and I billed any more hours to the file.

But when I arrived at Daniel's office, I found it empty. I went in search of Madeline, his secretary, and found her hunched over her desk weeping over a stack of unopened mail. Babbage, she explained in a halting whisper, had been rushed to the emergency room in the middle of the night. She wrote down the number of his room at Billings Hospital and I trudged back to my office filled with a sense of resignation mingled with dread. For some reason, instead of making it easier, news of Daniel's illness made bowing out seem cowardly and impossible. From that point on there was no turning back.

DAGNY CAVANAUGH CAME TO the door of her lovingly restored brownstone dressed in a pair of jeans and a sweatshirt. She looked about sixteen. After learning of Daniel's relapse, I'd called her and asked for an urgent meeting and she'd agreed to see me that evening provided that I'd be willing to come to her house. She had, she explained, another commitment, but she thought there would still be time for us to talk. Besides, she'd added cryptically, there was a good chance I'd find it interesting.

"Welcome to the Mount McKinley Expedition planning meeting," she said with a smile as she swung the heavy oak door wide. From somewhere inside the house I heard the faint tinkle of laughter. "We're just finishing up and then we'll have dinner. I hope you haven't eaten yet. Here, let me take your coat. Why don't you take your shoes off, too? We're very casual in this house."

"I didn't realize that you live right across the street from your father," I exclaimed, handing her my coat.

"Oh, it's even worse than that." Dagny laughed. "It's hard to see in the dark, but Philip and his wife, Sally, live in the brick house next door to Dad and Lydia lives right across the street. Eugene's house is next to Dad's on the other side. My grandfather may not have known how to run a company, but he knew a bargain when he saw one. He bought all the property at the end of the Depression for pennies on the dollar."

"When Daniel told me that you were a close-knit family he wasn't kidding."

"After today it's beginning to feel like a variation on a Sicilian knife fight. You know, where they take two guys who want to kill each other, tie them together by their left hands, and give them each a very long dagger for their right. We're having some problems with one of our chrome plating lines. I spent the whole afternoon locked in the conference room with my father and brothers. Right now we're very long on blame and very short on solutions. Anyway, enough about that. Come on in and meet the gang and I'll get you a drink."

The house was very pretty, with floors of polished oak and beautiful woodwork that had been meticulously stripped and refinished. There was a gorgeous stained glass window that I glimpsed at the top of the stairs.

"When I said Mount McKinley Expedition I wasn't kidding," Dagny declared as we came to the end of a long hall. "I don't know how I got talked into taking a bunch of juvenile delinquents on a climbing trip this summer, but that's what I'm going to do—provided the three of them can figure out how to read a topographical map between now and then."

In the large, open kitchen three teenagers pored over a set of maps that had been unfurled on a central island. An oval rack hung with gleaming copper pots was suspended above them.

"Meet the next generation of Superior Plating and Specialty Chemicals," Dagny announced jovially.

"Oh please, Mom," complained a pretty girl of sixteen.

"Kate Millholland, this is my daughter, Claire Gilchrist. I'd also like you to meet my niece, Mary Beth Cavanaugh—she's the oldest of my brother Eugene's brood. And this is Peter McCallister, my sister Lydia's son."

I pronounced myself happy to meet them all. Claire and Mary Beth seemed to be about the same age, though Dagny's daughter was obviously the livelier of the two. Peter was a good-looking, but sullen young man of fifteen.

"We're planning a technical ascent of Mount McKinley as soon as school's over," Claire explained while her mother went over to the stove to give something a stir. "We've been planning it for months.

We even did some technical climbing in Arizona over Christmas break and we didn't do too badly."

"If you don't count the crevasse where Peter slipped, got tangled in the rope, and practically hanged himself," teased Mary Beth, beginning to roll up the maps.

"If you had been keeping your mind on the belay and not drooling over that French climber that passed us . . ." whined Peter, sharply reminding me of Lydia.

"Come on, guys," Dagny admonished. "We're a team, remember? We all make mistakes. Remember all the equipment we had to leave on top of Flatiron because you insisted that you'd figured out a way down, Mary Beth? Or how about the time I made you all get cleaned up in that lake when we were in Quantico and it turned out that the water was full of leeches?"

The Mount McKinley Expedition shuddered in unison at the recollection.

"That smells very good," I said. "Is there anything I can do to help?"

"No. It's all done. It's my home-cured corned beef. I make it from my grandmother's recipe. I told you, I'm having my dad and Peaches for dinner tomorrow night, so I'm using you guys as guinea pigs. Kate, why don't you just go ahead and have a seat over there?"

I did as I was bidden, taking my place with the rest of them at a round table of well-worn oak.

"If you'll just hand me your plates, I'll serve everyone. This platter is too heavy to pass," said Dagny.

"Aren't we going to say grace, Aunt Dagny?" Mary Beth inquired reproachfully. I remembered what Babbage had said about Eugene and his wife being deeply religious.

"Give me a break!" groaned Peter.

"Why don't you say the blessing, Mary Beth," Dagny replied equably.

"In the name of the Father, the Son, and the Holy Ghost," she said as Dagny and Claire bowed their heads and crossed themselves. Peter shot an angry look at Mary Beth, truculently bent his head, and began a minute examination of his fingernails.

"Bless us, O Lord for these, thy gifts, which we are about to receive from thy bounty through Christ the Lord," intoned Mary Beth. "And please speed the soul of Cecilia Dobson to thy safekeeping. Amen."

"Who the hell is Cecilia Datsun?" Peter demanded, reaching for the breadbasket.

"It's Dobson, you dope," Claire replied. "A Datsun's a car. For your information Cecilia Dobson was Mother's secretary—the one who dropped dead at the office."

"My dad said she died of a drug overdose," reported Mary Beth in an awed whisper.

"That's not the worst part," Claire chimed in. "Her family won't even pay for her funeral. Can you imagine?"

"So what's going to happen to her?" Mary Beth asked.

"She is going to have a very nice funeral tomorrow afternoon at four o'clock at St. Bernadette's Cemetery," Dagny informed her. "We've even persuaded your grandfather to close the office early so that the people who worked with her can attend." She handed me a plate of corned beef and cabbage. "I was wondering whether you might want to come, Kate."

"Of course," I said, my good manners getting the better of me.

"Is the company paying for it?" Peter demanded unpleasantly.

"No. I'm paying for it myself, not that it's anybody's business," Dagny replied tersely. I don't think she was annoyed with her nephew. It was just that there was something in the way that Peter had asked the question that once again brought his mother very sharply to mind.

*   *   *

"THEY SEEM LIKE NICE kids," I said, once we'd taken our coffee cups into the living room. A fire burned merrily behind the grate, the flames reflected in the polished surface of the baby grand piano. On the low table in front of us was a spray of dendrobium orchids in a crystal vase and a plate of chocolates. I helped myself.

"These are wonderful," I said, taking a bite.

"They're from Belgium. I have a climbing friend who sends them to me."

"I can't believe you're really taking your nieces and nephew up Mount McKinley."

"Oh, I'm not worried about the kids. In some ways they're better technical climbers than I am. They're certainly in better shape. Of course, the sport's changed so much since I was their age. Now they all go to the climbing gym and work out on the wall—they feel like they can climb anything. I'm just going along to slow them down."

"Claire seems like a neat kid. She looks like you."

"Do you really think so? I always imagine she looks like her dad."

"Where does he live?"

"We're not divorced. He died in a climbing accident before Claire was born."

"I'm surprised you still climb."

"I didn't for a long time. When Claire was little I was afraid. But when she got older she got interested. She's a lot like Jeremy, her dad, that way. I guess from time to time everybody has got to feed the rat."

"What's feeding the rat?"

"It's a climbing expression. The rat is that voice inside your head that whispers, 'Go for it. Take the risk.' Claire hears the rat loud and clear, just like her dad. You know, there were times when we were climbing in Arizona this winter, when I'd look up the rope at her and swear I was seeing Jeremy. There's something about their climbing styles that's very similar."

"It must be nice to be able to remember him that way," I said, feeling jealous.

"Daniel told me that you'd lost your husband to cancer. Was it long ago?"

"Four years this past November. We weren't married very long."

"Any kids?"

"No. There wasn't any time. He got sick right after we were married. You know, when he was first diagnosed I knew that it would be terrible—his illness, his death. In some ways these last years have been worse. At least during the crisis you have the crisis to deal with. I was completely unprepared for . . . the emptiness that followed."

"I understand completely. It was the same way after Jeremy died. A numbness sets in. I was five months pregnant when he died and everyone kept talking to me about the baby—telling me that that's what I had to live for. They were right, of course. But at the time the baby was still an abstraction. Only my loss was real. I remember I used to go to the mailbox and there'd be mail for him—come-ons, solicitations, just junk. I'd stand there with grocery circulars in my hands and cry."

"I still wear Russell's old shirts sometimes when I'm just bumming around at home. I know it's crazy, but they're all that's left."

"Do you still keep in touch with his family?"

"His mother and I go to the cemetery together every year. She's this old Polish lady who doesn't speak any English, but we go and lay flowers on his grave and cry together. I know it doesn't do either of us any good, but we can't stop going. Everybody tells me that I have to move on. . . ."

"You already are, you know. You don't know it but you are. You take one breath and then another. You get up and you go to work. You eat and you sleep and you do what you have to do. It's not the life you planned, but it's a life. And in a while you're going to look back and realize that it's not so bad. It just takes time."

"And you never married again?" I asked.

"No."

"Ever tempted?"

"Not really. Well, maybe once—the Belgian who sends me the chocolates. We still climb together once or twice a year."

"But that's it?"

"I've gotten used to doing things my way, making my own decisions, having my freedom. I have my work, my house, my daughter. . . . I have enough family for four lifetimes. I couldn't really see how I was going to be able to make a relationship work with a man who lives four thousand miles away in another country. In the end it turned out to be not as important as I thought."

"And are you happy?"

Dagny thought a minute before answering.

"Yes," she said finally. "I am happy. And who's to say what life would have been like with Jeremy? For all I know he might have turned out to be a womanizer or a drunk. Maybe I'd have come to resent having a globe-trotting rock climber for a husband once I had a house full of kids. That's the problem with being widowed young. You mourn not just the man, but the ideal of the life you were going to share together. You never had a chance to find out if your Polish mother-in-law would have driven you crazy or if you and your husband would have fought like cats and dogs. In the beginning everything is perfect. You look at your life and it seems complete . . . and then in an instant, it all gets taken away."

9

The fire had died down. The bottle of wine and the plate of chocolates were empty. Mary Beth and Peter had been gotten home safely and Dagny's daughter, Claire, had long since gone up to bed. Outside, it had started to snow.

"What can I tell you about my family?" Dagny sighed. "They're my family and I love them. But that doesn't make me stupid. I think I can see them for what they are. My father is a stubborn son of a bitch who has been getting his way for so long that he's come to believe that if he wants something to happen, it will. And you've got to hand it to him. The number of things he's accomplished and overcome just by sheer force of will is staggering—his alcoholic father, a fire that leveled the plant the first year he turned a profit, an all-out war with the Teamsters—I'll never forget it. I was still a teenager. They blew up Dad's favorite Cadillac in front of our house but he still wouldn't give in. In all those years there's only one thing that's ever defeated him."

"What's that?"

"My brother Jimmy's death. Did Daniel tell you we had an older brother? He died when I was thirteen."

"Daniel told me about what happened."

"Losing Jimmy is the one thing that Dad can't change or fix, and every time he looks at my brother Philip you can see the disappointment in his face."

"How sad for Philip."

"Yes. He's spent his whole life being the good son who's never been good enough. I'm the first one to admit that Philip is not an easy man to get along with. He's petty and humorless and has a mean streak like the stripe down a skunk's back. But I don't think there's been a day since the accident that Philip hasn't wondered if he'd just been able to swim a little faster, if he'd just been a little stronger, tried a little harder, Jimmy would still be alive. The irony of it is that of all of us, Philip and my dad are the most alike. But Philip's been in Dad's shadow for so long it's robbed him of his self-confidence. After more than twenty years of working together Philip is totally unable to communicate with Dad. He's actually very accomplished. Did you know he has degrees in chemistry and mechanical engineering?"

"I had no idea."

"He's done incredible things with our specialty chemicals division over the last ten years. It's been his baby. Last year specialty chemicals accounted for more than twenty percent of revenues."

"That should make your father happy."

"You'd think so, wouldn't you? But it doesn't. It makes him feel threatened. Plating is what he knows, and dammit, what's good enough for him should be good enough for his son. It doesn't help that Philip's biggest successes have been new compounds that have nothing to do with plating—a solvent for industrial cleaning, a special lubricant for pumping equipment, and a new surfacting agent for a large specialty market." She sighed. "I know it doesn't make any sense, but nobody ever said that families are logical."

"How does Eugene fit into all of this?"

"Even though Dad feels that neither of his surviving sons measures up to Jimmy, he's always been very protective of Eugene."

I thought about the ramrod of a man with the snake tattoo on his wrist. He hardly seemed in need of anyone's protection, so I asked Dagny to explain.

"It all goes back to when we were children. Eugene was nine when Mother died—she developed a blood clot after Lydia was born. One day she was fine, proudly showing off the new baby. The next day she was dead. Of all of us, Eugene was the most affected. As soon as she died he stopped speaking, literally—not one word came out of his mouth.

"Dad took him to all kinds of doctors. They all agreed it was the shock—now they even have a name for it, post-traumatic stress syndrome—but none of them knew how to help him. Doctors, psychiatrists, priests, they all said he would get better eventually, but a year after Mother died, Eugene still hadn't said a single word.

"It was a terrible time in the family. Dad was spending all of his time at the plant, and when he wasn't working he was drinking. We had one housekeeper after another—nobody could handle five kids including one who wouldn't speak but woke shrieking from nightmares four or five times a night."

"So what happened? How did Eugene finally get better?"

"It was Jimmy who did it," recalled Dagny. "He decided that the psychiatrists were all wrong. They were saying that Eugene wouldn't talk because he was so sad about Mother dying, but Jimmy decided that it wasn't grief that had struck his little brother mute, it was fear. Confronted with the realization that someone you love can be taken away from you at any moment, Eugene was literally scared speechless."

"So what did Jimmy do about it?"

"He never left Eugene alone, not for one single minute. It was summertime and we were all out of school. Jimmy stuck to Eugene like glue. They ate together, slept together, went to the bathroom together. By the time August rolled around, nobody could shut Eugene up."

"What an amazing story."

"Yes. But it just made it worse when Jimmy died. Naturally Eugene worshiped him. He followed his big brother around like a dog. We used to joke that Jimmy had a shadow. . . . After Jimmy died, it was like something broke loose inside of Eugene. He started to get into trouble. He was thrown out of four different schools in two years, including some military school in Virginia where they specialize in straightening out the incorrigible. I know that on more than one occasion he got into trouble with the police. Dad'll never talk about it, and of course Eugene leads such an exemplary life now, what would be the point?"

"So what straightened Eugene out?"

"Believe it or not, it took a judge. He gave Eugene an ultimatum—enlist in the military or go to jail. Eugene signed up with the marines. The structure and discipline of military life agreed with him. While he was in the service he met Vy—her dad's an artillery instructor so she was living on the base. Vy's very religious and she got Eugene involved in the church. Mother was also a very devout Catholic, so it's not surprising that one of us would have inherited her deep spirituality. But I guarantee you that there were quite a few years there when no one would have guessed that it would be Eugene.

"It turns out that Eugene learned a lot about managing people in the marines. I can't see Philip going to work on the plant floor every day and supervising a bunch of high-school dropouts, half of whom don't speak English. But Eugene is good at it. He's tough, but fair. The workers love him. We've cut turnover in half since he took over as plant manager."

"How do Philip and Eugene get along?"

"They're so different, which makes it hard. Philip looks down his nose at Eugene because he's not educated. Eugene, on the other hand, has a kind of chip on his shoulder from being a marine. I mean, Philip's been to graduate school, but Eugene's parachuted out of an airplane at night. Philip thinks Eugene's coarse. Eugene thinks Philip is weak. It'll never change."

"So what does all this mean if we manage to get your father to agree to buy Lydia's shares? Do you think we can at least count on Philip and Eugene to present a united front, to go along and not try to change his mind?"

"I think so. What you have to understand is, the biggest obstacle to a buyback is not going to be my brothers. It's going to be my father. It's like the whole fight about giving Lydia a seat on the board. Did Daniel tell you about it? . . . No?

"Well, seven years ago Lydia moved back to Chicago from California. Her marriage to her second husband, Rick, was breaking up—he was a plastic surgeon at Stanford; take a look at her nose sometime—she's had her breasts done, too. She'd spent three years in California and she'd had the total California experience: flotation tanks, meditation training, religious reawakening by walking on hot coals, Tibetan gurus, bending spoons, channeling, crystals. . . . Lydia did it all—anyway, her marriage was over and she was completely adrift, so Dad told her she had to come home."

"Did she want to?"

"Who knows? My little sister is a life member in the analyst-of-the-month club. She hasn't the first idea what she wants, but Dad told her he'd cut off her checks from the company if she didn't come back to Chicago, so she did. Dad had hatched this plan of putting her on the board and getting her more actively involved in the company.

"Naturally, the rest of us were all against it. I remember telling him, 'Lydia has failed at her life and made a mess of her two marriages. Now you are trying to wave a magic wand and make it all right. It's fine to want to help her, but don't use the company to show her your love. The company is what *you* love. She loves you. Talk to her, tell her you're there for her, show her you love her that way—not by putting her in a business situation she knows nothing about.' "

"What did your father say?"

"He said, 'I want Lydia on the board. I want Lydia working for the company.' He told me that he wanted to do something to help Lydia mend her life since she felt that so much of what was wrong was his fault."

"How was it his fault?"

"It wasn't his fault!" Dagny insisted. "It's never been his fault. It's never been anybody's fault but Lydia's. You can't believe the stuff she's put us through. Take our last board meeting as an example. Did Daniel tell you about what happened?"

"No, he didn't mention it."

"Well, it was originally scheduled for February eighth, which was a Wednesday. Dad, Philip, and I had kept our calendar clear six weeks ahead of time; Daniel, too. Eleven o'clock on Tuesday night Dad gets a call from Lydia. She's still down at Tall Pines and she can't make it back for the meeting and we're going to have to reschedule."

"Was she in Georgia on vacation?"

"Worse than that. Her therapist told her that women who have her kinds of emotional problems were very often molested as children, but have repressed the memory. The therapist told Lydia that she needed to dig into her past. I'll never forget it. Lydia kept on trying to draw one or the other of us off into whispered interrogations about whether we'd seen anything happen to her when we were all children. I couldn't believe it, but Dad lent her the plane so that she could visit Nursey. She's the woman who took care of us after Mother died. It turns out Lydia wasn't having any luck with Nursey, so she wanted to stay a couple more days to see if she could pry anything else out of her. The whole thing was deeply, deeply sick."

"And did Lydia ever discover any evidence that she'd been molested?"

"No. Of course not. And that's what's so infuriating. Aren't there enough real victims in the world without someone as privileged as Lydia going around trying to invent misfortune?"

"So why didn't you hold the meeting without her or even conference her in by phone?"

"Dad wouldn't hear of it. We're a family company and he said we should be flexible. Yeah, right, we're flexible. Let me tell you how flexible we are. Lydia deigned to return to Chicago that Friday evening, too late to hold a meeting. When she got home she informed us that she was leaving early Sunday morning for two weeks at Canyon Ranch—that's a spa in Tucson—which meant that we had to hold the board meeting on Saturday. Normally that wouldn't have been a big deal, but that Saturday was Dad and Peaches's first wedding anniversary and I was having a hundred people to my house for dinner that night. Of all the days of the year that Saturday was absolutely the most inconvenient one possible for me, but as usual, Lydia got her way. And then, to top it all off, when we finally did hold the meeting, Lydia sat at the conference table and paid her bills. You had to have been there. Philip was doing this little show-and-tell on a new surfacting agent that the specialty chemicals division is going to start marketing and Lydia was busy writing out checks and licking stamps. We met for two hours and Lydia did not say one single word the entire time. I've got to tell you, Kate. I was so furious I could have strangled her with my bare hands."

BY THE TIME I left Dagny's house, it had begun snowing in earnest, and I was grateful for the fact that once I got to Wacker Drive, there was hardly any traffic. To my left lay Lake Michigan, brooding and unseen in the darkness. To my right, the city was lit up and gloriously peaceful, like a fairy-tale town in one of those glass globes that you shake up. The Wrigley Building, like an enchanted wedding cake, glittered in the distance; the Art Institute with its juxtaposition of old and new buildings, and the Field Museum, solid and magnificent, stood sentinel to my passing.

It had, I reflected, been a long day filled with Cavanaughs, but it had ended well. I'd enjoyed getting to know Dagny and I was beginning to understand what Daniel Babbage found so satisfying about representing family businesses. He built his relationships with his clients over decades, not deals. Unlike the constantly changing roster of lawyers and executives I usually worked with, Babbage and Jack Cavanaugh went back more than thirty years.

I looked forward to developing that kind of relationship with Dagny. It was more than the fact that I felt an easy kinship with her. I also got a sense, looking at her, that I was seeing what I might become in ten years' time. She had taken what life had dealt her—good and bad—and built something with it. She had chosen hard work and happiness as surely as her sister, Lydia, had chosen self-pity and neurosis. At a time when I was beginning to feel the need for my own forced march from the past, Dagny's accomplishments stood out for me like a beacon.

PARKING MY CAR IN the alley behind my apartment, I was glad to see the light on in the kitchen, which meant that my roommate was home. Claudia was a surgical resident at the University of Chicago Hospitals. She worked long hours and spent every third night in the on-call room. In addition, she'd lately begun seeing someone, a dermatologist at the same hospital. While I didn't keep track of her comings and goings, my sense was that recently she'd been out of the apartment more than one night in three.

Claudia and I had met when we roomed together our freshman year at Bryn Mawr, thrust together by fate in the form of the housing office computer. We knew each other for all of fifteen minutes before we realized that we had absolutely nothing in common.

Claudia was from New York City. Her parents, both professors at Columbia, had embraced radicalism in the sixties and never let go. Claudia had grown up boycotting grapes, picketing in sympathy with striking union workers, and marching against nuclear power. She didn't care about being pretty, or popular, or what other people thought. Her entire approach to life seemed to be "who says I can't?"

Naturally, we became best friends.

I let myself in the door and dust balls scattered in every direction. Petra, our Czech cleaning lady, had walked out right after Christmas. Indeed, the first indication I had that she spoke any English was when she told me that she was quitting.

Claudia was sitting cross-legged on the floor dressed in hospital scrubs. Her long hair, which she invariably wore in one braid long enough to sit on, was casually thrown over her shoulder. She was drinking a beer.

"Do you ever get the feeling that you just have to change your life?" she demanded without looking up.

"I don't know," I replied, disconcerted by the question. Like most surgeons', Claudia's approach to life had always been straightforward and not particularly introspective. "Why do you ask?"

"I just think all of it is starting to get to me."

"All of what?"

"The work, the hours, being up to my elbows in blood all the time. I get to hospital in the morning before the sun comes up and I leave long after it's gotten dark. I can't remember the last time I saw the sun."

"It's hard this time of year. It gets dark so early," I offered lamely. I'd never known Claudia to be discouraged about her choice of professions, and frankly, I was alarmed.

"It's gotten so that the hospital is my whole world. I'm either in the OR, or in the clinic, or crashed in the on-call room."

"What about Geoff? Don't you guys go out when you're both off?"

"Yeah, but when's that? The last three months we've been on

conflicting schedules—when I'm off he's on and vice versa. And the few nights we've been able to spend together I'm so tired I don't want him to touch me. Isn't that terrible? I've reached the point where sleep is much more attractive than sex. It doesn't help any that Geoff's a dermatologist. Believe me, God never made a rash that couldn't wait until tomorrow. And it's not as though seeing patients in the derm clinic is what I'd call tough. Not like being on your feet for twelve hours in the OR. Last time we were together I think he was planning on telling me that he doesn't want to see me anymore, but I fell asleep before he had a chance to get around to it."

"So what's your alternative?" I asked. "You've got another year to go in your residency."

Claudia shook her head and drained her beer.

"Do you know that I've lost my beeper, my lab coat, my stethoscope, and two pairs of glasses—all in the last week."

"That's just a sign that you're focused on what's really important—your work," I said. "Believe me, if I didn't have Cheryl, I'd do the same thing. Actually, I have Cheryl keeping track of me and I still lose things and forget what day it is."

"It's worse than that," complained Claudia. "This afternoon I assisted on a bowel resection; it was my fifth or sixth case of the day, I can't remember. The attending asked me to go out to the waiting room and talk to the family and let them know how everything went. So I take off my bloody scrubs and go out into the family waiting room and go up to a middle-aged woman and her two grown daughters. I tell them that the procedure went well, the resection was without complication, and their loved one was in post-op and doing just fine."

"So what happened?" I asked, dreading the answer. The currency of Claudia's work—and her stories—was so often life and death.

"Tonight, after evening rounds, I finally got off my rotation. I put my coat on to go home and I was walking through the lobby when the middle-aged woman I'd spoken to earlier walks up to me. 'Doctor,' she says kindly, 'I just thought you'd like to know that our son was in surgery for a hip replacement operation, not a bowel resection.' "

"You're kidding!" I exclaimed. "I can't believe she let you go on about the wrong surgery. Why didn't she say anything when you were going on about the bowel resection?"

"I asked her that," Claudia replied with a weary shrug. "She told me she didn't say anything because she felt sorry for me—I looked so tired."

10

The phone woke me from the darkness. I blinked, struggling to focus on the glowing numbers on the clock radio. It was a quarter to six.

"Hello," I croaked.

"Have you read this morning's *Wall Street Journal*?" It was Jack Cavanaugh. He did not sound happy.

"No. I don't read in my sleep. Besides, I have it delivered to the office."

"Well, you'd better go and get yourself a copy," he barked as a prelude to slamming down the receiver.

"Shit," I mumbled, forcing myself out of bed and dragging myself into the kitchen. Claudia was already gone, her episode of introspection ended by the inevitability of patients that would not—could not—wait. I could never be a doctor, I reflected numbly as I stumbled into the kitchen. It wasn't the crushing hours—I worked almost as many hours as Claudia. It was the early starting times.

Fumbling with the water and the filter, I managed to put some coffee on to brew. While I waited I leaned up against the kitchen sink and glared through the steel bars of the burglar grille at the lone houseplant perched on the windowsill. It was a housewarming present from our landlord, and incredibly, three years later it still clung to life, fed only on cold coffee and neglect.

When there was an inch of dark liquid in the bottom of the pot I poured it into my cup while the fresh coffee hissed and sputtered onto the heating element. It took me two full cups before I was sufficiently conscious to get my sweats on and my running shoes laced up. On my way out the door I remembered to take a five-dollar bill out of my purse, fold it up, and slip it into my pocket along with my key.

The air was clear and cold, the sky still gray as the pale sun struggled to burn its way through the clouds. About an inch of new snow crunched under my feet. I touched my toes, decided that I'd done enough stretching, and set off at a slow trot toward the Museum of Science and Industry. By the time I got to Fifty-seventh Street, I was sufficiently awake to notice that I was freezing, so I picked up the pace. I pushed through the rest of my usual loop along the lake to Fifty-first Street, propelled as much by the cold as by my curiosity about what had prompted Jack Cavanaugh's wake-up call.

Panting and with a stitch in my side, I stopped at the newsstand under the viaduct at Fifty-third Street and bought that morning's *Wall Street Journal.* Walking slowly, I crossed Lake Park and scanned the front page for whatever might have set Jack Cavanaugh off, but I didn't see anything. I tucked the paper under my arm and walked the half block to Starbucks and ordered a double latte. Then, cup in hand, I retired to a stool at the counter by the window to search the paper in earnest.

I found what I was looking for on page fourteen. It was a small item that ran under the headline SHARES OFFERED IN ILLINOIS PLATING AND SPECIALTY CHEMICALS COMPANY. The article went on briefly to describe Superior Plating's operations and assets. It also quoted Mark Hoffenberg, Lydia's investment banker from First Chicago, as saying that "Ms. Cavanaugh-Wallace is actively soliciting buyers for her shares in the company." In the stripped-down jargon of the business press, it was Lydia's formal announcement that she was serious about selling her shares. Under the circumstances, I found it impossible to decide whether Lydia's decision to sell her interest in the family business was an act of self-immolation or revenge.

LEAVING CHERYL TO FEND off hysterical Cavanaughs as best she could, I stopped at the hospital on my way to the office to see Daniel Babbage. After Jack Cavanaugh's wake-up call, I was anxious to hear whatever advice Daniel might be able to offer about how to handle his old friend.

I eased my car into a quasi-legal parking place on the "other side" of the Midway, the wide swath of grass that separates the law school from the rest of the University of Chicago. Now covered in snow, it lay like a white carpet at the feet of the University, which stood majestic and incongruous in the pale morning light—quadrangles of medieval splendor in the heart of the city.

But all the gargoyles in the world don't change the fact that once you walk through the double doors on Cottage Grove, you're in a large, urban teaching hospital. I hadn't been there since Russell died and my reaction was visceral and overwhelming. My step slowed. Memory squeezed my chest so fiercely that for a split second I fought for air. I didn't need to ask directions to the oncology service. I knew the way by heart. Indeed, on bad nights, I still walked it in my dreams.

Visiting hours were still half a day away, but in my suit and high heels I went unchallenged, taken no doubt for some sort of administrator. I found Daniel's room with no difficulty. One of the partners at Callahan was a trustee of the hospital and consequently Babbage had been assigned the equivalent of the presidential suite—a double room that held only one bed and boasted cheesy aqua curtains on the window and industrial-grade carpet of the same shade on the floor. Everywhere you looked there were flowers and cards from friends filled with best wishes.

Daniel had clearly taken a turn for the worse. His cheeks seemed to have caved in and his skin was unmistakably yellowed by jaundice. I knocked softly on the door frame. His eyes opened in an instant.

"I was just pretending to be asleep," he said, struggling to sit up a little. "Damn nurse always comes and tries to poke and prod every time I turn around. I don't see why they can't just leave me to die in peace. The doctor says he's going to come by and talk to me about some new chemotherapy protocol. Doctor! You should see him. He's just a kid. Ten to one he doesn't shave yet. I told the nurse I don't want to see him. I won't be turned into a guinea pig. I just want to be left alone."

"Is there anything I can get for you?"

"How about a bottle of single-malt scotch and a good cigar, though I don't think they'll let me smoke it."

"There's a lounge on the seventh floor where I know you can smoke. I'll talk to the nurse. I'll bring the cigars and we'll get you down there."

"You've got a deal. How are things going with the Cavanaughs?"

"It depends on which Cavanaugh you're talking about. I had dinner last night with Dagny. It was one of the nicest evenings I'd spent in a year. I also met with Lydia yesterday morning."

"So how did that meeting go?"

"On a scale of one to ten, with one being as normal as you and me talking and ten being a conversation with a hallucinating psychotic in a straitjacket, it was about a six."

"Did she come alone or did she bring Arthur with her?"

"She brought him. You know, if I were trying to invent the man most likely to annoy Jack Cavanaugh, I'd end up with Arthur Wallace."

"Why else do you think she married him?" countered Babbage with a little bit of his usual elfishness. "But you know, when it comes to the present generation, Jack Cavanaugh should consider himself lucky if she marries someone of the same color and the opposite sex! Fathers like Jack always hate their sons-in-law. They invariably think that they're gorillas—hairy, stupid men who marry their babies for their money. I have to tell you, Lydia's seemed much more well-adjusted since she married Arthur."

"That can't be possible. I spent an hour with her yesterday, and after the first two minutes I could tell she is one seriously disturbed individual. I can't even imagine what she must have been like if this is an improvement."

"You should have met her right after her second divorce. She was a total malcontent. On her bad days she would lash out at anyone and everyone. On her good days she would sink into a terrible depression. She had absolutely no idea how to go about leading her life. It was frightening to witness. Whatever Arthur's motives, he's the first one who's given Lydia the attention and emotional stability that she craves."

"But at what price?" I reached into my purse, pulled out a copy of that morning's *Wall Street Journal,* and read him the piece about Lydia and her shares.

"Has Jack seen this?" Daniel demanded when I'd finished.

"He called me at home this morning and woke me up."

"You have to admit that it was clever of the boys from First Chicago to get her to agree to an item in the *Journal*. It just makes it that much harder for her to back down. What did Jack have to say?"

"I haven't discussed it with him. I wanted to talk to you first, but from his brief call this morning I'd guess he's furious. I have to be honest with you. I don't have any sense of how to handle all of them. It's like herding cats. They all have their own agendas."

"Let me tell you what the engine is that really drives a family-owned business. It's a combination of three parts: love, power, and habit. Jack loves his children, he holds great power over them, but he is in the habit of seeing them in the same way as he did when they were little. He is a shrewd businessman, but he's got this one big blind spot and that's his family. Sometimes I think it's a universal trait that parents don't ever seem able to see their offspring for what they really are. Maybe that's what keeps parents from murdering their children—who knows?"

"But if Jack insists on refusing to believe his daughter is really going to sell her shares and she does go ahead with it—and with Mark Hoffenberg and First Chicago behind her, you've got to admit that they'll generate quite a bit of momentum—Jack Cavanaugh is going to have a much more painful reality to confront than the fact that his daughter no longer cares to be a shareholder."

"Do you really think that they'll be able to find a buyer?" asked Daniel, struggling to reach the plastic water jug on his bedside. I poured him a glass and handed it to him. He drank it while I pretended not to notice how badly his hands shook and how much the simple task of raising a glass to his lips seemed to exhaust him.

"That depends," I said. "Granted, I do agree with you that the piece in this morning's *Journal* is a clever negotiating tactic—a way to light a fire under the rest of the Cavanaughs and possibly push up the price. After all, there aren't a tremendous number of investors who'll find a minority interest in a family-owned company an attractive opportunity. But there's been quite a bit of renewed interest in manufacturing companies and Superior Plating is an attractive operation. For someone who's not looking to make a killing in the short term, someone who might be looking to gain control of the company in five or ten years, it could be a smart move. I've got to tell you, Daniel. I have a bad feeling about this. If Jack doesn't get on the stick and at least talk to Lydia about this in a realistic way, he's going to be sitting across the table from some stranger who owns twelve percent of his company."

"Don't worry. He'll come around. When is Dagny planning on giving him her ultimatum?"

"Tonight. She's invited her dad and Peaches to dinner. The question is, will it work?"

"Given the choice between losing Lydia as a shareholder and Dagny as a chief financial officer, I think Jack will stick with Dagny."

"And if he doesn't?"

"Then you'll have to find some other way to convince him. I have to tell you, Kate, there will be no peace in the Cavanaugh family until Lydia is out of the company."

"And if Jack won't buy her out?"

"Then believe me, there will be no limit to the price he will be asked to pay."

I SPENT THE REST of the day trying to push ahead on other matters, but every time the phone rang it was another Cavanaugh. Philip, furious, reported that his phone was ringing off the hook with investment bankers either volunteering their services or requesting information about the company. Jack called twice, and even though I spent more than half an hour on the phone with him, each time I hung up wondering why he'd called, other than to vent his frustration. I even talked to Peaches, who suggested in her sweet southern drawl that I knock some sense into her stepdaughter Lydia before she drove Jack into coronary arrest.

I didn't hear from Dagny until lunchtime and then it was only to remind me about Cecilia Dobson's funeral, which I had already forgotten about completely.

"I was hoping you wouldn't mind swinging by the plant and picking me up," Dagny ventured. "That way I'd have an excuse for not going with my father or Philip. They're both insane about the article in the *Journal* this morning and I'm frankly sick of hearing about it."

"I'd be happy to. What time do you want me to be there?"

"I'll wait for you in front of the building at three-thirty," said Dagny. "You won't even have to get out of the car."

I ASKED CHERYL TO hold my calls and I shut the door. I kicked off my shoes, dragged my disc player out from my bottom drawer, and pulled a CD from the pile—The Smiths, as it turned out. Cranking up the volume, I happily immersed myself in the Frostman Refrigeration file—a dull-as-dishwater corporate restructuring, blessedly devoid of any and all family entanglements.

When it was time to leave and pick Dagny up, I'd gotten the Frostman memo and a full third of the other tasks off my most urgent to-do pile. So it was with a much lighter heart than at any other time in that horror show of a week that I set off to Cecilia Dobson's funeral.

As I drove south on State Street, with its odd assortment of auto parts stores and wig emporiums, it occurred to me, not for the first time, that I really needed to get rid of my old Volvo and buy a new car. Russell and I had picked out the station wagon, a wedding present to ourselves that we planned on filling up with dogs and kids. For a long time after his death it really was sentiment that made me hang on to it. Recently, I realized, it was more like entropy.

I honestly couldn't remember the last time I'd had it washed. The man in the parking garage in my building offers—no, I take that back—begs me to let him wash it. But I've let it go for so long that I'm almost afraid of what I'll see once all the layers of urban grime are rinsed away. Besides, if he washed the outside, then I'd have to do something about the interior, too.

I glanced over my shoulder at the backseat. I saw old newspapers, a dirty blanket, a crumpled bag from Harold's Fried Chicken, and so many empty diet Coke cans that every time I hit a pothole I heard a tinny clang. If a car could have mice, I concluded, mine would.

I pulled into the Superior Plating lot, grateful for being a few minutes early. The lot was almost completely empty and I remembered what Dagny had said about closing early in order to let employees attend the funeral. I spent the next few minutes frantically cleaning up the worst of the mess in my car, including some McDonald's wrappers of uncertain provenance and more empty bags of M&M's than I'd like to confess to. That done, I checked the front door, but there was no sign of Dagny.

She had said that the cemetery was close to the plant, so I waited a few more minutes, growing increasingly uncertain. Perhaps I'd gotten the time wrong or misunderstood her directions about where to meet. There was a reason, I realized, that I usually left these kinds of arrangements to Cheryl. I picked up my car phone—a concession to the firm's obsession with having partners constantly available—and dialed the Superior Plating number, but got their after-hours recording.

Finally, not knowing what else to do, I got out of my car and went into the building to look for Dagny. The front door was open, but the reception desk was empty. I made my way through the deserted administrative wing toward Dagny's office, passing no one. The door was closed. I knocked.

"Dagny?" I called.

There was no answer.

Afraid that I'd hopelessly screwed up, I turned the handle and pushed the door open. I could not believe what I saw.

Dagny Cavanaugh lay on the floor of her office—facedown.

CHAPTER

11

For a minute, maybe longer, I just stood there. It was all too much to absorb. Dagny Cavanaugh sprawled facedown on the carpet. Just like Cecilia Dobson.

Then she moved.

Her arms and legs jerked as if she were a rag doll being shaken by some invisible hand. Suddenly her limbs twitched in an uncoordinated spasm. Then, just as suddenly, they were still.

Relief flooded through me. At least she was alive.

I ran to her side, dropped to my knees, and rolled her onto her back, calling her name. She didn't respond, but she didn't look all that bad. Her cheeks were pink. Her skin was warm. There were flecks of white foam on her lips and her eyelids fluttered uncontrollably. I checked her throat for a pulse and found none. I watched her chest and put my hand above her mouth—but no air moved and as I put my face near hers the unmistakably sour smell of vomit mingled with her perfume.

I shouted for help, but knew that no one would hear me. They'd all gone to the funeral. I willed myself to be calm. I had to call 911 before I began CPR.

Suddenly Dagny's arms shot out and she clutched me in an iron grip. Startled, I cried out. My heart was beating wildly. I looked at Dagny. Her face was convulsed in terrible pain, her mouth moving as if she were trying to speak. I bent closer in order to hear her.

Without warning, her back arched up off the floor as if her body were being electrified by some internal agony. Her head jerked up violently, hitting mine and knocking me back onto my heels. From her mouth came a hideous, wordless roar that seemed to rise up out of her throat from some primitive source. It was a sound I shall never forget—a rasping, whooping cry like a rusty door being pulled from its hinges, like a desperately wounded animal giving voice to unspeakable torment.

And then she fell silent, her body completely slack. Frantically, I bent over her and called her name. Her eyes were open but vacant. In them I searched desperately for some glimmer of the woman whom the night before I'd rejoiced in as a friend. Instead, all I saw was the face of a corpse. Blue eyes fixed under half lids in an expression of vague wonder, like a flustered schoolchild to whom the logic of a simple equation has just been revealed. It was the same look of sudden, silent comprehension that I had last seen on the face of Cecilia Dobson.

I WATCHED IT ALL like a movie I had seen before—the tube down the throat, the IV drip, the same futile search for pulse, reflexes, respiration. I stood out of the way, an onlooker on these last pointless efforts. Sweat was pouring off my face and the thin silk of my blouse was as cold and wet as if I'd been caught in the rain.

This time I did not go to the hospital. Despite their best efforts to convince me that I really should have a doctor look at the bump on my head, I explained as calmly and as firmly as I could that I would just stay right where I was and wait for the police.

A pair of uniformed officers arrived just as they finished shoveling Dagny onto the gurney. They listened attentively as I explained about finding Cecilia Dobson dead in the same way in the same place three days before. I told them about all of the other employees being at St. Bernadette's Cemetery for the funeral. With a shiver I acknowledged that that was where they'd find Dagny's family.

When I finished, one of the officers got on the radio while the other began stringing yellow police-line-do-not-cross tape across the doors. I found a folding chair that someone had left in the hallway outside Dagny's door and sat down on it. At some point I began shaking as if from some terrible cold. The officers who had taken my statement had disappeared, but other people began arriving—a police photographer, a man in overalls carrying heavy-equipment boxes marked COOK COUNTY CRIME LAB—and from the waiting room came the faint crackle of two-way radios.

I heard Eugene Cavanaugh before I saw him. Bellowing unintelligibly, he charged toward Dagny's office, oblivious to the scrum of blue uniforms attempting to restrain him. His face was terrible to see—almost disfigured by anguish and disbelief. I saw him and could think only of the little boy who'd lost his mother and his power of speech; his brother and control over his life; and had struggled so hard both times to regain what had been lost.

Finally, the cops managed to turn the tide of his progress and led him back down the hall toward the reception room. For a long time after that I heard him through the thin plastic paneling.

"Oh my God, not Dagny!" he wailed over and over again.

WHEN I MET DETECTIVE Joe Blades for the first time at the hospital after Cecilia Dobson died, I hadn't really paid him much attention.

But this time I found myself observing him much more closely. Suddenly he was a man from whom I expected a great deal.

At first glance he looked almost too young to be a policeman, and certainly a homicide cop. Tall and thin, he had a reddish-gold beard and a quiet, almost scholarly manner. He pulled up a chair from behind another desk, turned it around, and sat on it so that his hands rested along the top of its back. Without saying a word, he fished for something in the pocket of his tweed jacket and pulled out a Hershey bar.

"You'd better eat this," he said. His voice was cultured and deliberate.

"I'm not hungry."

"I know. But it'll still do you good. You've had a shock. In the bad old days I would have given you whiskey."

I took the candy bar, but would no doubt have preferred the whiskey. My hands were shaking so badly that it took me a few seconds to get the chocolate out of its wrapper. Self-consciously, I ate the whole thing. Even under the most appalling circumstances, I find chocolate impossible to resist.

Blades took off his gold-framed glasses and began to polish them slowly with the fat end of his tie. Without them he looked even younger, a high-school kid who'd somehow managed to produce a beard.

"What happened to your forehead?" he asked. "I should have one of the EMTs come back and have a look at you."

With trembling hands I reached up and touched my face. Slippery with sweat and blood, the lump in the middle of my forehead was definitely getting bigger. I winced at my own touch.

"Her head hit me. . . ." I stammered in explanation. "She had this seizure . . . at least I think that's what it was. Her body arched up and I remember falling backward. . . ."

"Why don't you just take it from the beginning and tell me what happened here today," he suggested, pulling a small notebook from the pocket of his jacket.

I tried to begin, but I could not organize my thoughts. Events were jumbled with emotion and my body and my brain were seemingly disconnected. In frustration, I forced myself to imagine that I was standing in one of the big lecture halls in law school, having been called upon to recite the facts of a case. It worked. Focusing on the main points, laying out events in a clear voice, I managed a semi-coherent account of what had happened—the story of two apparently healthy women who died suddenly in the same office, one during the funeral of the other. By the time I was finished, Joe Blades looked grim.

I had felt something turn inside of me as well. The sweating had stopped. So had the shaking. The panic, the shock of what had happened, had receded. But in its place was something else, something that gripped me by the entrails and would not let go. Clear and pure, unadulterated by ambiguity, unmitigated by circumstance, what I felt was anger. What I wanted was revenge.

ACCORDING TO ELLIOTT ABELMAN, the Monadnock Building is the perfect place for a private investigator's office—halfway between the courthouse and the jail. Nonetheless, the building is a strange landmark. Sixteen stories tall and occupying an entire city block, it was built by John Root in 1891 as the tallest structure ever erected using wall-bearing masonry construction. At its foundation the walls are six feet thick. But less than a dozen years after its completion the technique of steel-frame construction was introduced and the sky was opened up to architects. John Root's accomplishment had become obsolete.

Like the building, Elliott Abelman defied easy categorization. The son of a Chicago homicide cop, Elliott had broken with tradition. Decorated for valor during the last, ignominious days of the Viet Nam War, he chose law school over law enforcement, only to find after a stint in the prosecutor's office that like his father, he was really an investigator at heart.

The lobby of the Monadnock is long and narrow, a gallery with shops on either side. An iron staircase of ornately wrought metalwork runs up the center of the building like a knobby Victorian spinal column. Consulting the computer screen that serves as the building's directory, I learned that Abelman & Associates occupied a suite on the second floor. I decided to take the stairs.

It was after hours and the hallways in the upper floors were dark. But the door to Abelman & Associates was made of smoked glass set in an oak frame with the name of the firm lettered onto it, and light shone from within. The cozy waiting room was deserted, the armchairs unoccupied, the magazines unread, but beyond another door I could hear the clack of keyboards and the ringing of phones.

Someone came up behind me and took my arm. I jumped in fright. I might have shouted, too. Who knows? At that point my nerves were all over the place. I wheeled around and Elliott put his hand gently over my mouth.

"Shhh," he said, his face illumined by an enormous, wolfish grin. "You'll frighten the detectives." He caught sight of the bump on my forehead and turned serious. "Jesus Christ, what's happened to your face? Did someone hit you? You look like you've had a beating."

I opened up my mouth to explain, but no words came out. His hand stayed near my cheek. He softly brushed a strand of hair off my face, tucking it behind my ear. I felt the heat rush to my face.

"You'd better come into my office," he advised, putting his arm around my shoulder and ushering me inside. "I'm going to get you an ice pack and a cup of coffee—or maybe you'd prefer something stronger."

"Yes, please," I whispered as he guided me into a comfortable chair.

"I'll be right back," he said.

The internal wall of his office was glass. Beyond it, in a large, open space laid out like a police squad room, only with nicer furniture, were half a dozen people who I supposed were operatives who worked for Elliott. A gray-haired woman was talking on the phone and furiously scribbling notes. A man with a ponytail dressed in the greasy coveralls of a mechanic was reading a file that was spread out on the desk in front of him. Two or three meat-faced men with spreading guts and ex-cop written all over them filled out the assembly.

Elliott returned with two glass tumblers filled with amber liquid over ice. Under his arm was tucked a chemical cold pack. He handed me my drink, set his down on the desk, gave the cold pack a twist and a shake, and then handed it to me. I took a long drink and held the icy compress to my forehead.

Dressed in khaki pants and a perfectly starched white button-down shirt, Elliott looked like he'd fit better in my office than his own. About my height, or give him an inch and say six feet, his soft brown hair and warm brown eyes did little to distinguish him from the rest of the briefcase-toting hordes. He was good-looking in an unassuming way—a Winnetka Galahad, nothing more. But I'd seen enough of him to know that he was a man capable of taking people by surprise. He always managed to keep me off balance as well.

"I'm impressed," I said, wincing as I applied the cold pack to my forehead. "I always imagined you in a tiny office with a bottle of bourbon in your bottom drawer and a cheap but loyal blonde for a secretary."

"Who says loyalty is cheap?" Elliott countered with a grin. His smiles were a minor phenomenon. Between them and the scotch I was beginning to feel a little bit better. "Now why don't you tell me what happened to your face. Please tell me that boyfriend of yours did this to you. You know I'd like nothing better than to go over there and teach him a lesson."

As usual, I let the crack about Stephen Azorini pass. For the second time in as many hours I told my story about what had happened, first to Cecilia Dobson and then to Dagny Cavanaugh. With Elliott I went into even more detail than I'd managed with Detective Blades, explaining how I'd come to take over as counsel for Superior Plating from Daniel Babbage, laying out the particulars of Lydia's decision to sell her shares, and providing as much information about personality and family history as I could cogently serve up.

By the time I was finished, it was dark outside and I felt nothing but emotionally spent.

"So you obviously don't think that the two deaths are unrelated," Elliott concluded.

"Do you?"

"I'm sure it's mathematically possible," he offered.

I was in no mood for discussions of mathematical possibility and told him as much.

"I wonder if there might be something wrong in the office, in the room itself—some kind of gas leak maybe?" he speculated.

"I've thought of that, too. But wouldn't something like that have turned up at Cecilia Dobson's autopsy?"

"It depends on what the pathologist was looking for. The medical examiner's office can't test every case for everything. There are thousands of substances that, under the right circumstances, can poison you—aspirin, drain cleaner, table salt, cocaine. . . . They don't have the time or the money to check for every one. Instead they test for anything that seems likely based on the physical evidence. From what you've told me, it sounds like the cops figured she died of an overdose."

"At the time it seemed the likeliest explanation. Now of course, I'm not so sure."

"What if both women were drug users? It would certainly explain what happened. They shared the same shit and met the same end."

"If you'd met Dagny, you'd realize that's impossible," I protested. "She was an intelligent, educated, highly charismatic business executive. I don't know how else to say it, but Cecilia Dobson was white trash. I don't think the two women could have had much in common."

"Maybe they didn't," countered Elliott. "But Cecilia worked for Dagny. As her secretary they worked in the same office, handled the same papers, had lunch in the same place. They may not have had much in common, maybe only one thing. But it was that one thing that killed them."

CHAPTER

12

I dragged myself out of bed when my alarm went off at five-thirty. In the bedroom mirror I examined the variable landscape of my face. The bump on my forehead where Dagny's head had struck mine during her last terrible moments was less swollen, but there were bruises under my eyes that a lack of sleep and a surplus of tears could only partially account for.

I dressed for the office in a hurry, jumping into the first thing that I pulled from my closet. On my way out the door I stopped to stuff some ice cubes into a plastic bag. I figured I'd try holding it up to my face when I stopped at red lights. I didn't want to take the time to do it at home. I had to get to the hospital before Daniel Babbage woke up. I didn't want him to learn about Dagny Cavanaugh's death by reading about it in the newspaper.

At the hospital everything was quiet. The silence of the oncology wing was interrupted only by the intermittent beeping of unseen monitors and the much louder clatter of my high heels on the brightly polished linoleum of the floor.

One look at Daniel and I knew that he had turned onto that last twisted curve on a piece of bad road. He seemed shrunken in his hospital bed and the jaundice of his skin was vivid against the white fabric of his pillowcase. There was the smell of decay in the air that no flowers or antiseptic could completely mask.

I walked quietly into the room, not wanting to disturb him. Daniel's eyes were open and unfocused, staring blankly in the general direction of the radiator. His pupils were constricted to pinpoints from whatever they were pumping into him for the pain. I pulled a chair up to his bed and took his hand in mine.

"It's me—Kate," I said softly. His skin was hot to the touch. Not a good sign. On the tray in front of him was a blue plastic emesis basin and a hospital-issue box of tissues.

"Did you bring the cigars?" he croaked, slowly turning his head toward me.

"No. I'll bring them by later."

"You'd better hurry," he advised, trying for a smile. "There isn't much time."

Tears sprang to my eyes. I busied myself by filling his cup with fresh water from a plastic jug and helping him to drink.

"You came to tell me about Dagny, didn't you?" he rasped, falling back onto his pillow.

"Yes. I didn't want you to hear about it from a stranger."

"Eugene came to see me last night. He's my godson, you know. He told me everything. Do the police know what happened to her yet?" His voice was weak and he spoke very slowly, every word an effort. I had to bend my head close in order to hear him.

"They won't know until they do the autopsy."

"How is Jack?"

"I don't know. I plan to talk to him today. Last night I went to see a private investigator I know. I want Jack to hire him. The police are good, but I don't want to take any chances. If six months or a year from now Dagny's death is still an open file—just another unexplained death—Jack won't be able to live with himself, and frankly, neither will I."

"Leave it to the police," Daniel said sharply. "You and Jack will have enough to worry about."

"Don't you think that Lydia will let this business about her shares drop? At least for a little while?"

Daniel gripped my hand. "Expect the worst from Lydia," he counseled. "I guarantee she'll never let you down."

I LEFT THE HOSPITAL with limbs like lead and grief pushing on my chest like a wrestler's fist. When I got to the office, Cheryl, whom I'd phoned from the car to tell her about what had happened, was especially solicitous, bringing me a king-size bag of M&M's with my coffee and parrying all of my calls without complaint. Heartened by her kindness, I did what I always do when I feel the earth shift beneath my feet. I crawled into the solid refuge of my work and stayed there until the worst of the tremors passed.

I took the top file off of the stack and dove in. When I finished with that one I moved on to the next—phoning, dictating, delegating. The practice of securities law is not earth-shattering stuff. But I find a certain satisfaction in sorting out the conflicts and confusion of commerce, a kind of harmony in making all of the pieces fit together. There are days when you just have to hang on to whatever sense of peace comes your way.

At noon Cheryl knocked softly on my door and told me that Jack Cavanaugh had called. He was at his house on Astor Place and wanted to see me. Jack Cavanaugh was my client and we had matters of importance to discuss. But I had been dreading his summons nev-

ertheless. I spent the entire cab ride wishing I were going somewhere else.

As I climbed the steps to his front door, I could not help taking a
backward glance across the street at Dagny's house. The curtains
were all drawn and I felt a fresh stab of compassion for her father,
whose windows would forever look out onto his loss. Willing these
morbid thoughts from my head, I stepped up and rang the bell.

Peter McCallister, Lydia's son, came to the door. Awkward in
his grief, he accepted my condolences and led me to his grandfather's study. He told me, in response to my question, that Claire
had been under sedation ever since she learned of her mother's
death.

Jack Cavanaugh crossed the room like an old man and took my
hand. His pale skin was clawed by grief, his shark's eyes red-rimmed
with tears.

"I'm so sorry for your loss," I said. The words sounded hollow and
inadequate and I felt unprepared for the situation I found myself in. I
had neither Daniel's wisdom nor experience. I had, after all, become
a lawyer expressly to avoid dealing with emotions.

"The police were here last night and again this morning," Jack
told me in a beaten voice after we both sat down. "They told me
how you found her. But they wouldn't tell me . . . they couldn't tell
me . . ." He struggled for the words. "They didn't say whether she
suffered."

"She didn't suffer," I lied, adding, "It was all over very quickly."

"The police are asking whether there could be some kind of
chemical leak from the plant that killed them both. They're so stupid.
It's true that there are poisonous compounds used in plating, but
they would have to be mixed with acid in order to turn into gas. If
that happened, the first person who'd be killed would be the fool
who'd done the mixing. But they won't listen. They're shutting us
down. Philip's there right now with the health department. It's a
shame. He should be with the family. . . ."

"So they still have no idea yet what happened?" I ventured.

"I told you, they're fools."

"I know a man," I said, unsure how to begin. "He's a private investigator and he's very good. He used to be in the prosecutor's office. I spoke with him yesterday. He said that he'd look into it for you if that's what you wanted. Even if the police can't, he'll find out what happened."

"No one can bring her back," he whispered, not looking at me.

"No," I said, thinking of Claire. Her mother had been a woman who didn't flinch from what life threw in her face. I hoped that she'd passed a little of that on to her daughter. Lord knows she was going to need it. "But I think that you all need to know what happened. I think Claire needs to know."

Jack didn't say anything. I couldn't tell whether he was thinking or he'd just gone numb. Finally, he turned toward me.

"Call him and tell him he's got the job," he said.

BACK AT THE OFFICE I stood at Cheryl's desk, listening to her run through the list of my phone calls, shaking the snow off of my shoes.

"Sandy Morgenstern called. They've scheduled the Frostman Refrigeration deposition for tomorrow at three."

"Call him back and tell him I can't make it. See if he can move it to next week. If not, I'll have to send someone in my place. I'm flying down to Georgia tomorrow afternoon."

"To Georgia? Why?"

"The Cavanaughs have a place down there called Tall Pines. That's where Dagny's going to be buried. Jack Cavanaugh wants me to come down for her funeral."

"But what about your grandmother's birthday party?" demanded Cheryl. There were lots of times when my mother blamed her for my shortcomings. My secretary did not seem eager to take the fall if I didn't make it to Grandma Prescott's eighty-third birthday party.

"I'm flying down with the Cavanaughs on their plane tomorrow afternoon at four, so you've got to book me on a commercial flight out of Tallahassee that gets back to Chicago in time for the party on Saturday."

She nodded and made a note.

"Philip Cavanaugh called while you were out," she said, not raising her head. "He said it's urgent."

"Get him on the phone for me."

"He said it has to be in person."

"I'm not leaving the office again today," I replied wearily. "Call and tell him that if he needs to see me in person, he's got to come here."

"Are you going to be okay?" Cheryl asked, looking up and cocking her head to one side.

"I guess I'll live."

"Good," replied my secretary, flashing me an impish grin. "It's a real pain being so nice to you. I'm not sure how much longer I'll be able to keep it up."

PHILIP CAVANAUGH WALKED INTO my office looking haggard and defeated. The expression on his face was of someone who sees an incredible catastrophe approaching but is powerless to stop it.

"What can I do for you?" I asked after he'd taken a seat and Cheryl had come and gone offering coffee.

"The police came to my house this morning," he reported. "They were asking all kinds of questions."

"It's just routine. They have to talk to all the members of her family."

"They were asking about Cecilia Dobson." He gave one of his dry little coughs.

"That's only to be expected. Your sister's death puts what happened to her secretary in a new light."

"What do you mean?"

"Well," I answered, puzzled that he needed to have it spelled out for him, "two apparently healthy young women who worked in the same office died under almost identical circumstances. Don't you think there must be some sort of connection?"

"I don't know what to think!" Philip wailed. "Isn't it bad enough Dagny's dead and now I have no one to help me run the company? The police showed up at my house this morning and started asking all sorts of embarrassing questions—"

"What kind of questions?" I demanded, something in his voice setting off alarm bells in my head.

"Stupid questions," Philip answered warily.

"Give me an example," I said, thinking I didn't have the stomach for coaxing it out of him.

"You know. Questions about who knew her. What she did outside of the office."

"What Dagny did outside of the office?"

He shook his head.

"Questions about Cecilia, then," I continued.

He nodded mutely. The stamp of misery on his face was unmistakable. In an instant enlightenment dawned.

"Were you seeing Cecilia outside of the office?" I demanded, trying to keep the incredulity out of my voice.

He nodded wretchedly, acknowledging it to be true.

"I was going to break it off," he said finally. "Honest. We were going to have dinner tonight. Sally—that's my wife—plays Bonko with some of the ladies from church on Thursdays. I was going to take Cecilia out to dinner and tell her that we were through."

"Why?" I asked, with a mounting sense of alarm. All I could think of was what this was going to look like to the police.

"She'd started asking for money. Hinting that she really needed

a nicer apartment, that I should buy her a car. She thought that because my family owns the company that I must be rich. I tried to
explain to her that the house, the car, all of that belongs to my father. But she wouldn't believe it. God knows what he'd have done if
he found out I was sleeping with one of the secretaries." He gave
an involuntary shudder at the thought. "And she was getting so
bold. She started wearing these sexy outfits to work. Some days
she'd just walk into my office and start flirting. It scared me to
death. I've never done anything like this before. The whole thing
was like a sickness. You know that it's wrong. You know that it's
dangerous. You're terrified and yet you can't help yourself. You go
ahead and do it anyway. And then, after a while, the thrill wears off
and all that's left is the fear—the fear that you'll get caught and
you'll have ruined everything that you've worked your whole
life for—"

"You have to go to the police and tell them," I broke in—no-
nonsense advice that was much easier to give than to receive.

"I couldn't possibly," Philip stammered spinelessly. "What if it
turns out there's something funny about the way they died? I can't be
involved in that."

"You're already involved," I countered, deliberately taking a very
tough tone. If Philip came to me expecting a sympathetic confessor,
he'd been mistaken. "And believe me, if there's 'something funny,' as
you so eloquently put it, about the way they died, the longer you wait
to tell the police, the worse it will look."

The expression on Philip's face was hard to read—mulish and
miserable.

"But she's dead," he protested. Philip Cavanaugh, master of the
obvious.

"The police don't care whether you were cheating on your wife," I
told him. "But believe me, they'll care a great deal if they find out
you've been withholding information."

"What difference can it make?"

"To you? A great deal. If they find out that you lied about Cecilia Dobson, they're going to assume that you're lying about other things—and they're going to assume there's some reason. If you think they were asking embarrassing questions at your house this morning, wait until they find out you lied to them. Besides," I added, taking another tack, "don't *you* want to find out what happened to them? You probably know things about Cecilia that nobody else knows, things that might be relevant to how she and your sister died."

"She had a boyfriend, you know," said Philip, tossing off the information like throwing a bone to a dog. "He's some sort of musician."

"Did she say anything else about him?" I asked.

"Not really. Only that he was the jealous type."

BEFORE I ARRANGED FOR Philip to give his statement to the police, I called a criminal lawyer I am friendly with. I wasn't sure what Philip's confession about Cecilia meant, but of one thing I was sure: I know less about criminal law than your average felon in the street, and I was sorely in need of advice. At the very least I was hoping that Elkin Caufield would be able to arrange for one of the associates in his office to accompany Philip on his visit to the police.

"I don't think that would be such a good idea," Elkin concluded once he'd heard me out. "Not unless you think there's some possibility of your client being arrested and charged in the future."

"Let's not get ahead of ourselves. At this point we don't even know how they died."

"That's exactly my point. If he goes marching into police headquarters with a criminal lawyer in tow, the only thing that'll happen is that the cops will assume he's guilty of something."

"But . . ." I began to protest, some vague recollection having to do with the right to have an attorney present stirring in the back of my brain.

"I know. It's not what they taught you in law school. But believe me, even though you think he'd be acting prudently if brings someone from my office with him, the cops will just think he's acting guilty."

"He's already acting guilty," I interjected. "Talking to him, you'd think he was the first man on the planet to ever cheat on his wife. He's like a little kid who sticks his hand into the cookie jar and comes out with a handful of snakes. At this point he's feeling so guilty that I'm afraid he'll confess to anything."

"So you're his lawyer." Caufield laughed. "*You* go with him. If he starts taking credit for the Lindbergh baby, shut him up. If not, let him talk. Besides, a trip to the police station will do you good. You guys at Callahan need a taste of what real lawyering is all about."

A BURLY POLICEWOMAN WITH a face like the back of a bus ushered us into a windowless room the size of two parking spaces. One wall was mirrored and I wondered who was watching us from beyond the dark glass. From the way that voices died in the air, I guessed that the room was soundproof. I thought about Elkin Caufield and did not see how this could possibly be doing me any good.

Joe Blades made a casual entrance, a cup of coffee in one hand and a stack of forms in the other. He sat down at one end of the scarred wooden table and laid the papers down in front of him.

He began by thanking Philip for coming in, assuring him that the police were truly grateful for any information that might assist them in their investigation. I looked over at my client. He was so nervous he wasn't shaking—it was more like he was vibrating.

Detective Blades began reading questions from the form in front of him, laboriously filling in the blanks as Philip answered. Orderly and reasonable—like a doctor taking a medical history from a patient with an embarrassing complaint—he struck an attitude of weary routine that was remarkably effective with Philip. Names and dates, times and places—the rhythm of the interrogation resembled nothing more than the filling out of a bank application, and the story that it revealed was scarcely more interesting.

Man Sleeps with Secretary—ho-hum. According to Philip, it had been Cecilia who'd instigated the affair, offering to stay late and behaving provocatively until she finally succeeded in seducing him one night in his father's office. Soon they were meeting once a week on his wife Sally's Bonko nights. The only person I could think of who would find that interesting might be one of Lydia's shrinks.

"What kind of person was she?" asked Blades, in a voice that invited friendly confidence. Philip Cavanaugh actually smiled.

"She wasn't educated and she wasn't sophisticated, but she was smart. She was always talking about wanting to improve her situation."

"Do you know if she took drugs?"

"I don't know. I never saw her do it. But she was the kind of person who might—I mean, she liked to have a good time."

"Do you think your wife knew about your relationship with the deceased?"

"No," Philip bleated. "I was very careful. Sally has a naturally suspicious nature. . . ."

I thought I detected a flicker of a smile pass Joe Blades's lips, but it was gone in an instant. All in all he didn't seem overly impressed with Philip's indiscretion.

When he was finished with his questions Blades asked Philip to read and initial each page of his statement.

"Is that it?" Philip asked as he slid the initialed sheets back across the table toward the detective. He sounded almost disappointed.

"That's all. Thank you for your time, Mr. Cavanaugh. You're free to go."

Philip rose, but as I followed suit Joe Blades reached across the table and took my arm.

"I was wondering if I might have a word in private with your attorney."

13

C ops as a rule don't make me nervous, but there is something essentially unnerving about any conversation conducted in a homicide interrogation room.

"Thanks for getting Philip Cavanaugh to come in," Detective Blades began, equably enough. "We'd have found out about him and the Dobson woman eventually, but anytime somebody can save me half a day's dragging around town, I'll take it."

"This is hard for a man like Philip Cavanaugh," I said. "He feels very guilty about their affair—ashamed actually. But all the Cavanaughs want to cooperate with the police in any way they can."

Blades took a slow sip of his coffee, no doubt long grown cold. His skin was so pale that it seemed almost translucent, and now that I had a chance to look closely I could see the first strands of gray hair mixed in with the red. He sat quietly for a minute, seemingly measuring me for something while I squirmed inwardly, worried about what had prompted this cozy chat.

"So," he said finally. "Tell me how you know Elliott Abelman."

So that was it. I hadn't expected the police to be ecstatic about the Cavanaughs hiring a private investigator. But I also hadn't expected the news to get out quite so quickly.

"It's not that the family doesn't have complete confidence in the police. . . ." I ventured, managing to sound lame and lawyerly at the same time. But Blades acted as if he hadn't heard me.

"Is it just professional between the two of you?" he asked. "Or is there something else going on?"

"No," I replied, taken aback by his question. "What makes you think there is?"

"Just the way Elliott talks about you. He gets this goofy look on his face I haven't seen since he first started seeing Janice."

"Who's Janice?" I asked, in spite of myself.

"She works for the *Wall Street Journal*. They split up right around the time Elliott left the prosecutor's office."

"Is that why they broke up?" I asked, imagining that some women might be less than supportive when they learned that the man in their life intended to jettison his legal career in order to hang out his shingle as a PI.

"Nah, that's not it. Elliott wanted kids. Janice wanted to wait. At some point Elliott started wondering what exactly she was waiting for. Then one day he comes home and finds Janice waiting for him, all excited. She's got a bottle of champagne in one hand and two glasses in the other."

"Was she pregnant?"

"No. She'd just been named chief of the paper's Hong Kong bureau."

"Ouch."

"It took a little while, but after that it was pretty much over. There really hasn't been anybody since then."

"Why are you telling me this?"

"Because Elliott is my friend. We play basketball together"—Detective Blades stroked his beard thoughtfully—"and I think he has a thing for you."

"I'd really rather not discuss my personal life."

"From what I've heard, you don't have much of one," Blades countered, not unkindly.

"That's my business."

"Elliott's a nice guy. You could do a lot worse."

"So I take it you don't object to his involvement in the case?"

"I'll take any help I can get, especially from someone with Elliott's brains. Who knows? If he's got the family's cooperation, he may be able to get to people in a way that I can't."

"Do you know what killed them yet?" I asked, not sure whether he'd say even if he knew.

"It's too soon to tell. The health department hasn't turned anything up in the office itself, though I've ordered that it remain under seal until they get all of their test results back. They still haven't done the autopsy. Jack Cavanaugh's been on the phone all day, pulling strings, trying to get it moved up. I understand him wanting to make funeral arrangements, but unfortunately, there was a triple murder in the Robert Taylor homes yesterday and two uniforms showed up at a domestic call last night to find both combatants ten-seven. They're a little backed up at the medical examiner's office."

"What does it mean to be 'ten-seven'?" I asked, curious.

"Police communication code for 'out of service,' " replied Blades, with a grin meant to forgive his own callousness. "There's no way you can do this job without developing a diseased sense of humor. No offense. Why did you ask Elliott to come in on this thing? What's your interest?"

"I'm the lawyer for the Cavanaughs' company. I was there when both women died. That in and of itself should be enough for me to take an interest. But there's more to it because of Dagny. I didn't know her for very long, so it's hard to explain. But if you'd met her, you'd realize she was the type of person who, no matter what the circumstances, would know exactly what to do. I know that doesn't seem like much, but there are so few people like that in the world. Maybe that's why her death seems such a loss to me—that and the fact that I really liked her. I just don't want her death to be one of those things that just falls through the cracks."

"What about Cecilia Dobson?"

"It's all part of the same thing, don't you think?"

"It sounds like you think they were murdered."

"I don't know what to think. But whatever happened, I don't think it was a coincidence."

"You live in a lawyer's world," Blades said carefully. "Where you live, actions have consequences and riddles have answers."

"What's that supposed to mean?"

"Nothing. I just want you to be prepared for the fact that this business with Dagny Cavanaugh and Cecilia Dobson may not end up the way you think."

"Why? How do you think it's going to end up?"

"I'm a policeman. I'm not paid to think. I'm paid to find out."

Before I could press him for an explanation, a red-faced man opened the door just wide enough to stick his head in. Between his beefy shoulders and the door frame I could see that he held a man in handcuffs by the scruff of the neck. The man was bleeding profusely from his nose, which resembled nothing more than a quarter pound of raw ground round. I could hear the faint *pat, pat, pat* of drops of blood landing on the tile.

"Wordell Jones says he wants to talk to you about the Jonavich shooting," the red-faced man said.

"Put that worthless piece of shit into the big interrogation room and tell him he'd better not bleed all over everything before I get there or I'll tear him a new asshole," Blades snarled.

The head withdrew and the door closed.

"You have quite a way with people," I said.

"It's the job." Blades grinned. "It teaches you the subtle art of conversation."

IT WAS ALMOST MIDNIGHT before I got home from the office. The time it was taking to deal with the Cavanaughs was cutting into the rest of my cases to the point where I dreaded even the sight of Cheryl's carefully typed to-do list. I drove home fighting exhaustion, slipping an old Warren Zevon tape into the player and turning the volume all the way up so that I could sing along with "Lawyers, Guns and Money" in order to stay awake.

The apartment was empty when I got there, the red light on the answering machine blinking in the dark. I switched on a light and pushed the button to rewind the tape—one message. I kicked my shoes off and began gratefully shedding the trappings of the workaday world—earrings, jacket, panty hose—as I stood listening to Elliott Abelman's voice asking me to meet him for breakfast at the Valois at seven the following morning to discuss the Cavanaugh case.

THE NEXT MORNING I chose the grubbiest running clothes I could find—a pair of stretched-out leggings that sagged dramatically in the rear and an old turtleneck in a pustulent shade of green that I'd bought in college to wear as part of my Halloween costume the year I went as an iguana. I crowned the whole ensemble with a hot-pink baseball cap advertising an ulcer medication made by Azor Pharmaceuticals. When Elliott looked at me he was going to see the name of Stephen's company directly above my face.

On the steps in front of my apartment I stretched my hamstrings. The sun was out—brilliant and warm. The snow was melting into little rivers on the sidewalk. Birds seemed to have appeared from nowhere, along with a half ton of rapidly thawing dog shit. Aaaah . . . springtime in the city.

I launched myself into a five-mile loop that took me south through the university and back up again to Fifty-third Street. Pushing it the whole way, I managed to cut three minutes off my usual time and arrived at the restaurant, sides heaving and soaked with sweat, at five minutes to seven.

Elliott was already waiting for me, leaning up against a parking meter in jeans and a worn jacket of soft brown leather. He had the *Tribune* open to the sports section, which he closed when he saw me.

The Valois is a neighborhood institution. True Hyde Parkers pronounce the name of the storefront restaurant so that it rhymes with *boy*. As long as anyone can remember, the "See Your Food" cafeteria has served up hot, cheap food to the students, bookies, cops, pimps, and petty thieves that parade through its doors daily—home cooking for people who barely have a home.

Pete, the surly Greek short-order man, was behind the counter taking orders, flipping pancakes, and shouting at Adele, his nemesis at the cash register. Elliott ordered two eggs over easy, grits, biscuits, coffee, and orange juice.

"What you want?" demanded Pete, turning his rheumy eyes on me.

"Coffee, please."

"You don't want nothing else? No eggs? No potatoes?"

"No thank you."

"Come on, honey, you got to put meat on those bones," urged the woman who stood between Pete and Adele serving up the biscuits. It looked to me like she had enough "meat" for both of us.

"I don't like breakfast," I said, resenting having to explain.

"Then what you doin' here?" demanded a good-natured voice from behind me in line.

"You be nice to her, now," joked another. "She looks like she had herself a rough night."

"Fine," I said definitively. "I'll have two eggs, scrambled, and a biscuit."

"No grits?" demanded Pete, pressing his advantage.

"Absolutely," I replied. "A double order, if you please."

As Pete cracked eggs onto the well-oiled surface of the hot griddle, Elliott took two trays off the pile. As he wiped them carefully with a napkin the butt of his Browning automatic peeked out from the holster under his arm.

Miraculously, three cops got up from their table just as we finished at the cash register. At the Valois a group of regulars takes up the tables between the front door and the pay phones, nursing their coffee and making book, so seating is generally at a premium.

"I went to see Jack Cavanaugh yesterday. He didn't object to hiring me. He seemed pretty out of it. Most of the time he let his wife do the talking."

"Peaches?"

"I'd heard that she left Channel Seven to marry some old guy. I knew her when I was working in the prosecutor's office. She was having trouble with an obsessed fan. Lots of women in the public eye have that kind of trouble—men, too, for that matter. There are a lot of sick people in this world and not a lot you can do about it. Most people just hire a bodyguard, change their routine, keep their fingers crossed, and chalk it up as one of the unpleasant realities of success—you know, like divorce and liposuction." He flashed me one of the wonderful grins that transformed his face and—I hate to admit it—made my heart beat faster.

"But the guy who was stalking Peaches took it a step further. He broke into her apartment one night while she was on the air—went through her underwear and stuff. Most people would have freaked out, but Peaches is one tough lady. Smart, too. She got the station to agree to let her do a series on celebrity stalkers. They ran it during sweeps month, and ratings went through the roof. Needless to say, she did a segment on what had happened to her. Lit a fire under the cops, who miraculously arrested the guy in time for the chief of police to get an interview on the eleven o'clock."

"Daniel Babbage told me that Peaches was smart, that I shouldn't be fooled by her fluff-girl act. Have you talked to the family yet?"

"I thought I'd wait until this afternoon—give the cops a chance to finish up. In the meantime I've been doing a little checking on Cecilia Dobson."

"So what did you find out?"

"I decided to pay a call on her landlady. It turns out that your friend's secretary was hardly a model tenant—even by Uptown standards. By all accounts she was a real party girl—late on the rent, lots of loud music, male visitors, and empty bottles in the trash."

"So Philip wasn't the only guy she was seeing."

Elliott smiled again. "Joe told me that you managed to sweat a confession out of Philip Cavanaugh yesterday."

"Yeah, right. He came into my office practically beating his breast in contrition."

"You know what they say. The Jews may have invented guilt, but it's the Catholics who first used it to its full potential."

We both laughed.

"I met Philip's wife, the lovely Sally, when I went to see Jack Cavanaugh about taking the case," Elliott continued. "I must confess, I can hardly blame Philip for playing around."

"Why? What's she like?"

"Church lady. You know the type—starched hair, sensible shoes, can spot a sin before it's committed."

"Philip told me that Cecilia had another boyfriend—somebody regular," I said. "Did you find anything out about him?"

"Richard Cooper, age twenty-six, plays drums with a band called Spastic Cantaloupe. I have the name of a guy who might know where I can find him. He works in a body-piercing parlor over on Halsted, but it doesn't open until noon. You want to come?"

"I'll pass."

"Cecilia also had a small-time criminal record. Did Joe tell you? Two busts for shoplifting. She was also picked up once in a prostitution sweep but was never charged."

"Any drug arrests?"

"No. But that doesn't mean she wasn't using, just that she was never caught. The landlady let me take a look at her apartment. It looked like a druggie's place—mattress on the floor, a ripped couch that looks like she got it off of someone's front lawn—but I didn't see any drug paraphernalia around. You have to wonder. She had a job, she was probably getting money off of Philip and some of the other guys she was seeing. Where was it all going if it wasn't going up her nose?"

"Philip says he didn't give her money. Though he says she asked."

"His wife probably keeps track of every dime."

"He says that's why he was going to end the affair. That and the fact that he was worried that his wife would find out."

"So you think Philip might have killed her?"

"Aren't we getting a little ahead of ourselves? For all we know, Cecilia died of a drug overdose and Dagny Cavanaugh had an undiagnosed brain tumor."

"Yeah, and I'm Sheena, Queen of the Jungle."

"Even if we assume that Cecilia Dobson was killed, and if we completely ignore what happened to Dagny Cavanaugh, you still have to ask yourself why Philip Cavanaugh would have to kill Cecilia? He said he was going to break it off with her. From what you've told me, she doesn't exactly sound like she was particularly attached to the guy. What motive would he have?"

"Fear," replied Elliott, flashing one of his megawatt grins. "Believe me, Kate. I've met his wife. I know what I'm talking about."

CHAPTER

14

I said good-bye to Elliott Abelman on the sidewalk in front of the Valois. As I walked toward my apartment I found myself thinking about what Joe Blades had said about Elliott having a "thing" for me. No doubt the private investigator and I had our moments—times when the spark of mutual attraction crackled between us—but that was all. Elliott was a professional and I sent a great deal of business from Callahan Ross his way. He was smart enough and gentleman enough to leave it at that. Crossing the street at Lake Park, I found myself turning my conversation with Joe Blades over and over in my mind. I decided that I resented the homicide detective giving speech to what I had long chosen to ignore. When you came right down to it, I liked my life simple. Now, suddenly, everything was getting complicated.

I made a quick stop at Big Jim's Tobacco Shop under the bridge beside the train station. The backbone of Big Jim's trade was rolling papers and boxes of blunts—cheap cigars that the neighborhood dopers soaked with whiskey, hollowed out, and filled with hash. But he was happy to sell me two of his best cigars, Paul Garmierian double coronas, each in its own pale cream cylinder, sealed with red wax.

Back at my apartment I showered quickly, dressed for the office, and twisting my still-wet hair into its usual French twist, packed as best as I could for my trip to Georgia. I had no idea what Tall Pines plantation would be like and, under the circumstances, had nobody I felt comfortable asking. I chose a dark suit for the funeral and then tried to cover the rest of the bases as best I could, stuffing everything into the hanging bag I used for overnight trips.

I flagged a cab down in front of the apartment and had the driver stop at Billings Hospital. I told him that I wanted him to keep the meter running. I had a ten o'clock meeting with the in-house counsel for Azor Pharmaceuticals and the lawyers from the firm that was representing Gordimer A.G. in the pending joint venture with Stephen's company—but I wanted to see Daniel before I left for Georgia.

I stood in the doorway of the hospital room, clutching the cigars, and I knew instantly that he'd never smoke them. Daniel looked like he was sleeping, but I could tell from listening to him that it was unlikely he'd ever awaken. His breaths were slow and shallow—after each one I waited, straining to hear if there would be another. When he finally exhaled it was with a rattle from deep in his throat.

A nurse was with him, busily checking his blood pressure.

"How is he?" I asked.

"Are you a relative?"

"No. Just a colleague."

"He's resting comfortably."

I nodded, knowing full well what that meant.

I ARRIVED AT AZOR'S corporate headquarters on South Michigan with my briefcase in one hand and my suitcase in the other. I parked the suitcase with Tamara, the beautiful Eurasian woman who manned the reception desk and made almost twice what Cheryl did because Stephen thought that she went well with the Art Deco decor.

Stephen did not come to the meeting—it was lawyers only—but he caught me in the hall before I went in and drew me around the corner, away from the attorneys for the Swiss. I stood against the wall between two abstract paintings that I particularly disliked. Stephen rested one of his massive hands on my shoulder and I felt overwhelmed by the sheer size of him.

"Cheryl told me that another woman died at Superior Plating. What happened?"

"Nobody knows. It might have been some sort of industrial accident."

"Are you okay?"

"I'm hanging in there," I assured him, wondering whether it was concern for me, or for the negotiations with Gordimer, that had prompted the question.

"Come home with me tonight," he said, dropping his voice to one notch above a whisper, his baritone so deep that some of the softer notes got lost. "I'll make you dinner."

"I can't," I answered with real regret. "I'm flying down to Georgia for Dagny Cavanaugh's funeral. But I'll be back in time for the party for Grandma Prescott."

"Promise?"

"Promise."

I WAS DEEP INTO a mind-numbing conversation about the relative capital depreciation structures of the United States and Switzerland when Stephen's secretary slipped me a note to call my office. I excused myself and ducked into a small room that had been set up with a desk and phone for just such occasions.

"I'm sorry to bother you, Kate," said Cheryl, who'd obviously been waiting for my call, "but I've got some guy named Cliff Schaeffer on the phone. He says that he's Lydia Cavanaugh's attorney and he will not take no for an answer. He says it's urgent and he absolutely has to speak to you."

"Can you connect him or do I have to call him back?"

"I think the switchboard here can connect you. Hang on."

I waited through dead air and a series of clicks before a male voice bellowed, "Schaeffer here."

"Hi, Cliff. It's Kate Millholland. What's the crisis?"

"The first round of documents that Superior Plating is required to furnish to my client under section eleven-eight of the Illinois Shareholder Protection Act were due on my desk at nine o'clock this morning. I have no choice but to interpret their nondeliverance as a sign of bad faith on your part."

"Hold your horses, Cliff. First of all, I don't think that 'nondeliverance' is actually a word. Second, I don't know how closely you've been in contact with your client, but in case you haven't heard, her sister died on Wednesday."

"I fail to see what that has to do with it."

"Well, for one thing, Dagny Cavanaugh was the chief financial officer of Superior Plating and Specialty Chemicals, and since most of the documents were in her safekeeping, I'd say that her death slows things down a bit."

"Don't tell me she was the only one who knew how to work the photocopier," Schaeffer snapped sarcastically. Lydia's attorney had a reputation for being a hyperactive pit bull of an advocate, a man whose glaring personality defects were only justified by his ability to get results. He was pugnacious, argumentative, and suffered from an inflated opinion of his own skills, and I was in no mood to take his shit.

"Don't pull this plaintiff's lawyer crap with me, Schaeffer," I hissed. His indignation may have been an act designed to rile me, but there was nothing artificial about my anger. "I won't get into the gutter with you. In the end you'll be in the dirt all by your little self. I'm going to say this really slowly so that I'm sure you understand. Dagny's death is going to slow things down. If you don't think your client can live with that, I suggest you call her and ask her. But I'd do it soon. She leaves at four o'clock to fly to Georgia for the funeral."

"For your information, Ms. Millholland," he said, dragging the first syllable out until it sounded like a buzz saw, "I just got off the phone with my client ten minutes ago and she says that if you try to use her sister's death as an excuse to delay production of the information we've requested, she wants me to file suit. Now, would you like me to repeat that for you slowly, or did you get it the first time?"

I FOUND KEN KURLANDER giving shorthand to his secretary in a voice that carried the seriousness of a benediction. He made a great show of interrupting what he was doing on my account. Ken was one of those partners who have been with the firm so long that they actually believed their corner offices imbued them with sovereignty. All those old guys are the same with their acres of calf-bound law books and their monster views. They drive me crazy.

"Did your secretary deliver the copy of Dagny Cavanaugh's will that I gave her?" he asked.

"Yes, she did. That's what I wanted to talk to you about. I was wondering if you knew what was behind Dagny's decision to name her brother Eugene executor of her estate?"

"As you say, he was her brother," Kurlander replied, playing coy.

"I know. But I'd have thought that Philip would be the more obvious brother to choose. After all, we're talking about managing a considerable number of assets, not the least of which are the shares in Superior Plating. Assuming that Dagny believed it likely that she would survive her father, Philip is the only other family member that has the financial skills for the job. And if I know you, Ken, you laid that out pretty straight with her. So the question remains—why didn't she choose Philip?"

"Eugene's wife, Vy, took care of Claire from the time she was an infant so that Dagny could go back to work. Claire is exactly the same age as Vy and Eugene's oldest daughter, Mary Beth. From what I gather, the two girls are almost like sisters. In Dagny's mind there was never any question that Eugene and Vy would be named Claire's guardians."

"I understand," I replied, wondering whether Kurlander was being deliberately obtuse. "That's not what's bothering me. Let me put it another way. Dagny Cavanaugh was the chief financial officer of a large manufacturing company. In short, exactly the sort of person you'd expect to be a very savvy testamentary planner. So why did she leave control over her only daughter's financial future to the least educated, and arguably least capable member of her family? Why not give guardianship to Eugene and Vy, but name Philip executor?"

"Dagny and I did discuss that possibility at length, but in the end she decided against it."

"Was she afraid that there would be friction between Eugene and Philip over what was best for Claire?"

"There is always that danger when one person has the authority to make decisions about matters of travel and education and someone else controls the money, but that wasn't the overriding concern."

"What was?"

Kurlander clasped his hands together and leaned forward across the polished surface of his desk. "Dagny did not want her brother Philip to control that many shares of Superior Plating stock, even temporarily," he breathed confidentially. "She was afraid that if her father died and left his shares divided among his four children, and then she passed away before Claire turned eighteen, Philip would have effective control of fifty percent of the shares if he were Claire's trustee."

"And she felt that would make him too powerful in the company?"

"She feared that Philip would make any kind of deal he could with either of the surviving siblings in order to gain complete control of the company—even if it meant not acting in Claire's best interest."

I thanked Ken for his time and walked slowly back to my own office. The Medicis, I reflected, did not live in a world more filled with intrigue.

CHAPTER

15

I t was an awkward group that gathered in the passenger lounge of the executive terminal at Midway Airport. Earlier in the day Jack and Peaches had taken the Superior Plating jet to accompany Dagny's body to Tall Pines. Jack had chartered a plane to take the rest of the family down, and confronted with the Cavanaughs en masse, I was sorry I wasn't flying alone on some anonymous, commercial flight.

Philip's wife, Sally, acted as self-appointed hostess, making introductions and filling me in on the details of the travel arrangements. We were, she pointedly explained, still waiting for Lydia and her family. From her tone of voice it was clear that waiting for Lydia was something at which the rest of the Cavanaugh clan had a great deal of practice.

Sally Cavanaugh was everything that Elliott had said—a stern, large-knuckled woman with parade-ground posture and disciplined hair. Looking at her, I couldn't decide which was more incredible—that Philip had waited until meeting Cecilia Dobson to seek the comforts of another woman, or that he'd gotten up the courage to do it at all. He actually seemed careful when he was near her, the way you would be around a large, bad-tempered dog.

I had not seen Eugene since those few moments right after Dagny died. He still seemed pulled taut by grief, and my heart went out to him. He paced restlessly along the perimeter of the waiting area, a pair of hunting dogs slavishly at his heels. Eugene's wife, Vy, a girlish woman with long brown hair and a simple cotton dress, sat quietly in the background, surrounded by her children. I counted six—from the oldest, Mary Beth, who was Claire's age, all the way down to a little boy, still in diapers, who toddled happily between his father, the dogs, and the rest of his family, a toy truck clutched in each chubby fist. Between Vy and Mary Beth sat Claire. The three women seemed ill with grief.

When Lydia finally arrived it was like the circus pulling into town. Three taxis drew onto the tarmac outside the gate. Arthur emerged from the first as soon as it came to a stop, sauntered disinterestedly into the waiting area, and wordlessly pulled a cellular phone from his pocket and began dialing.

Lydia was left to supervise the unloading of what looked like enough paraphernalia for a yearlong cruise—strollers, car seats, boxes of diapers, duffel bags, tricycles, and one of every piece of luggage made by Louis Vuitton. Two-year-old twins seemed to escape from one of the taxis, their faces smeared with chocolate, and were pursued by their harried au pair. Peter brought up the rear, sullen and wretched. Vy made room for him beside his cousins—a heart-wrenching reunion of the Mount McKinley Expedition.

Lydia made her entrance preceded by three hyperactive shih tzus, whose barking escalated to a frenzy at the sight of Eugene's dogs. The pointers, who had turned to assert their domination over the newcomers, dropped to the floor at a single word from Eugene. In the meantime Lydia's dogs ran in circles around each other, threatening to hang themselves on their leashes.

By the time we all finally boarded the plane, the Jet Stream, it was packed to the bursting point. In the air, the twins seemed intent on occupying every minute of the flight running up and down the aisle with their grimy hands and runny noses, alternately taunting their exasperated relatives and their mother's yappy little dogs. By the time we touched down in Tallahassee, we were all scrambling over each other to get off the plane.

Three identical minivans had been sent to pick us up. Lydia's family took the first one while Vy and Eugene loaded their well-mannered brood and Claire into the second. I rode with Philip, Sally, and Lydia's overflow baggage.

Up until this point my entire experience of the South had consisted of trips to my grandmother's house in Palm Beach and one wild, sketchily recollected road trip to the Kentucky Derby with three friends during college. I found myself completely unprepared for how beautiful it was. After the eternity of the Chicago winter and the indifference of the Chicago spring, the warm Florida air was like a fragrant blessing. I rolled down the window of the van and drank it in.

Once we were ten minutes from the airport, the road narrowed to two lanes and traffic dwindled to an occasional pickup truck. On either side of us the soil was a vivid terra-cotta, red like a gash between the blacktop and the grass. Above us, trees shot up, their dark branches bursting with new leaves and swinging with Spanish moss. The buildings grew sparser and disappeared completely save for the odd shack of weathered planks and tarpaper that we glimpsed in flashes through the trees.

We'd been driving for half an hour before we turned onto an unpaved road. The trees were so thick that they blotted out the sun, casting the rutted red soil of the road in perpetual shadow while suicidal rabbits dashed in front of the car. Every hundred yards or so I'd see a metal sign, nailed high up onto a tree near the road. For about ten minutes they all said the same thing: POSTED—BRADFORD. Abruptly they changed to POSTED—CAMERON. I asked what it meant.

"It's shorthand for 'posted, no trespassing,' " explained Sally. "All the property we're passing through is Ken Cameron's land. Next we'll go through Fran Goldenberg's until we get to Tall Pines, which is all Cavanaugh property. They put up the signs so that the poachers won't be able to use the excuse that they didn't know whose land they're on."

"Not that it stops them," complained Philip.

"Tall Pines is more than sixty thousand acres with only one road through it. Now all the locals have four-wheel drive, so there's no stopping them."

"You can't begin to imagine the damage they do. Last year Eugene caught the three Grisham boys drunk as skunks, hunting deer at night with assault rifles."

"It was a mercy that no one was killed," added Sally, shaking her head.

"You can say that again," chimed in the driver, speaking for the first time. "They must have caught one of Eugene's charitable moods."

THE WORD PLANTATION CONJURES up images of Tara, of white-columned mansions set at the end of tree-lined drives. Tall Pines was wilder than that—a plantation for hunting rather than for cultivation—but there was a rugged beauty to the place that made me understand why Dagny Cavanaugh would choose it for her final resting place. From a sudden clearing in the trees I caught my first glimpse of the main house, an attractive low-slung building that I realized, as I got closer, was in reality two houses connected by an airy, covered walkway with a rustic pine-hewn railing and a terrazzo roof.

The van I was riding in stopped just long enough for me to extract my bags from the rest of the luggage and then continued up the
road to where Philip and the other Cavanaugh children had their
houses. Peaches met me at the door of the house she shared with
Jack. She looked tired but even more striking in jeans and half the
makeup she'd worn when I'd seen her in Chicago.

"I hope you had a good trip down," she said. There was more
Georgia in her voice now, but none of the animation that I remembered from our first meeting. Dagny's death, I reflected, had torn the
heart out of every member of the family.

Peaches led the way into the house, which, though large, was un-
pretentiously furnished in the style of a hunting lodge. I would be
staying in the guest wing, which, Peaches explained, was the newer
end of the house.

"How's Jack managing?" I asked as I followed her through the
breezeway.

"It's very difficult," she replied, shaking her head. "About an hour
ago I finally convinced him to take a sleeping pill. He's been so wound
up, fighting with everybody about releasing the body and screaming
at the people at the funeral home."

She stopped at a door of polished wood and pushed it open. My
room was large and L-shaped, with a high-beamed ceiling and long
windows commanding a spectacular view of rolling hills dotted with
dogwoods and magnolias in full flower. I set my suitcase at the foot of
the four-poster bed and pronounced the accommodations lovely.

"I was wondering if you'd like to go for a ride with me before dinner?" Peaches asked, almost timidly. "Now that Jack's asleep and
doesn't need me, I thought I'd call down to the barn and have them
saddle up my horse. Do you ride?"

"Some."

"Then why don't you come with me. There's really no better way
to see the place," she urged. There was no mistaking the loneliness in
her voice.

"I think I stuck a pair of jeans into my bag," I ventured, unsure.

"Good, it's settled, then."

THE STABLES WERE ABOUT two miles from the house, down the same dirt road that we'd taken from the airport, but in the opposite direction. Peaches drove us in a white Jeep Cherokee with Georgia plates, pointing out Lydia's house as we passed it. It was incongruously modern, all angles and panes of glass. On the lawn was an enormous sphere of polished brass at least eight feet in diameter.

"I wish that Lydia would keep her taste for modern art in Chicago, where it belongs." Peaches sighed. "They had to take all the seats out of the plane to get that thing here. Of course, all the people down here who work on the plantation refer to it as the bowling ball and laugh at her behind her back. Now, back over that rise you can see Eugene's house."

I saw a rambling house built of logs with a porch running all the way around it.

"It looks more rustic from the outside than it really is. It's actually gorgeous inside. Eugene did most of the work himself."

Peaches stopped the car in front of a functional and well-kept barn next to a neat paddock. Opening the door, I smelled the familiar scent of horses and heard the cacophonous barking of dogs.

"That's the kennel over there," said Peaches, pointing to a white-washed building that looked like a big henhouse. "We keep about fifty hunting dogs. I love the horses, but the dogs are Jack's pride and joy."

A jeaned and cowboy-booted farmhand brought out mounts, a set of reins in each hand. Peaches took the bridle of a pretty palomino, stroking its neck and talking quietly as she led it out into the sunshine.

"You'll be likin' Scarlet, ma'am," the hand advised me with a self-conscious pull at his cap as he handed me the reins to the bay. "She's a real push-button horse. You don't need to be tellin' her what you want more'n once." He laced his fingers together to give me a leg up. I put my foot into his palms and managed to hoist myself up on the first try, giving a grunt as I swung into the big western saddle.

"Water's real high over by the river, Mrs. Cavanaugh," he advised Peaches as he shortened up my stirrups. "And them banks are gettin' real soft on account of all the rain we've been gettin'. I'd take the path that leads out by the big pond if I was you."

"We'll do that, Tom. Have you heard anything about the weather?"

"More rain's supposed to be comin' through tomorrow afternoon."

"Well . . ." Peaches sighed. "Let's just pray the Lord keeps the rain away until after the funeral."

Then she turned her horse and gave him a kick.

IT HAD BEEN A while since I'd last been on a horse, and for the first few minutes I fought down the uneasiness that comes from sitting on the back of an animal much bigger—and stupider—than yourself. But after a few minutes I found my seat and fell into a comfortable slow trot beside Peaches. Jack's wife, obviously at home on a horse, turned her high-spirited palomino onto a rough track that ran through fields planted with alfalfa.

We rode for a while without talking, adjusting stirrups and shifting saddle blankets. I am, as a rule, a city girl at heart. There is something undeniably frightening about the country. It is full of shadows and secret places, natural violence, and no one to hear your cries for help. But after everything that had happened over the last few days, I found in the silence and the space of the Georgia countryside a kind of relief.

"The police said that you were there both times," said Peaches, finally breaking the silence. "I hope you don't mind my asking, but I can't discuss it with Jack. It's too painful for him. But even if we don't talk about it, it's all we think about. What do *you* think killed them?"

"I wish I knew, but I'm convinced that whatever it was happened to them both. The similarities were just too striking for it to be otherwise. Dagny was lying on the same place on the floor in virtually the same position as Cecilia was when we found her. It was almost as if Dagny was trying to copy her secretary. . . . I don't know. The whole thing is eerie."

"When the police came to the house they kept asking us if Dagny ever used drugs. We kept on telling them no, but I'm not sure they believed us. I know what cops are like from when I used to do the news. All they deal with all day long are lowlifes, addicts, and thieves. Still, if it wasn't drugs, what was it?"

"I don't know. I guess we'll just have to wait until the test results come back."

"But what I want to know is how do we live until then?" Peaches demanded bitterly. "Jack is drinking too much and he can't sleep without pills. I don't think Claire has eaten since her mother died. Vy and Eugene are doing their best, but they were both close to Dagny and they have their own grief to deal with. Their pastor, Father O'Donnell, is coming down tomorrow to say the funeral mass and Vy wants us all to talk to him, but honestly I can't imagine what he'll say. . . ."

I knew what he'd say. I'd heard everything that anyone ever said to the grieving. None of it ever helped, but I thought it best not to say so.

"There's a good place for a gallop coming up," Peaches announced suddenly. "There, just over the rise. Do you feel up to it?"

"Absolutely," I said, and gathered up the reins.

IT IS AS CLOSE as I'll ever come to flying, that glorious combination of speed and freedom that comes when you're standing in the stirrups, balanced over the withers of a galloping horse. We thundered up a gentle hill, along a grass-covered earthen dam, and the entire way around a large pond. The water was so glassy and still that we could see our reflections. When Peaches finally reined in the palomino and I followed suit, slowing to a walk, it was with a real pang of regret. It was only after we'd walked for a minute that I realized I was winded, felt the horse's heaving sides beneath my legs, and saw the flecks of foam along its flanks. We must have galloped for miles, but in my mind it had only taken seconds.

I looked up at the sky. The sun had dropped lower on the horizon. Clouds were gathering.

"This is the place where Jack's oldest boy drowned," said Peaches. "I've only been down here once or twice. Jack won't go near the place. Dagny's dying has brought it all back to him as if it were yesterday. You can't imagine the hurt."

"I can't imagine anything worse than losing a child," I said. "Now Jack's lost two."

"And the ones who are left hate my guts," said Peaches in a voice ripe with bitterness. "When I fell in love with Jack I didn't expect the world to understand. It's not just that he's so much older, but he's also a hard man and rough around the edges. I know what people think—you're blond and you work in TV, so you must have the intellectual capacity of a hamster. But I'm not stupid, and I really thought I was ready for what the world was going to throw at me when I decided to marry Jack. So the whispers didn't bother me, or the assumption that he must have left his wife for me. But the one thing I never anticipated was the extent to which I have been vilified by his children. I never expected them to run to me with open arms and call me Mommy. But the level of their animosity never ceases to astonish me. Dagny was the only one who was ever fair to me, and now she's gone. I can't even begin to imagine what we are going to have to endure from Lydia over the next few weeks."

"You never know," I offered. "Sometimes it takes a tragedy like losing Dagny to bring a family together, to make them realize what's really important."

Looking out over the still water of the pond, I found myself fervently hoping that what I'd just said was true, that the Cavanaughs would somehow find a way to pull together in the wake of their loss. But I knew from experience that the physics of tragedy more often works in the opposite direction.

16

I swung my leg across the saddle and slid down to the ground, feeling suddenly short after having surveyed the world from the top of a horse for the last two hours. Following Peaches, I led my mount up to the hitching post, not surprised to find that I'd developed the rolling cowboy gait that I knew preceded a pair of very sore legs. Standing with one hand on the saddle horn and the reins in the other, I was startled to see Eugene Cavanaugh charging across the stable yard toward me, his face distorted with fury.

"Who said you could ride that horse?" he demanded furiously.

I was completely taken aback. It was Peaches, emerging from the shadow of the barn with a bridle over her arm, who answered him.

"I asked Tom to saddle Scarlet for Kate," she answered with a steely edge of warning to her voice.

"That's Dagny's horse! How dare you take it out without permission!"

"Whose permission?" Peaches inquired with studied sweetness.

"I was under the impression that all of these horses belong to your father, or am I wrong? Maybe you and I should go back up to the house and ask him whether it was okay for me to let Kate ride one."

Eugene stood mutely rigid, furious at the rebuke but unable to reply. Peaches may have married into a nest of vipers, I reflected, but it was obvious that she was more than able to defend herself.

A battered pickup appeared around the bend in the road and pulled up to the barn. Two men in overalls and baseball caps jumped out of the rear, the backs of their necks sunburned from hours behind the wheel of a tractor.

"Howdy, Mr. Cavanaugh. We just come back from checking the road over by the grave just like you asked. I'm thinkin' maybe we should put down some of that sand we've got bagged up in the yellow barn on account of there's bad mud in a coupla spots, but it's up to you."

Peaches took the reins from my hand and led my mount into the barn. I followed her, not eager to be caught in further conversation with Eugene.

"Sometimes I just can't abide any of them," Peaches announced from between gritted teeth as she bent to unbuckle the double straps of Scarlet's girth. "He thinks that because when he says 'jump' the factory workers all answer 'how high?' that he can order everyone else around as well. It's sickening how they're all always assuming. . . . And it's not just Eugene. Take Philip. It's true that he's going to be the boss after Jack's dead, but the greedy little bastard just can't wait."

I reached up and pulled the saddle off my horse's back with a grunt, staggering a little under the sudden weight.

"It goes in the tack room, over there. You'll see the spot," Peaches instructed, clipping a lead line to the horse's halter and leading it toward the paddock behind the barn. I lugged the saddle into the dusty tack room and followed her outside, blinking in the sunlight.

Lydia's son, Peter, was standing with one Doc Martened foot on the split-rail fence, chewing on a piece of hay.

"I was wondering if you could give me a lift back to my mom's house?" he asked. "I was going to go with Tom and J.T., but Uncle Eugene's sending them back to the barn to get some sand and they can't take me until they're done."

"That shouldn't be a problem," Peaches replied. "What have you been up to?"

"Actually, I've been trying to avoid my mother. We all have. When Uncle Eugene asked me to help out with the new puppies, I jumped at the chance. But I have to get back and get cleaned up for dinner. Mom's invited Nursey, so we all have to be on our best behavior and pass inspection."

"Nursey's the old housekeeper who came to work for Jack after Eleanor died," Peaches explained. "Her husband, Lucas, was killed in a fire and so she agreed to come up to Chicago and help Jack with the children. She lived with the family until Lydia went away to college. Now that she's retired she lives down here with her sister."

"My mom always says that Nursey's her real mother. Don't you think that's a weird thing to say?" Peter inquired, kicking the dirt.

"I'm sure she means it as a compliment," Peaches replied firmly. "Her real name is Henrietta Roosevelt, but everyone calls her Nursey, even Jack. She really is a part of the family, especially for your mother. She must be eighty if she's a day—and half-gaga, but still, terribly sweet."

"More like terribly gaga and half-sweet," grumbled Peter, sticking his hands in the back pockets of his jeans and heading toward the car.

IT WAS OBVIOUS THAT Jack Cavanaugh had already put away a fair amount of bourbon before dinner. It wasn't that he was acting drunk, but he had the slow, measured speech of a man who's taking pains to appear sober.

"You know what I'm going to miss most about Daniel Babbage?" he asked, pouring himself another drink. Peaches had turned in early with a headache. Someone had made us a couple of bacon, lettuce, and tomato sandwiches for our dinner. Jack's sat on his plate, untouched.

"What?" I asked, putting my hand over the top of my glass, indicating that I was still fine.

"Babbage understands guys like me. Now, I'm sure that you're one hell of a lawyer—Daniel'd never have asked me to hire you if you weren't. And I know that you're going to make sure that all my *i*s are dotted and my *t*s are crossed. But from what everyone tells me about your background, it sounds like you've been handed every single goddamn thing in your whole life. Am I right?"

I had learned from experience that there's no answer to that question, so I said nothing.

"Nobody ever handed me anything," he continued. "I was seventeen when my father died. He was killed in a bar fight in an argument over a woman. Not many people know that. He left me a factory that was practically falling down, half a dozen other pieces of property that he owed back taxes on, and about two thousand dollars in bar debts—which in those days was considered a fortune. From that I built one of the biggest plating operations in the country. I have two hundred employees, a house in Chicago and this one down here and a plane that gets me between the two of them. You want to know how I did it?"

"Yes," I said. I really did want to know.

"I told my customers any lie that would get me their business and then I did whatever it took to make good on my promise. We didn't have OSHA back then, or the damned EPA. We dumped our waste chemicals at night and had an accounting system that would have done credit to a call house. I stayed up nights working on a second ulcer trying to figure out a way to keep the unions out and the bank from shutting me down. Ask Daniel, he'll tell you what it was like. He and I have been through a lot together. It's hard to believe that we're not going to be together through this."

"I went to see him before I left," I said. "I know that if he could be here, he would."

"You know, I used to worry all the time that Dagny would get killed doing that rock-climbing stuff. That's how her husband died. Slipped and bounced against the side of a cliff like a yo-yo. He was dead when they brought him down. I could never understand how she could do it, why she wasn't afraid. She always told me that it didn't scare her because she never thought about falling. She was always looking ahead of her, thinking about the next piece of rock she was about to climb. She was concentrating so hard on getting where she needed to go that she didn't have time to worry about what would happen if she didn't make it.

"That's what running your own business is like. It's not about rules and briefs and working in a fancy office on LaSalle Street with hot-and-cold-running secretaries. It's about getting where you have to because you're too stubborn or too stupid to listen to anybody who tells you that you can't do it.

"Dagny loved the business. More than any of my children, she was the one who loved it the way I love it. They wanted her to go to Harvard, you know. Offered her a scholarship, the whole thing, but she wouldn't go. You want to know why?"

"Why?"

"Because she didn't want to leave Chicago. She went to Northwestern so that she could still work for the company on the weekends and over vacation. She's been keeping the books since she was nineteen years old. I can't believe we're going to be putting her into the ground tomorrow. . . ." His voice cracked and faded away.

I got up to get myself another drink. Not because I wanted one, but because I wanted to save him the embarrassment of my watching him cry.

I promised myself that this was the last case like this I was ever going to take. I liked meetings in conference rooms with lawyers who screamed and called you names. Lawyers who, when the negotiating was done, wanted to know whether you were free for lunch on Friday. This was too personal—too painful.

"She liked you, you know. She told me that the morning that she died. Philip and I were arguing about some stupid thing or other—I can't remember; we're always fighting—it doesn't matter about what. We've been fighting so long we don't know how to do anything else. Dagny came into my office and told me she thought you were a good lawyer—a good choice for the company—that you'd be able to handle this mess with Lydia and all the rest of it."

"Have you talked to Lydia at all since then?" I asked.

"She's beside herself," Jack replied. "She and Dagny were like this." For a brief instant his two hands made a token marriage. "I'm sure that she's completely forgotten that whole business about her shares. . . ."

I remembered my conversation with her lawyer earlier that day, and his satisfaction in telling me that he'd just gotten off the phone with Lydia, who was determined not to allow her sister's death to interfere with the sale of her shares. I looked at Jack Cavanaugh and could not tell him. It was an act of charity that I would soon come to regret.

BACK IN MY ROOM I took a long, hot shower. Riding exercises muscles that get no other use and I suddenly found myself aware of each and every one of them. I took two Advils and combed all the snarls out of my wet hair while I waited for them to work. I finished and changed into a pair of clean gray sweatpants and a white T-shirt, but I was still so sore that I knew I'd never be able to sleep, so I set off toward the main house to see if I could scare up a stiff scotch or, at the very least, some more of Jack Cavanaugh's bourbon.

I was surprised to find all the lights on in the house and an ample woman with a stiff beehive of teased hair at work in the kitchen.

"Howdy," she said. "You must be the lawyer lady that's come down from Chicago. I'm Darlene. What can I get for you, hon?"

I explained about the scotch and she obligingly pulled a bottle of single malt from a cupboard in the pantry and fetched me a glass.

"I sure hope the weather holds for the funeral tomorrow," she volunteered as I poured. "You wouldn't know it from all the sunshine we had today, but we've been having more rain than anyone knows what to do with. My Tom said that when he ran into Chuck Zellmer over at the feed store, Chuck told him that he's got twenty acres already under six inches of water. Now, Zellmer's property lies closer to the river than Tall Pines, but I can tell you if we get much more rain, we're going to see flooding as bad as we saw in sixty-nine—you mark my words."

"What happened in sixty-nine?" I asked, not wanting to seem rude.

"Snake Creek went right up over its banks and the dam over by Chapaloosa didn't hold. Half of Tall Pines was waist-deep in water. We had so much water in this here kitchen you couldn't see the tops of the counters. Then, of course, when it finally went back down the mud was worse than the water. The men had to come down in here with shovels. There was dead catfish in Mr. C's bedroom. Lord, you can't believe the mess. Let's just pray that don't ever happen again, but I'll just be happy if the rain holds off until after Miss Dagny's funeral."

"Is that what you're baking all these pies for?" I asked, looking at the half dozen or so that sat cooling on the counter.

"Yes, ma'am. Last time I baked this many pies it was for the party we had for Miss Lydia's wedding. Her second one, that is, not the first—nor the third neither, for that matter. And the time before that it was for Mr. Jimmy's funeral." She put her hands on her hips and drew a deep breath.

"You worked for the Cavanaughs back then?" I asked, pulling a stool up to the counter where Darlene was rolling out pastry with a rolling pin.

"My mama kept house for Mr. Cavanaugh until her arthritis got too bad for her to get around. I've been helpin' out 'round this house since I was big enough to swing a broom. I was just a little slip of a girl when Jimmy died, but I remember it like it was yesterday. We all do. Mama and I stayed up all night right here in this very kitchen baking pies and cookin' for after the funeral. We cried our eyes out, we did. It was such a terrible thing. He was such a fine young man. We thought Mr. C. would die from the shock."

"It must have been terrible for the girl's family as well," I said, thinking that there seemed to be a forgotten victim in every tragedy: the girl who'd tried to kill herself and ended up taking Jimmy Cavanaugh to the bottom of the pond with her; Cecilia Dobson, whose death would seem forever eclipsed by the loss of Dagny Cavanaugh.

"I don't know if they felt nothin'." Darlene sniffed. "According to my mama, the Swintons was the worst sort of white trash there is. They all moved away right after it happened. Grace's mama ran off when she was just a baby and her dad was an old drunk who only held down a job for as long as it took to get money for his liquor— that's when he wasn't out poaching or moonshining. . . . Grace was a pretty thing, though. I remember that. Big blue eyes and hair like corn silk. She sure was something to look at. I remember how Edna Tibbets was always squeezing lemons onto her hair and sitting out in the sun until she drew flies, trying to get her hair to go the same color as Grace Swinton's. . . ."

"Why did she kill herself?" I asked, thinking about the pond where we'd galloped earlier in the day. I was suddenly struck by the fact that, sitting in the middle of Tall Pines plantation, inaccessible by any road, it would make a rather inconvenient spot to choose for taking your own life.

"There was lots of talk, of course. There still is, for that matter.

You'd think that folks'd have better things to do than to sit around and jaw about what happened all those years ago—but you know what folks are. And after what happened to Miss Dagny, the old talk will start right back up again. Just this morning I heard 'em talking out there at the Dairy Pik over by Pinkerton about how the Cavanaugh family is cursed."

"So what do they say about the girl who killed herself?" I asked.

"They say that Grace Swinton was carrying Jimmy Cavanaugh's baby," breathed Darlene conspiratorially.

"And was she?"

"Nobody knows," Darlene replied, wiping floury hands on the front of her apron, "least of all the folks that's doin' all the talking. The only people who really know are Grace Swinton and Jimmy Cavanaugh and they're both dead. But—"

I never found out what else Darlene was going to tell me because she stopped in midsentence. Just then, from the other end of the house came the unmistakable sound of a woman screaming.

17

Darlene ran into the main section of the house, through the living room, and down the hall. I was right on her heels. We met Peaches coming from the opposite direction, clutching her pink satin bathrobe around her throat and shrieking like a freight train.

"What's happened?" I demanded. I had seen too many emergencies in too few days and my heart was in my throat.

"There's . . . there's . . . there's . . ." she gasped, pointing in the direction of the bedrooms.

"There's what, sugar?" asked Darlene, putting a motherly arm around Peaches's shoulder.

"A . . . snake!" she managed to blurt.

"Where's the snake?" Darlene demanded. Relief flooded through me.

"In our bathroom," Peaches replied, struggling to regain control of her breathing. "I went in to brush my teeth. . . . I heard it behind me, rattling."

"Did you get bit?" Darlene looked Jack's wife up and down.

Peaches shook her head no.

"Where's Jack?" I asked. "Is he all right?"

"He's in the bedroom. He's on the phone calling one of the men."

Jack marched into the hall and slammed the door quickly behind him. He was wearing black pajamas and knee-high rubber boots.

"Are you okay, honey?" he asked his wife, his voice still slurred from the bourbon. "It's nothing to get upset about. Just a big old rattlesnake. Someone must have left a door open, that's all."

Peaches nodded, pulling her thin robe around her shoulders. Jack turned to me.

"Kate, you take Peaches into the kitchen." he ordered.

"I'll heat up some water and make y'all some tea," Darlene offered as we made our way toward the kitchen. "This time of year if we get a lot of rain, the snakes come looking for dry land," she explained, filling the kettle from the tap. "Remember the time Mr. Philip had one?"

"Sally was in the kitchen," said Peaches, smiling in spite of herself. "She turned around and there was a rattlesnake—it must have been as thick as my arm—slithering across her white tile floor."

"They heard her screaming all the way down to Chapaloosa." Darlene laughed.

"But what I want to know is how this one got into my bathroom?" Peaches demanded anxiously. "I'm so glad I decided to leave Snuggles in Chicago."

"That little dog of yours would have been that snake's dinner," said Darlene.

"Ugh!" Peaches shuddered. "I hate to think of that horrible snake slithering through my house."

We heard a car door slam outside and Darlene scurried off to greet Tom, the farmhand who had driven our van from the airport. He appeared in the kitchen wearing overalls over a bright red union suit and a pair of high boots. In one hand he held a long pole with a loop of rope at one end. In the other he carried a big blue plastic bucket with a lid. He scratched his head sleepily.

"Where's the snake at?" he demanded. In the country, people go to bed early, and Jack's call had obviously awakened him. His hair stood up comically on his head.

"It's in the bathroom, right this way," said Jack, bringing up the rear.

"Stay here with me, Kate," Peaches begged. I was all too happy to comply. The men disappeared, and Darlene, not wanting to miss out on the action, followed.

"How are they going to catch it?" I asked.

"Tom'll slip that loop over its head—it's a kind of lasso for snakes. He'll pull the rope tight and then just pick it up and drop it into the bucket."

"It sounds like they're prepared for this."

"They do catch rattlers, especially this time of year. Tom's got a lot of experience with them on account of the dogs."

"Why's that?"

"When they have a new litter of hunting dogs that they're starting to train, one of the first things they do is catch a rattlesnake and kill it. Then they run an electric wire through its body. After that they let the puppies loose and let them come sniffing around. When one of them touches the snake they get an electric shock."

"How terrible!"

"Not as terrible as being killed by a snake," Peaches countered reasonably. "A hunting dog with a good pedigree costs thousands of dollars, and then they spend hundreds of hours training it. If the first time the dog goes out to flush game it gets killed by a snake, it's a terrible waste."

From the bedroom we heard Jack's booming voice. "Okay Tom, on the count of three!"

Safe in the kitchen, Peaches and I sat perfectly still, listening like

stowaways. After a minute we heard a crash and then a bump followed by a shout of triumph. Jack led the procession, carrying the
pail through the house. We could hear the angry rattle of the snake's
tail through the blue plastic.

"Don't you ladies worry now," Tom advised shyly. "We've got this
feller where he won't be doin' nobody any harm."

"You're not going to be letting that thing loose near the house,
are you?" Peaches asked anxiously.

"No, ma'am. I'm going to take it back down to the kennel. It'll
come in handy with those new pups. Just today J.T. caught a rattler
up by Snake Crick, but he mustn't have put the lid on real good because it got away before he got around to killin' it. You just be careful
about leavin' those doors open, you hear? These rascals are on the
move on account of it bein' so wet, and there's more rain in the
forecast."

I felt the hairs on the back of my neck stand up as he took his
gruesome prize out into the night.

DAGNY'S FUNERAL WAS SMALL and sad. As a light rain fell, Father
O'Donnell, who had, as a parish priest, offered Dagny Cavanaugh her
first communion, spoke movingly about eternity while the mourners
huddled tearfully underneath their umbrellas. Besides the family
there was a cluster of local residents, people who worked at Tall
Pines, like Darlene, and had also known Dagny since she was a little
girl. People who'd stood in much the same place and watched them
lower her brother Jimmy into the ground.

Claire stood bravely between her grandfather and the aunt who
had helped raise her. Before them, the fresh-turned red of the Georgia soil stood out like a wound against the damp green of the grass.
Behind her, Eugene wept openly, and even Philip could not contain
his grief. Lydia, dressed like a cross between Morticia Addams and
Coco Chanel, wore a heavy mantilla of black lace and hovered over an

old, frail black woman whose rheumy eyes never strayed from the casket. The twins had blessedly been left at home.

After the final prayers were said, an elegantly athletic man of forty with a shock of black hair and a dark Armani suit walked with Claire back to the house. When I asked who he was, Peaches explained that he was Dagny's rock-climbing friend from Belgium. I remembered the night we spent talking before the fire in her living room and the chocolates we had eaten the night before she died.

Here, under the graceful awning of willow trees, it might seem easy to imagine that it was some gentle hand that had laid claim to Dagny Cavanaugh. But for me, nothing would ever obscure the final agony of her death or my anger at seeing her taken from her family.

Back at the house I did not join the others for pie and coffee, but instead went back to my room to pack and organize my papers. Earlier that morning, as we prepared to leave the house for the funeral, Jack Cavanaugh had surprised me by announcing that he'd called a family meeting for one o'clock.

He refused to answer any of my questions about what he intended to discuss, and under the circumstances I'd felt uncomfortable pressing him. But all morning long I'd felt a sense of impotence mingled with foreboding. Try as I might, I could think of no good that could possibly come of a face-to-face meeting of all the Cavanaughs.

I WILL NEVER FORGET the strain and pretense in the room that afternoon after Dagny's funeral. My experience in corporate work had not prepared me for what emotions, laid raw by the death of one daughter and the dark heart of another, could whipsaw through a family bound together by blood and business. I'd seen CEOs plead with directors for their jobs and corporate officers beg bankers for mercy. I'd been bullied and screamed at, and had listened to whispered threats. None of it compared with Jack Cavanaugh pleading for his children's love under the thin guise of corporate unity.

I knew that words did not come easily for Jack Cavanaugh. He doled them out carefully, as if each one exacted a price. Yet he managed to speak movingly about his dream of having his children work together in the business he'd labored his entire life to build. He begged them to put aside their differences and work together, if not for his sake, then for their children's. He spoke of Dagny's love of the company and her dedication over the years, and told them that Superior Plating's continued success would be the most fitting of memorials.

As he spoke I watched the faces of his family. Eugene fiddled with his collar like a little boy being forced to sit quietly in church. Philip's face was impassive, a mask of attention hiding endless calculation. Beside him on the couch sat his wife, Sally, her knitting needles clicking out her wordless disapproval.

Lydia, the red lipstick of her mouth set in an expression of discontent, did not even bother to feign interest. Instead, she rearranged her hair in the reflection of the polished brass of a nearby lamp or methodically lined up the bracelets on her wrists. Of all of them, Arthur Wallace was the only one who listened. He sat motionless at his wife's side, hands clasped on his lap, his eyes never leaving his father-in-law's face.

How many years, how many wrong turns had it taken to bring a family to this? I wondered, wishing, not for the first time, that Daniel Babbage were here.

Jack Cavanaugh finished and pulled a sheet of white paper out of his pocket. The rattle of the paper seemed unnaturally loud. He cleared his throat to begin what I assumed was the formal portion of the meeting.

"Dagny's loss has left us with a serious gap in the management of the company. As chairman of the board and CEO, I have made some decisions that I feel will not only help fill the vacuum but will also equalize responsibility across the management team so that we can move the company forward confidently for the next generation."

Sally paused in her knitting. In the strained anticipation in the room, it seemed almost difficult to breathe.

"First," Jack Cavanaugh continued, "Lydia will be appointed to the newly created post of director of communications, accompanied by an increase in salary. At the same time Eugene will be promoted to the position of vice-president in charge of operations with responsibility for purchasing, procurement, and procedures. My son-in-law, Arthur Wallace, will assume the position of acting chief financial officer."

By the time he got to Arthur Wallace, all the color had drained out of Philip's face. He stared at his father with a look of undisguised disbelief. However, the same shock that had paralyzed Philip propelled his wife, Sally, to her feet.

"How can you do this?" she demanded. Her voice was loud and shrill. "When you told us you were going to have a family meeting, we all assumed you were finally going to step down and turn the company over to Philip like you've been promising all these years. Now you're telling us that you're going to just lay more burdens onto his shoulders and load up the payroll with more dead wood. He's worked sixteen hours a day for twenty years for half of what he'd earn at any other company, and this is what he gets? You talk about family unity, but what you really want is for Philip to kill himself so that everyone else can have a free ride. You expect everyone to lie down while you walk all over them!"

"Sally, please," implored Peaches.

"You stay out of this!" Philip snapped savagely to his stepmother. "This is none of your business."

"What else are you going to let Lydia get away with?" Sally demanded. "What about next time? A year from now, when Princess Lydia decides she wants to sell her precious shares again, what are you going to do? Are you going to tell Philip he has to step down so that Arthur can be president of the company?"

"I just can't believe that you'd do all this without consulting me!"

Lydia shouted, clearly unwilling to see the spotlight fall on her sister-in-law. The role of family bad girl was clearly hers and she set out to reclaim it. "This is exactly why I want my money out of this stupid company. You think that you can treat me like a child for the rest of my life, Daddy. But you're wrong. You can't just make these edicts about what we're going to do. Arthur has his career, his clients. You can't expect him to drop everything and come to work for you just because you snap your fingers."

Jack Cavanaugh's features turned to granite as he watched the family meeting disintegrate into a shouting match, with each child clamoring to have his or her own point of view heard, but none seemingly willing to listen. Looking back, I still can't believe that I did it, but I climbed up and stood on the seat of my chair, put two fingers into my mouth, and let out an earsplitting whistle.

Astonished faces were lifted toward me.

"Dagny would have been ashamed of all of you," I declared indignantly. "And you should be ashamed of yourselves. Now go home, all of you. Your father will reconvene this meeting when everyone has had a chance to come to their senses."

To my utter astonishment, they all got up and left, including Jack Cavanaugh, who said not one further word to me the rest of the time I was down in Georgia.

I WAS SNAPPING THE catches shut on my briefcase, silently berating myself for that afternoon's debacle. I didn't know what Daniel Babbage would have done to avert the total meltdown of the Cavanaugh family, but I was pretty sure he would have done something. After five years of practicing in one of Chicago's most high-powered law firms, I thought I'd begun to acquire a certain confidence in my own abilities. A little less than a week's acquaintance with the Cavanaughs had eroded it badly. I found myself wondering, once again, what had prompted Daniel to choose me for the Superior Plating file.

Dagny's daughter, Claire, slipped into the room, quiet as a ghost.

"Jules is going to do the Mount McKinley climb with us this spring," she said without preamble from the doorway. "He was Mom's climbing partner. I think they used to sleep together. What do you think?"

"I think you should definitely climb Mount McKinley," I replied, not knowing which question she meant and choosing the safer one. "Nothing would please your mother more than the thought of you standing at the summit. She'd be happy to know that you'd managed to get up to the top without her."

"It's so hard to believe she's gone. I keep pretending that she's just gone away for a few weeks, like the times she'd go climbing in the Alps with Jules. I don't think that I can face the thought of her not coming back. I can't believe she'd do this to me."

"She didn't do this."

"I know, but who did? Nobody will tell me anything. They just keep on patting me on the head and telling me that my mother would want me to be strong. My mother would want to be alive, dammit. What happened to her?"

"Don't worry. We're going to find out."

"Now you're patronizing me, too!"

"No, I'm not. I'm just telling you what I've been telling myself. I know it's frustrating, but I promise you we'll find out what happened to your mother."

"How? By sitting back and waiting for the police to do their job like Uncle Philip says, or should we follow Aunt Vy and Uncle Eugene's example and just pray for enlightenment?"

"I don't know whether I'm supposed to tell you this, but your grandfather has hired a private detective to help the police. I know him and he's good. Believe me, in the end we'll find out how she died."

"Then what was the big fight about with all the adults? And don't tell me nothing. I just got off the phone with Peter and he says that his mother's storming around the house screaming and throwing things into suitcases. They were supposed to stay down here until Tuesday, but now they're leaving in the morning. When I walked past Sally and Philip's house on the way over here, I heard them arguing. Does all this have something to do with Mom dying?"

"Yes and no. Do you know what's going on with your Aunt Lydia and her shares?"

"No. Mom never said anything about it."

"Well, now that you're a shareholder, I think you need to know."

As simply as I could, I filled her in on Lydia wanting to sell her shares in Superior Plating.

"Grandpa says I have to go and see some lawyer back in Chicago when I get back on Monday. Is that what it's about?"

"I don't think so. You're probably going to see one of my partners by the name of Ken Kurlander. He's the lawyer who prepared your mother's will. I'm sure he wants to explain the arrangements she made for you."

"As long as I get to live with Aunt Vy and Uncle Eugene, I don't care about the rest. According to my mom, I inherited enough money for college when my dad died. I don't want anything to do with Grandpa's stupid company. All it does is start fights and cause trouble. You can't believe the stuff that goes on—just one big fight after another. It's so immature. It's like a bunch of little kids who can't share. Sometimes I feel like I must have been adopted. I mean, the way they act, it's just so *stupid.*"

"You don't get problems this big when people are stupid," I replied sadly. "You get these kinds of problems when intelligent people decide to use their skills against each other."

18

When I got off the plane in Chicago I was surprised to find Elliott Abelman waiting for me at the gate.

"What are you doing here?" I asked as he took my heavy trial bag out of my hand and fell into step beside me.

"I have something I wanted to tell you."

"How did you know when I'd be here? Who told you what plane I was taking?"

Elliott flashed me a major-league smile. "I'm a detective, Kate. I find things out for a living."

"So what did you find out that you had to come out to the airport to tell me?" I asked.

"The medical examiner just ruled on a cause of death for Cecilia Dobson and Dagny Cavanaugh."

"And?" I demanded.

"It turns out both women died of cyanide poisoning."

"What?" I cried, my feet slowing involuntarily to a stop. Harried airline passengers, eager for their luggage, streamed past us down the concourse. "How can that be possible? If it was cyanide, how did they miss it when they autopsied Cecilia Dobson?"

"They just didn't look for it. According to what Joe tells me, the Cook County Medical Examiner's Office doesn't routinely test for cyanide. It's too expensive to test every case. Usually the medical examiner has to request it."

"So they requested it for Dagny Cavanaugh, but not Cecilia Dobson?" I demanded.

"No. It was just an accident that they tested Dagny Cavanaugh. You see, even though they don't test everybody for cyanide, they test every fifth case for everything."

"What?"

"It's part of their quality-control program. Any case with a number ending in a five or a zero gets a full toxicology screen—that's every toxicology test they can do, including the one for cyanide. Cecilia Dobson's case number ended in three, which is why she wasn't tested. In her case, the ME suspected an overdose of street drugs, so they only ordered her checked for opiates. But since Dagny Cavanaugh's number ended with a zero, she got the full treatment. According to Joe, they sometimes turn up an unexpected overdose that way. This is the first time they've turned up cyanide."

"So how did they find out about Cecilia Dobson?"

"After they got the test results for Dagny Cavanaugh, Joe asked them to test the Dobson woman."

"But she was already buried!" I protested.

"Whenever they issue a pending death certificate, they save and freeze blood and tissue samples."

"So when did they find all this out?"

"About an hour ago."

"Have they told the family yet?"

"You'd better leave that to Joe. He told me in confidence and that's how I'm telling you."

We walked through a set of automatic doors into the indoor parking garage. Elliott's car was parked in the towaway zone, a Chicago patrolman's hat prominently displayed in the back window. I asked him about it.

"It was a present from my dad. Cops don't give other cops parking tickets, at least not in this town," he said, unlocking the door and holding it open for me. "Why don't we go someplace where we can talk? Joe gave me a copy of the autopsy report, but I was in such a hurry to meet your plane I haven't had a chance to look at it."

I looked at my watch. "I can't," I said. "I've got to get home and get dressed to go somewhere."

"Hot date?" Elliott asked. I thought I detected a note of something other than professional inquiry in his voice.

"A birthday party for my grandmother," I answered sweetly. "If you don't mind giving me a ride back to Hyde Park, you can read the report out loud to me while I get ready."

Traffic was heavy heading into the city as suburbanites swarmed downtown for a good time on Saturday night. After the near summer of the Georgia spring, Chicago seemed cold and dreary. But when we swung around on the Stephenson and I caught the first glimpse of the rugged promontory of the downtown skyline, I felt the same quiet thrill I always do.

"So what do the police think?" I asked, turning in my seat to look at Elliott while I talked. He drove fast but easily, skirting construction barrels and keeping his eyes on the road. He was wearing the same jacket of chocolate-colored suede that he'd worn to breakfast at the Valois. Underneath, he had a plain white T-shirt and a pair of jeans. His hands were both strong and elegant, resting lightly on the steering wheel. I wondered why I had never noticed them before.

"The police aren't saying what they think, at least not yet," Elliott replied, seemingly oblivious to my scrutiny. "But if I know Joe, he's not jumping to any conclusions, though I can tell just from talking to him that he still hasn't ruled out the possibility that the two deaths were accidental."

"How could they be an accident? Cyanide isn't exactly the sort of thing you find lying around."

"If you work in a metal plating plant, it is. Joe says they get the stuff in fifty-pound shipments at Superior Plating every week. It's the same stuff that you read about jealous wives slipping into their husband's coffee in murder mysteries. According to the medical examiner's office, there was enough cyanide in both women to have killed an elephant. I stopped over at Superior Plating on Friday while the guys from the health department were there. You can't believe the number of poisonous chemicals they have just lying around. The company is required to keep something called an MSD book—a looseleaf notebook with a sheet for every hazardous chemical they use in the plant, with information on where it's kept and what to do in case it's accidentally spilled or swallowed. It's as thick as a phone book. If you worked there and wanted to kill someone, you'd have your pick of poisons."

"Come on. They must take precautions. I can't believe the cyanide's just left lying around where anybody has access to it."

"No. It's not. It's kept in the hazardous chemicals room, which is actually a locked closet at the end of the hall between the administrative offices and the plant. A little old lady could kick down the door."

"Were there any signs that it was broken into?"

"None that I could see. Joe's going to go back over there tomorrow to see if he can nail down who had keys, whether any of the stuff was missing, that kind of thing. He's also planning on bringing back the crime-lab boys to go through the place with a fine-tooth comb. For all anybody knows right now, someone could have accidentally filled the sugar bowl with cyanide and Cecilia Dobson and Dagny Cavanaugh liked their coffee sweet."

"You've got to be kidding."

"Don't laugh. It could be as simple as that."

"And what if it's not?" I demanded as Elliott pulled up to the curb in front of my apartment—another no-parking zone. "What if someone deliberately poisoned them?" I got out of the car and said across the hood of his car, "No, I take that back. What if someone deliberately poisoned one of them?"

"You mean that one of them was the intended victim and the other was what—some sort of accident?"

I dug through my satchel bag for my keys, fumbling through the half dozen or so that were on the ring. Every lock in our building took a different key. According to the landlord, it made the apartment more secure, but I always felt that it increased my chances of being mugged on my own doorstep as I went from key to key.

"Call it what you want—accident, camouflage, dress rehearsal," I offered, finally managing to get us into the apartment. "The two women had almost nothing in common. What reason could there be to kill them both? It almost reminds me of the Tylenol poisoning case. I've never bought the police explanation that it was some demented lunatic who just wanted to kill people. The cops could never figure it out, so that's the explanation they had to settle for. It always seemed much more likely to me that one of the people who died was the intended victim and the others were just window dressing. It would be so easy if you really wanted to kill somebody and not get caught, provided that you didn't care how many other innocent people you murdered, too."

"Yeah, and it was probably a calculating attorney who slipped the cyanide into the Tylenol capsule—talk about cold. Do the people at work know you think about stuff like that?"

I checked the time. I had a little more than forty-five minutes to get myself showered, dressed, and able to pass muster with my mother.

"Listen. I'm going to run into the shower. Make yourself at home; help yourself to anything that doesn't have mold on it."

Elliott looked around the living room dubiously. I knew that he was a meticulous housekeeper. Dust bunnies admonished me from every corner. I turned my back on them and headed for the bathroom.

I emerged ten minutes later wrapped in a white terry-cloth bathrobe with damp hair wrapped in a towel, turban style. Elliott was stretched out in the black leather Eames chair that had briefly had a home in the library of my mother's house. Dad had bought it for himself, arguing that it was good for his back, but in less than a month it had been banished by my mother and her decorator.

"It's weird the things you find out from an autopsy report," said Elliott, looking up.

He looked at me and something passed between us, a moment lasting a heartbeat, maybe two. I knew that everything that Joe Blades had said about his friend was true and the same stab of attraction that I'd felt in the past for Elliott was not a fluke. Furthermore, in the heat of our discussion about what had happened to Cecilia Dobson and Dagny Cavanaugh, I'd made a mistake: I should never have had Elliott come back to my apartment. In my head I heard the unmistakable bell of warning. I chose deliberately to ignore it.

"So what did you find out?" I asked, slowly rubbing my hair with the towel. Elliott took a breath. I saw him choose to let the moment pass.

"Cecilia Dobson had an old fracture of her right femur, probably from when she was eight or nine years old. She'd had rhinoplasty—that's plastic surgery on her nose—one or two years ago. She'd also had breast implants and her tubes tied. Her last meal was a cheeseburger, french fries, and a milkshake—strawberry."

"Is that where the poison was? In the milkshake?"

"They're running the tests on the stomach contents today. Joe expects the results sometime tomorrow."

"What about Dagny Cavanaugh? What did she have to eat before she died?"

Elliott flipped through the photocopied sheets in his lap.

"That's weird," he said finally. "It says here that her stomach was almost completely empty." He flipped back to the page he'd been reading from before. "Cecilia Dobson ate two and a half to three hours before she died, but it looks like Dagny had nothing to eat at all the day she died. What time did she die?"

"It was close to four o'clock," I said. Somehow it didn't seem real to be talking about it this way. Dagny Cavanaugh had died in my arms, and here I was, five days later, standing and discussing it in my bathrobe with Elliott Abelman like it was some sort of abstract exercise in deduction.

"Why would she have gone the whole day without eating?" asked Elliott, who, I knew, liked his meals regularly.

"Maybe she wasn't feeling well," I offered. "Or maybe she just got busy. There are lots of days I'm so busy I wouldn't get a chance to eat if Cheryl didn't bring me a sandwich. Don't forget, Dagny didn't have a secretary anymore. Besides, you've been to the Superior Plating plant. The neighborhood's not exactly a mecca for restaurants."

"But if she didn't eat anything, what was the poison in?"

"Won't the tests they're running tell us? Why don't you come and talk to me while I put on my makeup?" I asked, keeping my eye on the time. Elliott extricated himself from my father's chair and followed me down the long hall to my bedroom. The apartments in Hyde Park were built in the twenties, railroad style—living room and kitchen in the front, bedrooms along a single hall like a railroad car.

Elliott perched himself gingerly on the end of my unmade bed and tactfully ignored the piles of clothes on the floor. The warning bells were louder now, but I told myself that if I were a male attorney discussing a client with a private investigator, there would be no awkwardness. I pulled my makeup bag out of my suitcase and went into the bathroom, leaving the door ajar for the sake of conversation.

"It still doesn't make any sense," came Elliott's voice from the bedroom. "If Dagny didn't eat anything the day she died, how was she poisoned?"

"Maybe she drank something. Don't you always read about putting cyanide in coffee to hide the bitter taste?"

I dotted my face with foundation, cursing my own clumsiness as I knocked the bottle over and quickly picked it back up. I was strangely nervous, and the more I hurried the worse I got.

I heard the rustling of pages.

"It doesn't say anything about coffee in either of them," he reported.

"I guess we'll just have to wait until tomorrow." I selected an eye-shadow compact at random from the bag. My entire inventory of makeup was composed of samples accumulated by my mother and passed along to me. I told myself that I liked the small sizes because I traveled so much, but the truth is that I hadn't been to a department-store makeup counter since becoming a lawyer and saw no reason to start now. "Let's just assume for argument's sake that only one of the women was the intended victim. Who would have wanted to kill Cecilia Dobson? Who would have benefited from her death? Have you managed to find her boyfriend yet?"

"I drove down to Champaign to see him yesterday. I think I told you that he plays in some kind of grunge band. They were performing in a college bar down there. I've got to tell you, I heard them play. It really made me feel like my dad—you know, the music's too loud, it just sounds like noise. . . . Anyway, the boyfriend didn't seem too broken up about what happened—though I'm not sure he really understood everything I was telling him. Either he's not very bright or he's ingested one too many illegal substances. All of which is beside the point, on account of the fact that he's got an alibi. It turns out he was in Iowa playing a gig the day she died. The other members of his band and the guy who owned the bar where they were playing backed him up."

"Was she insured?"

"The police are looking into it."

"So who else might have wanted to have her out of the way?"

"Philip Cavanaugh for one. He was having an affair with her and he wanted to break it off. What if she got nasty and told him she was going to go to his wife instead?"

"He could always have paid her off. From what you told me, she probably picked up with Philip in the first place thinking there was money in it for her."

"But what if she was asking for too much? Maybe little Philip decided murder was cheaper than blackmail."

"But then what about Dagny?" I countered. "After Cecilia Dobson died, everyone assumed that she'd just overdosed on drugs. No one would have known about the cyanide if Dagny hadn't died. Besides, Philip didn't have a motive to kill his sister."

"Why not? Maybe he resented the competition. According to what Joe's been hearing at Superior Plating, Dagny was the real brains of the outfit. Maybe he finally got tired of being shown up by his little sister."

"That's an awfully big stretch," I protested, holding my eyes open wide and stroking on the mascara. I looked at my watch. Six minutes. I abandoned the idea of doing anything special with my hair. Instead, I gave it a quick brush and wound it up into a French twist. I thought of the scene I'd witnessed that afternoon during the Cavanaugh family meeting. "I'm not going to tell you that these guys are the Waltons. It's actually pretty clear that they all hate each other's guts, but Dagny was the only one who seemed to have been generally liked and respected."

"You know that when we're spinning different scenarios for a motive, they all work much better with Dagny as the intended victim."

"Hold that thought," I said, closing the door and squirming into the midnight-blue cocktail dress I'd bought especially to wear to Grandma Prescott's birthday party. It was a Jil Sander, the German designer who was making a name for herself in this country with elegant, pared-down clothes. The dress was simplicity itself, a scoop neck and long sleeves, but when I'd first tried it on, it struck me that there was something almost magical in the way it was cut. I also remember thinking when I looked at the price tag that there had damned well better be. I leaned over the sink and put on some lipstick.

When I opened the door to the bathroom Elliott rose slowly to his feet.

"You look beautiful," he said in a hushed voice. Suddenly my bedroom seemed very small indeed. Elliott was so close.

"You missed a button in back," he said. "Here, if you turn around I'll get it for you."

"That's okay," I murmured hoarsely. There seemed to be something wrong with my voice.

"Come on. I won't bite," he urged, smiling.

Suddenly I felt prudish and silly. An overworked lawyer letting her imagination run away with her.

But when I turned and felt his fingertips brush the nape of my neck, I knew it had been dangerous to turn my back.

19

Only the doorbell saved me from doing something foolish. I heard the harsh sound of the buzzer and took a step away from Elliott. The moment dissolved into motion—Elliott stooping to pick up the copies of the two autopsy reports from the foot of my bed— me to the intercom panel in the front hall to buzz Stephen Azorini into the building.

The two men shook hands in the foyer. They had never met before and each eyed the other with suspicion thinly veiled by civility— two cats circling each other at their first meeting. Elliott knew I had a relationship with Stephen, but I had never offered to explain it, holding firm the line between personal and professional involvement no matter what sparks of attraction might sometimes flash between us. Stephen, on the other hand, clearly did not expect to come to my apartment on Saturday night and find another man there already.

I smiled radiantly at them both and gathered up the glittering excuse for a purse that I used for parties.

"Did you remember to buy your grandmother a present?" Stephen inquired in paternal tones.

The look on my face was most likely explanation enough, since he did not bother to wait for whatever excuse I might offer.

"That's okay." He sighed. "I did. We'll just sign the card from both of us."

As I preceded both men out the door I couldn't help but wonder what Elliott Abelman, private investigator, would deduce from that last exchange.

THE PRIVATE DINING ROOM at the Whitehall Club was almost as pretty as my mother's, though not nearly as large. She stood by the door greeting guests, flanked by my father and Grandma Prescott—a no-nonsense old woman who lived for fly-fishing and duplicate bridge.

"Happy birthday, Grandma," I said, kissing the papery skin of her powdered cheek.

"Thank you, my dear," she said, putting her hands on my shoulders and holding me at arm's length to look at me. "Your dad says that you've been working too hard and I won't tell you what your mother's been saying." She gave a wicked chuckle. Her voice was gravelly from a lifetime of cigarettes and scotch, almost as low as a man's.

"When did you buy that dress?" my mother demanded as I moved on to give my grandmother a chance to talk to Stephen. She liked to joke that she might be too old to do anything about it but she still liked at least to look at a handsome man.

"I was in Bonn this winter on business. One of the German attorneys working on the deal took me shopping."

"It's very attractive," my mother remarked, making the dress worth every single penny. I didn't even let it bother me when she criticized my hair.

Stephen and I did our duty during cocktails, saying hello to all the aunts and second cousins. Stephen was a much bigger draw than I was. No one ever knew quite what to say to me since I didn't fit into any of the neat pigeonholes of their limited experience—no husband, no country club, a career that frankly baffled them. Stephen, on the other hand, with his movie-star good looks, had undeniable appeal.

I drank less than I usually do at family gatherings, concentrating on the hors d'oeuvres, which were wonderful, especially the little puffs filled with a mixture of goat cheese and sun-dried tomatoes, which went a long way to compensate for the fact that I hadn't had lunch. I also found myself paying more attention to the family dynamics, which I had up until now taken for granted.

Grandma Prescott and my mother, though all smiles tonight, had never gotten along particularly well. My mother's mother had been an accomplished equestrienne and a crack shot in an era when women didn't shoot and they didn't ride. She'd grown up under the disapproving eye of her own socialite mother and a puritanical father, both of whom adored my mother and did everything they could to undercut my grandmother's influence over her.

In one corner by the fireplace I spotted my father, nodding amiably in agreement with his sister, Gertrude, who was one of the richest women in the world—and according to my mother one of the ugliest—on account of having married an elderly Van Buren shortly before his timely demise. She was a spectacular miser and had two sons, one who was completely estranged from her and another who had recently died of AIDS. Through his entire illness his mother had insisted defiantly to all of her friends that it was mononucleosis.

When we sat down for dinner I noticed that Mother had been careful to place the Prescott side of her family as far as possible from the Danforth side on account of a long-standing feud over the distribution of a family trust following my great-uncle Rawley's death. The dispute was over a relatively trivial sum—especially in a family where everyone invariably lived on interest—but the acrimony it caused had rankled for more than a dozen years.

At the head of the table I could see that my father was already drunk. Mother had kept a sharp eye on him until he'd delivered the toast she'd written for him to offer before dinner, but judging from the way he was listing to one side, he was now only a couple of gin and tonics from oblivion.

I thought about what Daniel Babbage had said to me about my own family the day he handed the Superior Plating file over to me. He was right. There was very little difference between my family and the Cavanaughs.

Dinner was trout meunière caught the day before by some old friends of my grandmother's from Canada and flown in specially. To serve it, white-gloved waiters placed large Villeroy and Boch plates in front of every person, each with a domed, silver cover. A waiter stood behind each pair of chairs, and at a discreet signal, the domes were simultaneously lifted to well-bred applause.

Stephen listened attentively to my cousin Gregory's droning stories about grouse shooting in Wales. On my left, my great-aunt Victoria, who was deaf as an adder, bellowed to the dinner partner on her other side. I played with my trout and found myself thinking about cyanide.

Perhaps I had been too hasty in assuming that there was no thread connecting Cecilia Dobson and Dagny Cavanaugh. They had worked in the same office, after all, both possibly privy to the same financial information. According to Jack Cavanaugh, Dagny had been keeping Superior Plating's books since she was in high school. Perhaps she'd been embezzling money or covering up some other financial impropriety that Cecilia had discovered. Neither Elliott nor I felt that Dagny's secretary had been above a bit of blackmail. Perhaps Dagny had killed her and then committed suicide in a fit of remorse. The police hadn't found a suicide note, but I knew that in more than half of the cases where a person takes their own life, they don't leave a note. Still, it didn't fit with my impressions of Dagny, but who could tell?

Or perhaps the two deaths were tied together in another way. Perhaps a disgruntled employee with a particular grudge against the financial side of Superior Plating had decided to extract their own brand of revenge. While I was pretty sure that the police would question the Superior Plating employees about the possibility, I made a mental note to have Elliott check through personnel records just in case something might turn up.

After the cake was cut, "Happy Birthday" sung, and the presents unwrapped—Stephen's gift of a set of hand-tied McGregor trout flies was the hit of the evening—we said our farewells. Stephen had an early meeting with his hematology research group the next morning and I was in a hurry to get back to Hyde Park. I wanted to stop at the hospital and see Daniel Babbage. To my surprise, Stephen offered to come along.

"What was that detective guy doing at your apartment?" he asked as we headed south on Lake Shore Drive. Every day I noticed more boats in the harbor—a sure sign of spring.

A number of answers to his question streamed past each other through my brain, not the least of which was "none of your business," but I opted for the truth.

"He's been hired by the Cavanaughs to help find out what happened to the two women who died at Superior Plating. He came to tell me that the medical examiner's office found out that both of them died of cyanide poisoning."

Stephen gave a soft whistle that rang through the dark interior of his BMW. We were passing through the no-man's-land between the projects and home. On our left, fires glittered on the beach.

"So do the police think it was murder?" he asked.

"I don't know. I guess there's a lot of cyanide used in plating, so it could have been an accident."

"Cyanide is bad stuff. It's odorless, tasteless, and a little goes a long way. You actually die of asphyxiation, which is what makes it hard to trace postmortem. Chemically, cyanide interferes with the enzymes that control the oxidative process. It prevents the body from using the oxygen in blood by crippling the cytochrome oxidase system that converts oxygen's energy to a form the body can use. That's why cyanide poisoning is sometimes referred to as internal asphyxia because even though the person may be taking in air through the lungs, it isn't being absorbed into the bloodstream."

"Which is why CPR doesn't do any good," I said, wrapping my arms around myself.

Stephen said nothing as we turned off the drive at Fifty-seventh Street and headed for the hospital.

IT WAS ELEVEN O'CLOCK at night, but in the emergency room at the University of Chicago Medical Center, it might as well have been noon. Most of my roommate Claudia's patients come to her through the ER, and while there's no such thing as a slow night in the combat zone of a big-city hospital, she, like most people who work there, is fond of predicting whether it will be busy based on all sorts of outside factors—hot weather, a holiday weekend, a full moon—all of which are held to add to the regular number of gunshots and overdoses, women in labor, and general gore that come through their doors.

Once the elevator carried us above the first floor, however, things grew quieter. Stephen, who'd done his medical training there, had lived five of the most intense years of his life in this building. Since then his work had carried him away from the hands-on practice of medicine. He said he didn't miss it, but looking at his face, I wasn't sure.

When we got to Daniel's room it was empty. The bed had been stripped down to the obscene black plastic of the hospital mattress. The cards and the flowers were all gone.

"Maybe he's been moved," said Stephen, quickly anticipating my alarm. "Let me go and see if his chart's at the nurses' station." He stepped out into the hall and turned back. "Are you going to be okay?"

I nodded mutely, staring at the vacant bed, not wanting to move. When Stephen came back the news was no surprise. Daniel had died at three-twenty that afternoon while I was in the air flying back to Chicago. I bit my lip. It had been no secret that he was dying. That was why I'd wanted to come to the hospital tonight and not wait until morning. I thrust my hands miserably into the pockets of my raincoat and felt the plastic sarcophagus of one of the cigars I'd bought for him.

Suddenly it all seemed so hopeless. Daniel was dead and so was Dagny. The rest of the Cavanaugh family seemed to have embarked on an unalterable course of self-destruction, and in the end what difference did any of it make?

"I want to go now," I said, wrapping my coat around myself against the sudden chill.

EVEN THOUGH HE LIVED only a few blocks away, Stephen rarely came to my apartment. His appetite for luxury was enormous and he lived so beautifully that when he came to my apartment he felt like he was slumming. But tonight he took me home without demur, coming in without being asked.

I knew that I did not love Stephen. I knew that if I did, my heart would not beat faster whenever Elliott Abelman was in the room. But tonight what I felt for Stephen was not about love. I had had a plateful of death and loss and sorrow. That night in my apartment I quite simply hungered for something else.

I know that women look at Stephen Azorini and imagine what he must be like in bed—what it must be like to possess and be possessed by a man like him. For Stephen and me, sex had always been the constant, the chemistry invariable and dramatic like indoor fireworks. That night, in my own bed, I was seized by the need to drive out the demons of the past week, to exorcise them with the sweat of sex.

By morning we did such a good job that I think Stephen was going to be hard-pressed to stay awake during his morning meeting.

I WOKE UP LATE and made myself coffee. There was a pair of size-six Nikes under the kitchen table. I realized Claudia must have come home sometime during the night—hopefully during one of the lulls in the action.

I went for a long run. The sun was out and I decided to brave a course through the cultural gardens behind the Museum of Science and Industry. I ran through the immaculately maintained Japanese garden and all the way to South Shore and back without incident. Then I came home and took a long shower. It was nice, I reflected, to spend the night at home for a change. It was nice to avoid that funky walk home on Sunday morning dressed in Saturday night's high heels.

After the emotional upheaval of the last several days, I finally felt at ease with myself. Whatever it was that I had been trying to drive out with the past night's exercise was gone. Strangely enough, I even found a sense of comfort in the knowledge that Daniel was finally dead. As long as he was alive, he had hovered over the Superior Plating file as I continually second-guessed myself, wondering how differently he would have chosen to deal with every new situation. Now the file was mine and I was ready to reassess and start from scratch. It was no use beating myself up over the debacle of the Cavanaugh family meeting. From here on in it wasn't Daniel's show, it was mine.

As I prepared to leave for the office I was surprised to see Joe Blades climbing the stoop to my apartment. His step was slow and his face pale with fatigue. Homicide cops, I guessed, just like ER docs, had busy Saturday nights.

"Detective Blades, what a pleasant surprise," I said. "What brings you to my neck of the woods?"

"Suspicious death call on Fifty-eighth Street. Turns out it was an eighty-seven-year-old piano teacher who died in her sleep. As long as I was in the neighborhood, I thought I'd look you up."

"Do you want to come in? I can make some fresh coffee," I volunteered, still uncertain whether this was an official or a social visit.

"Actually," he said, taking off his glasses and polishing them with the fat end of his tie, "I was wondering whether you might have a few minutes."

"Sure," I replied.

"Then, if you wouldn't mind taking a ride with me, there's somebody who wants to talk to you."

CHAPTER

20

"I assume Elliott already told you about the cyanide," Detective Blades remarked amiably from behind the wheel of his official police vehicle—OPV for short. Elliott had once pointed out that all OPVs had license plates beginning with the letters *QF*, thereby forming a code recognized by every small-time hoodlum in the city. This one was a sorry white Chevy Cavalier that smelled of spilled coffee and old cigarette smoke. Blades hadn't mentioned where we were going and I didn't ask.

"I saw Elliott yesterday. He told me that they were poisoned."

"What can you tell me about Dagny Cavanaugh's relationship with her secretary? Were they on good terms?"

"I don't know if they were on good terms," I hedged, strangely reluctant to say more. Somehow, in the light of what had happened, Dagny's irritation with her secretary seemed magnified and strangely out of proportion.

"The first time we met, the day that Cecilia Dobson died, as a matter of fact, Dagny told me that Cecilia was actually a very competent secretary."

"But she didn't like her."

"There were things about her behavior at work that Dagny felt were unprofessional."

"For example?"

"Cecilia had begun to dress provocatively."

"One of the secretaries at Superior Plating said that the day she died Cecilia had defied Dagny's standing order forbidding her from going down onto the plant floor. How did Ms. Cavanaugh feel about that?"

"I think she was annoyed," I said. "But so was her brother Eugene, who was in the plant giving me a tour—actually, he was furious. But I don't think their concerns were about Cecilia herself, but rather that her presence in the plant was unsafe. I don't think that any of it was personal, which is why I don't see what you're getting at. Believe me, lots of people get mad at their secretaries, but they don't kill them."

"Was it your impression that Dagny Cavanaugh was an emotionally stable woman?"

"She struck me as being exceptionally levelheaded."

"To the point of being calculating?"

I found myself getting annoyed, but I tried not to show it. After all, the man had a job to do. But I couldn't help wondering what it must be like to be married to a cop, a man whose job it was to wring the worst possible interpretation from the most simple declarative sentence. It would, I concluded, be even worse than marriage to a lawyer.

"I didn't know Dagny Cavanaugh very well," I continued patiently. "We'd only known each other for a few days, but in that time she seemed like a very intelligent and reasonable person—the kind who acts more from the head than the heart."

"Not the kind who would poison her secretary in a rage and then, three days later, swallow poison herself in a fit of remorse?"

"It seems far-fetched."

"Believe me, stuff like that happens all the time. Homicide is definitely on the rise in the workplace."

"I don't doubt it, but if you'd met Dagny Cavanaugh, you'd realize what a preposterous scenario that is. Dagny wasn't some dope-crazed lowlife psychotic living on the fringe. She was a successful executive. She was also one of the most sensible, down-to-earth people I'd ever met. The worst she would have done to Cecilia Dobson was fire her—and even then I think she would have regretted it. I'm telling you, I was with her the night before she died; we sat up until almost midnight talking. There was nothing she said or did that would indicate to me that she was capable of the kind of emotionally driven crime you've just described."

"I'll give you the fact that poisoning isn't usually a crime of passion—not like the guy who comes home, finds his wife playing hide the salami with the Maytag repairman, pulls out his trusty Colt forty-five, and blows them both away. Most people kill when they're angry or afraid or feel that they themselves will be killed. In addition, most homicides involve alcohol or drugs. Poisoning is the exception because it's almost always either an accident or a crime of premeditation."

"So which one was this?"

"At this point, Kate, I've got to tell you, your guess is as good as mine."

THE OFFICE OF THE Cook County medical examiner occupies a dismal bunker on a barren stretch of West Harrison. Minicam vans for each of the three major Chicago stations were parked at the curb in front of the entrance.

"What are they doing here?" I demanded, suddenly panicked at the thought that someone acquainted with Superior Plating and the Cavanaughs had contacted the press—Lydia, perhaps, in her thirst for ink. I could imagine the headlines: SERIAL POISONER TERRORIZES SOUTH-SIDE WOMEN. . .

"They're waiting for Violet Kramer."

"Who's Violet Kramer?"

"She was a fifteen-year-old girl who disappeared from the Old Orchard Mall two days before Christmas. Up until this morning she's been officially listed as missing. It's been all over the media. Don't you read the papers?"

"Only the *Wall Street Journal.*" Joe Blades shot me a look of disbelief before he continued.

"They found her body this morning in the woods near Ravinia. Somebody must have tipped the press that they were bringing her in. They're waiting to get shots of the morgue wagon for the six o'clock."

The security guard who occupied the grimy booth at the entrance to the parking lot waved us in without question, recognizing either Detective Blades, his official white Chevy Cavalier, or both. We parked behind the building across from the loading dock, where two men in orange coveralls lounged in front of the overhead doors, lifted and gaping, no doubt awaiting the mortal remains of Violet Kramer. I fell into step beside the homicide detective, who greeted them both by name as we passed.

Inside, the building was a maze of hallways and stairwells that seemed to have been connected at random in a clear case of municipal architecture gone wrong. The walls were painted the exact same depressing shade of mossy green I'd noticed at police headquarters; the city must buy the paint in quantity, probably from some alderman's brother-in-law in the paint business. The sickly smell of formaldehyde hung in the air. Beneath it lingered the suggestion of unbelievable stench.

Blades, obviously at home, led the way up a flight of stairs and down a long corridor punctuated by bulletin boards and office doors. From behind a few of them I heard voices, but no ringing of phones, which struck me as odd until I remembered that it was Sunday. The homicide detective stopped and knocked on one of the doors at the far end of the hall. Beside it on the wall was a brown nameplate that read DR. J. GORDON, ASSISTANT MEDICAL EXAMINER.

As we entered, the doctor looked up from a file on the desk in front of her and smiled.

Dr. Julia Gordon was a small woman, tiny in fact, with a short cap of blond curls and translucent skin that made her look, despite the authority of her lab coat, more like a novice in a convent than a person who made her living taking dead bodies apart with a surgical saw. She reached over the top of her desk to shake my hand and pronounced herself grateful that I'd come to see her.

Her office was small, crammed with books and periodicals. Even though it was only forty degrees out, an ancient air conditioner clanked in the window. Behind her on the wall hung diplomas and a framed photograph of two pretty blond girls hugging a Labrador retriever. Beside them was a large poster of gunshot wounds made by bullets of various calibers, illustrated with color photographs.

"I'm the pathologist who performed the autopsies on Cecilia Dobson and Dagny Cavanaugh," she said, after Blades introduced us. "As you know, when the toxicology reports came back both women had lethal levels of cyanide in their blood."

"Were the levels similar in both cases?" I asked.

"They were slightly higher in the Dobson woman, but I'd say both cases were in the same range—very high. . . . Cyanide poisoning is actually quite difficult to detect on autopsy," Dr. Gordon continued. "The signs are easy to miss. The blood that normally pools in the chest cavity after death is a very bright, cherry red in the case of death from cyanide poisoning. But you also see that same red color after a body has been refrigerated for more than a few hours. Unfortunately, last week we were very busy and both bodies were stored for some time before autopsy. You may also have heard about the scent of bitter almonds being present in the case of cyanide poisoning. The smell is much less pronounced in real life than it is in fiction, and indeed, not everyone can smell it. There's usually only one person in any medical examiner's office who's good at picking up that smell. In our office that's Dr. Margolick, but last week we had two cases going in the decomp room, and to be perfectly honest, it would be a miracle if anyone could smell anything else." She clasped her hands on the desk in front of her like a schoolteacher. "So, Detective Blades tells me that you were present at the time of both deaths. That's quite a coincidence."

"Not really. I'm the attorney for Superior Plating and Specialty Chemicals, the company where both women worked. I had a meeting with Dagny Cavanaugh the day that Cecilia Dobson died. The two of us were meeting in a conference room in another part of the plant. We went to pick up some figures from Dagny's office. When we got there we found Cecilia on the floor."

"And she wasn't breathing when you found her?"

"No. I also checked for a pulse. There was none. Now, of course, I realize that she was probably already dead when I started CPR."

"Yes," Dr. Gordon agreed matter-of-factly, "with the level of cyanide we found, I'd be surprised if death didn't proceed very quickly. If she'd taken a lower dose, you'd see a much more gradual progression of dizziness, gasping for breath, headache, nausea, and vomiting. Then, when blood pressure dropped, there'd be a period when the victim would experience unconsciousness and convulsions. But at the level of concentration that we detected in both victims, I'd be surprised if either of the two women was conscious for more than a minute or two after being poisoned."

"Dagny Cavanaugh was alive when I got there," I said, suddenly struck by the realization that if I'd gotten out of the car and gone looking for her a few minutes earlier, I might have found her . . . found her doing what? Taking poison?

"There's nothing you could have done," Dr. Gordon assured me, as if reading my mind. "With the amount of cyanide that we found in her bloodstream, even if you'd immediately administered amyl nitrate—which is the first part of the antidote—I doubt you could have saved her."

"But that means she must have taken the poison right before I got there."

"Yes. That's why I wanted to speak to you. I was wondering whether you noticed anything in the room. It was an office of some kind, I believe?"

"It was her office—Dagny Cavanaugh's."

"Did you notice anything unusual? Especially anything that might have struck you as being the same both times. A smell of some kind perhaps?"

"No," I said, trying hard to remember. "I honestly don't recall anything out of the ordinary." Except for the bodies on the floor, I thought to myself.

"Was there anything to eat or drink visible in the room either time?"

I thought before I answered. "No. But I can't say that I would have noticed the first time. With Cecilia Dobson, it was all a blur. I was so focused on trying to resuscitate her. I also went to the hospital with her, so I didn't have that much time to notice anything in the room. After Dagny died, I stayed at her office, but I honestly didn't see anything other than what you'd expect."

"A cup of coffee? A glass of water perhaps?"

"I didn't notice," I replied, chafing with frustration. "Do you think that maybe the poison was in something she drank?"

Dr. Gordon pursed her lips, raised her eyebrows, and let out a long sigh.

"Frankly, Ms. Millholland, I don't know what to think. The stomach contents of both women have been tested for cyanide. In both cases the tests came back negative. Detective Blades will tell you, when I do an autopsy I'm very thorough. I go over every inch of skin with a magnifying lens, and in both cases I found no cuts or abrasions and certainly nothing that even remotely resembled a needle puncture. I've got to be honest with you. I have two women who without a doubt died from a lethal level of cyanide in their bloodstreams. But I have absolutely no idea how that poison came to be in their bodies."

CHAPTER

21

I asked Joe Blades if he'd be able to drop me at the office. He asked if I'd mind if we made a stop on the way at Superior Plating and Specialty Chemicals. He explained that he had some questions he wanted to ask me about the way things were when Cecilia Dobson and Dagny Cavanaugh died. Besides, he added smoothly, Elliott Abelman was going to be there. Leave it to a homicide detective to play Cupid at a crime scene.

The Superior Plating parking lot was empty save for the crime-lab van and a couple of Chevy Cavaliers, both identical to the one Blades was driving. We followed the sound of voices into the administrative wing of the building. Just outside the door of Dagny's office a crime-lab technician was taking down the yellow police-line-do-not-cross tape, wadding it up in his hand as he yanked it from the door frame. Inside, it looked like a cop convention. Elliott Abelman stood in the middle of the room deep in conversation with a burly man with a salt-and-pepper mustache and dark eyes that looked like they'd seen it all.

"What the hell do you expect?" complained the man. "No matter what we do, the physical evidence is going to be fucked up. Hell, this room wasn't even sealed until after the second death, and even then the paramedics probably trampled anything that might have been of use to us. And if that wasn't enough, I just finished talking to the janitor, who tells me that a cleaning crew went through here every night as usual until the Cavanaugh broad turned up dead."

"Well, they sure as hell didn't do much," someone else observed from across the room, a heavyset man in a crumpled raincoat who was examining something in his latex-gloved hand. "We're still finding the Dobson woman's prints all over everything today."

"So what's the good word from the delectable Dr. Gordon?" demanded the plainclothesman with Elliott as he spotted Blades.

"Nothing new. They both definitely died of cyanide poisoning, but nobody has idea one how it got into them." In the bright light of the office Joe Blades looked, if anything, more exhausted than he had earlier that morning. His skin was so pale the freckles seemed to fairly leap off of it. "Kate Millholland," he said, turning to acknowledge me, "I'd like you to meet Tyrone Hackner, the department's ace physical-evidence expert and resident curmudgeon. Elliott Abelman you already know."

"Pleased to meet you," Hackner grumbled, enfolding my hand briefly in his enormous paw. From Elliott I received a wink and a smile.

"Miss Millholland is the witness I was telling you about. She's the one who was present at the time of both deaths."

"Okay, young lady," Hackner rumbled, "then what I want to hear from you is how the bodies were lying when you saw them."

"They were both facedown, with their heads toward the desk—"

"I know that. What I'm curious about is the angle."

"What do you mean?"

Tyrone Hackner looked me over, no doubt assessing my flannel trousers and cashmere pullover for what he was about to ask.

"Could you get down on the floor and show me the exact position in which Cecilia Dobson was lying?"

"You don't have to if you don't want to," Elliott interjected quickly. Blades flashed him a look, but it passed so quickly I didn't have time to decipher it.

"That's okay," I replied. I was willing to do anything that might help. I walked toward the desk, gauging the distance, and then got down on the floor. "I think this is where she was lying." I turned over on my stomach and arranged my arms and legs. "She was wearing a short skirt and it was hitched up over her left hip. Her underwear was showing."

"Any evidence of sexual assault?" Hackner asked Blades.

"No. Not in either case," Blades replied.

The rough nap of the carpet pressed into my face. I smelled the acrid stench of old vomit. Once the police had sealed the room, no one must have been allowed in to clean. When all of this was over they'd probably have to replace the carpet.

"Are you sure that's the direction she was facing?" Hackner demanded.

"Yes," I replied. Elliott got down on his haunches and held out his hand to help me up. "Why is it so important?" I asked, brushing the lint from my sweater.

"It's not so much a question of where they ended up," Blades answered, "but where they came from." Tyrone Hackner was already out in the hall giving orders to the crime-lab techs. "From your initial statement it was clear that both women were trying to get to the desk when they collapsed—presumably to use the telephone to call for help. But up until now we'd all assumed that they'd come into the office from the hall. Assuming that Dr. Gordon is correct and only a very short time elapsed between the time the poison entered their bloodstreams and the moment they collapsed, it makes a big difference in narrowing down where they might have been poisoned. From what you just showed us, it looks like both women were coming out of the bathroom, not the hall."

Two evidence technicians appeared with their gear and went into the small bathroom at the end of the office opposite Dagny's desk. I hadn't noticed it before. From the open door I could see them methodically taking every item from inside the medicine chest above the sink and putting them, one by one, into individual glassine bags.

"It's too bad," Elliott remarked. "From what Tyrone says, the bathroom is the one place the cleaning crew actually did anything. When they dusted for prints, the only ones they found were Dagny's."

"So you think the poison was in the bathroom?" I demanded.

"It's as good a place as any to start looking," Blades replied, stroking his beard. "Do you want to show Kate where the bulk chemicals are stored, Elliott?"

"Sure," said Elliott as his friend the detective tossed him a bunch of keys.

"You don't have to worry about touching anything," said Blades as we went out the door. "We're all done dusting for prints."

Elliott led me out the door and down the hall.

"How was your grandmother's birthday party?" he asked.

"Very nice."

We walked through the reception room and through the doors that Eugene Cavanaugh had first taken me through on my tour of the plant. On the other side of the wall that separated the manufacturing floor from the administrative offices, Elliott stopped at what looked like the door to a broom closet. It was covered with the same crummy plastic paneling as the rest of the wall and had a cheap brass doorknob, the kind with a lock in the middle.

"Anybody with either a screwdriver or half a brain could get into this thing," he commented as he slid the key into the lock.

"Any sign that somebody tried to break into it?"

"None. They lifted a bunch of prints, but they haven't ID'd them yet."

"In that case, I guess the question is who has the key?"

"According to Joe, there were only four keys and the only people who had them were Cavanaughs—Jack, Philip, Eugene, and the deceased."

"You mean Dagny."

"Yes. Dagny had a key."

"Are any of them missing?"

"Joe's going to check on it."

Elliott turned the handle of the door and held it wide so that I could see inside. He switched on the light. The whole thing was about the size of a large coat closet, with dozens of brightly colored plastic containers, each clearly labeled POISON in three languages.

"The yellow ones are chromic acid, the blue ones are the sodium cyanide." He pried the lid off one of the blue ones. It was filled with white granules that might have been sugar.

"Do I have to stand back or anything?" I asked. "What if you breathe it in?"

"You can't. Not unless you mixed it with an acid and turned it into a gas. Like this it's not dangerous. The security guard says the only reason he thinks they keep it locked up is so that somebody doesn't accidentally mistake it for sugar."

"So how much of this would it take to kill someone?"

"According to what Dr. Gordon told Joe, a quarter of a teaspoon, maybe less."

"You're kidding."

"Have you seen enough?"

I nodded. Elliott put the top back on the container, switched off the light, closed the door, and relocked it. We stood facing each other across the narrow and dimly lit hall, but there was no trace of the previous night's electricity. Elliott's features were stern—all business. Both of us were preoccupied with the riddle of the poison.

"I assume they're going to test all of the stuff they're taking from the medicine chest," I said. "Perhaps the poison was in some sort of medicine, eyedrops or a nasal spray. Might that not account for the fact that the stomach contents of both women had turned up negative for the poison? "How long will it be before they have the results?"

"My guess is a week or ten days. I'm sure Joe'll do what he can to speed things up. You should see if Jack Cavanaugh has any juice he can use to pressure them into moving on this. But between you and me there's only so much we're going to be able to do. The way things are right now we're in a catch-22 situation. So far the medical examiner's office has pended both deaths and I know for a fact that won't change until they've categorically ruled out the chance that both women were poisoned by accident. Unfortunately, as far as the Chicago Police Department is concerned, a pended case is not a murder. And if it's not a murder, then it doesn't go onto the homicide squad's list of open files and Joe Blades doesn't get taken out of the rotation to investigate it. It's up to the primary detective to investigate pending cases on his own. Believe me, Joe's a good cop and he's going to work it as hard as he can. But tonight he's going to report for his shift and the phone's going to ring and it's going to be a fresh murder. And after that it's going to be a steady stream of shootings, stabbings, overdoses, and autoerotic strangulations."

"So what are you trying to tell me?" I asked, knowing the answer already.

"I'm trying to tell you that the way things stand right now, unless we do something about it, this case is going to slip right through the cracks."

DECLINING A HALFHEARTED INVITATION for lunch, I had Elliott drop me a few blocks from my office. Under the circumstances, I felt like I needed the walk to clear my head.

It had been sunny when I'd gone for a run that morning, but that seemed like a lifetime ago. By now it had clouded over, and in the permanent shade of the office buildings on LaSalle Street there was a raw chill in the air. I shoved my hands deep into the pockets of my raincoat and pulled out the two cigars I'd bought for Daniel Babbage. I held them on my palm and looked at them for a minute. I closed my fingers tightly around them until I slam-dunked them into a filthy trash barrel on the corner of Monroe Street.

Callahan Ross was in its usual state of Sunday somnolence. On Sundays even the biggest grinds could be counted upon to stay at home, since no partner worth impressing ever crossed the threshold unless in the throes of a particularly heated transaction. Which, of course, is what made Sunday my favorite day of the week for getting work done. I loved the feeling of having the entire firm to myself. So I was surprised in my journey down the dark and silent corridor to see the light on in Daniel Babbage's office.

I don't know who I expected to see, but when I leaned into the open doorway to take a peek, it was Daniel's secretary, Madeline, who spun around with a small shriek of surprise. She was dressed in a pantsuit of lavender polyester and her hair was varnished into the same tortured bouffant that had greeted Daniel every day at the office. The only difference was that today her stern features were blotched and puffy from crying.

She had, she explained, been with him when he died. There had also been a sister who'd driven in from Naperville at his bedside as well. I usually try to steer clear of maudlin sentimentality, but I confess that I was glad to learn that Daniel, a self-proclaimed solitary in life, hadn't spent his last hours alone.

"How many years did you work for him?" I asked as she dabbed the corners of her eyes with a lacy handkerchief that she fished from somewhere within her ample bosom.

"It'd be thirty years this June. I came to work for the firm in the typing pool straight out of high school. In those days the firm used to look for girls from smaller towns downstate—they thought we weren't as coarse as the city girls, and would make better wife material. Back then, it was quite usual for a young lawyer to marry one of the secretaries. It was almost expected.

"So I came up here from Savoy—that's my hometown—and took a job with my friend Lucille. We lived in a ladies-only residence on Belmont, with no gentlemen visitors allowed beyond the front parlor. You girls have no idea how much the world has changed in the past thirty years.

"When I first came to work at the firm there was a secretary named Bernice Simmons who was a fully trained lawyer. She'd fought tooth and nail to get into law school at Northwestern—the only woman in her class. But after she graduated, the only job they'd give her was typing for Mr. Ross. She retired five or six years ago, just before you came. My friend Lucille ended up marrying a young man in the tax department, but it turns out secretaries were a hard habit for him to break and they ended up divorced. I worked for two years in the typing pool before I was assigned to Mr. Babbage. I've worked for him ever since. God knows what I'll do now."

"You didn't have to come in today," I told her. "I can't imagine that there's anything that can't wait until tomorrow."

"Oh, I'm not doing anything that couldn't wait until a year from tomorrow," Daniel's loyal secretary replied. "But when I got through with church this morning, I didn't want to go back to my empty apartment. Somehow it seemed better to come in here and get a start going through his papers. There's quite a bit of old material that will need to be put with the newer sections of the files. It'll take weeks to get it all sorted out. Besides, this was his favorite place," she said, indicating the office. "It just seemed right to be here today."

"Madeline, can I ask you something?"

"Of course."

"You probably knew Daniel better than anybody and I know he

discussed his cases with you. Did he ever talk to you about why he decided to give certain files to certain lawyers after he learned he was ill?"

"You mean, did he ever tell me why he chose you for Superior Plating?"

"Yes. Why me?"

"There were a number of reasons," she replied. "For one thing, he thought you and Dagny Cavanaugh would hit it off. Mr. Babbage believed that more than anything else when you were dealing with a family business, it was important that the lawyer and the decision-making family member have a good relationship. Over the years he and Jack Cavanaugh became very close. Mr. Babbage thought over time the same kind of relationship would grow between you and Dagny."

"But when you say decision-making family member, wouldn't that mean he'd want someone who'd get along with Philip Cavanaugh? After all, it's Philip who's going to succeed Jack as head of the company."

"Mr. Babbage told me that would never happen. He was convinced that Dagny would find some way to take over the company— or at least the main plating business. He assumed that after Jack died, Philip would spin off the specialty chemicals business—he never has had any real interest in plating, and according to Mr. Babbage, he has a real flair for the chemical business. He said you were the perfect person to structure that kind of transaction."

"He was probably right," I replied grimly. "Unfortunately, things haven't turned out like anyone expected. Dagny's dead and my relationship with the rest of the Cavanaughs feels suspiciously like a group-therapy session from hell. With Dagny out of the picture I honestly don't see what I bring to the party that's going to be of any use to the Cavanaughs."

"I know that Mr. Babbage wouldn't have agreed."

"What makes you say that?"

"He said there was something else that you had that the other lawyers he was considering for the Superior Plating file didn't have."

"What's that?"

"Forgiveness."

CHAPTER

22

All through the afternoon, as I worked at my desk, what Elliott had said about the police investigation gnawed at a part of me. I have been a lawyer long enough to have seen demonstrated with metaphysical certainty the fact that there is no force in the universe as powerful as the inertia of bureaucracy. I was chilled by the prospect of Joe Blades squeezing his search for the truth about what had happened to the two women into the odd moment between drug murders and domestic homicides.

I believed it when Elliott told me that Blades was a good cop. But even a good cop can't unravel one crime while he's interviewing witnesses at the scene of another. Every time Blades took another call, it was going to take time away from the Cavanaugh case. And time wouldn't be the only thing that would be lost. Physical evidence would disappear, memories would erode, and witnesses—if any had ever existed—would quietly fade away. It wouldn't be too long before whatever urgency Blades might feel would be invariably diminished by the red heat of fresh murders.

Of course that's why I'd urged Jack Cavanaugh to hire a private investigator in the first place. But as tenacious and well connected as Elliott Abelman might be, he was still working from the outside. There were some things you could only manage if you were a cop, people who you could get to talk only if you wore a badge.

The thing that rankled most—the thing that had rankled from the very beginning—was the leisurely pace at which the toxicology lab seemed to operate. They had stumbled upon the cyanide by accident. What if they hadn't? We'd still be waiting the two or three weeks for the toxicology results from Cecilia Dobson—which, when they eventually came back negative, would leave us exactly where we'd started.

Suddenly the thought of all the evidence I'd seen the crime-lab technicians take out of the bathroom at Dagny's office consumed me. Which of the little jars and vials in the bathroom medicine chest had contained the poison, if any? Once that was known, at least there would be a place to start. But how long was that going to take? A week? A month?

Somewhere in this town there was someone with the juice to get what needed to be done done in a day instead of a week. The question was who and how to get to them. I thought about calling Elkin Caufield, my defense-attorney friend, but decided that whatever influence he'd managed to salt away had to be cashed in for his clients.

Swallowing my pride, I reached for the phone to call Skip Tillman, the firm's managing partner. Skip played golf with the governor and tennis with several members of Congress. In addition, Callahan Ross had always coughed up generous contributions to both political parties in the pragmatic belief that it always pays to cover yourself both ways.

I dialed Skip's number but hung up before it rang. However juvenile and perverse it might be, I hated the idea of crawling to the firm's managing partner for a favor. I could just hear his well-bred, deprecating laugh as he explained to his lunchtime cronies what he'd managed to accomplish with a couple of phone calls. Besides, I suddenly thought of someone who was much better connected than Skip, someone who would be thrilled to have me owe her a favor. . . .

Which is why, when I picked up the receiver, it was my mother's number that I dialed.

STEPHEN CALLED ME FROM his office and asked what I was planning on doing for dinner. I looked at my watch; it was almost seven. I'd spent more than an hour on the phone with my mother—an all-time record, especially considering that we'd managed to remain on friendly terms throughout the conversation.

"I hadn't really thought about it," I replied honestly.

"Are you hungry?"

I thought about it for a second. "I'm starved."

"How about Chinese food? We could stop in Chinatown on our way back to Hyde Park."

"That sounds good. I just have to finish up one or two things. Can you pick me up in about half an hour?"

"Sure thing. I'll meet you out front."

Thirty minutes later, give or take the time it took me to make sure that Daniel's secretary, Madeline, had locked up his office and gone home, I found Stephen, good as his word, waiting behind the wheel of his dark blue BMW.

"Did you get a lot of work done?" he asked as he pulled away from the curb. The streets were deserted, the windows of the office buildings on either side of us dark and empty. I was probably the last person to leave work in the loop—just in time to have dinner, catch some sleep, and get up bright and early to begin another week.

"I did, but it's never enough," I replied, taking the pins from my hair and rubbing my scalp where it ached from the weight of my French twist. "It doesn't help that I'm burning all sorts of time on this Cavanaugh thing."

"You never told me what the funeral was like."

"It was awful. The worst part is that Dagny was the reasonable one in the family—the peacemaker. With her out of the picture, the Cavanaugh family is like a big driverless bus. I have no idea where it's headed." I went on to tell him in mortifying detail about the rapid disintegration of the Cavanaugh family meeting and how I'd resorted to climbing on a chair to restore order.

"Sounds like a load of laughs," Stephen remarked dryly, turning off of State Street onto Cermak.

"It was so awful I'm seriously considering giving up the practice of law," I said, groping in my purse for a rubber band and slipping my hair into a loose ponytail. "I've decided to work as a ticket taker at Disneyland for a year in order to restore my belief in the essential goodness of human nature."

"I'm sure your mother has some suggestions about what you could do with your time if you wanted to quit your job."

I stuck my tongue out at him, but I don't know if he could see it in the dark.

CHINATOWN IS JUST TWO miles south of my office, but to drive there is a lesson in the strange physics that governs the city of Chicago. Offices, lofts, town houses, and run-down but still respectable businesses give way to block after block of abandoned real estate—crack houses, junkyards, and vacant lots that after dark become open-air drug markets. Turning west onto Cermak takes you through some of the meaner streets of this city.

When it was built, the Hilliard Center Public Housing Project was heralded as a model of urban planning and contemporary architecture. But it's a good bet that none of the dignitaries who traded self-congratulatory smiles at the ribbon cutting have been anywhere near the place since.

Now the concrete walls have been spray-painted with graffiti and most of the windows shot out and boarded over. The little balconies that once had been lauded as a suburbanizing luxury were now covered over with chicken wire in an effort to channel traffic in and out of each building through the metal detectors at the single street-level entry.

This stretch of Cermak is one of the city's most shameful islands of hopelessness. A place where children play in the dirt in which some idealistic bureaucrat once dreamed of seeing grass, a place where violence is a more commonplace occurrence than employment, and even the most trivial of disagreements is settled by the exchange of gunfire.

Once you pass under the Twenty-third Street viaduct, everything about the landscape changes. At the corner of Cermak and Wentworth, an ornately carved and painted archway canopies the street and welcomes you to Chinatown. The signs are in English letters and Chinese characters and the language spoken in the shops is the same nasal patter you'd hear on the streets of Hong Kong or Beijing. It is a neighborhood known for its hard work and prosperity, a place for the newly arrived and the newly affluent as well as the shopping center for the city's burgeoning Asian population.

Crime is not tolerated here, at least not the kind that is so flagrantly apparent at the Hilliard Center four blocks away. By tradition, the Chinese gangs concern themselves primarily with gambling and protection. Yuppy round-eyes like Stephen and me, who come for the food, are safe as long as we stay on the right side of the viaduct.

While I was in law school a Canadian physician attending a professional meeting at McCormack Place, the city's enormous convention center, had grown impatient trying to flag down a cab in Chinatown and had decided to walk the ten blocks back to his hotel. The city that woke up to read about his murder in their Sunday papers the next morning was shocked but not surprised. Chicago neighbor-hoods form a checkerboard of anarchy and gentrification, well-known to residents, but seldom spoken of in any tourist guide.

Stephen and I always went to a restaurant called the Divine Palace. It was on the second floor, up a precipitously steep and nar-row set of stairs in violation of every known fire and safety ordinance. Indeed, the whole place had been gutted in a fire a few years before. Fortunately no one had been hurt and the owners had managed to rebuild, going so far as to duplicate the tacky red vinyl banquettes of the original dining room. It did, however, take a few months after the grand reopening for the smell of smoke and charred plaster to disap-pear and for the restaurant's full complement of roaches to return.

We were late enough to miss the worst of the dinnertime crowd. The old Chinese grandma who spoke no English but handled the seating showed us to our table. I didn't even bother looking at the menu. I always order the same thing: six pot-stickers, which I refuse to share, and an order of shrimp with tomato ginger sauce. Stephen, who is a tremendous food snob, always feels the need to remind me that they make the shrimp sauce with ketchup. That's probably why I like it. Stephen ordered shrimp toast, a whole sea bass with red chilis, and a Tsing Tao beer for each of us.

"So what did you do today?" I asked, taking a swallow of beer.

"Mostly tried to get caught up," he answered, holding his glass up to the light. Satisfied that it was clean, he poured his beer into it. "I've spent so much time going back and forth with the Swiss that I'm at least two months behind on everything else. I don't know why I let you talk me into turning the hematology division over to Richard. I still haven't been able to find anyone to take his place downtown."

Richard Humanski was Stephen's former personal assistant, a brilliant young man long overdue for promotion. The fact that I'd sug-gested that Stephen promote him to head the hematology research division had become a familiar lament. But the truth is, Richard had been turning down offers from Stephen's competitors for quite a while and it was only a matter of time before ambition overrode loyalty. Stephen knew full well that if he hadn't given Richard his own division to run, some other company would have. That didn't keep him from complaining to me about it whenever he felt overwhelmed at work, which was pretty much all the time.

Stephen took a long swallow of beer. "So what do you think is going to happen to that plating company?" he asked. "Do you think that there's any chance they'd want to unload their specialty chemicals division?"

"Why?" I demanded. "Are you interested?"

"Maybe. They make some very interesting proprietary compounds that we use in some of our hospital supply products. I might be interested if we could pick it up for the right price."

"If it comes up, I'll tell them you're interested," I answered noncommittally.

"From what I hear, it's a tidy little operation. But I don't see how it fits in with plating. Who knows? Maybe they'll need the cash if they're going to buy out that one shareholder."

Part of me felt uncomfortable discussing the affairs of one client with another. On the other hand, Lydia had advertised her intention to put her shares on the market in no less a public place than the *Wall Street Journal.*

"I've got to tell you," I said as our appetizers came, "I have no idea what is going to happen with this company. For all I know, Jack Cavanaugh is on the phone right now trying to find another lawyer to replace me. I'm sure my stunt standing on the chair impressed the hell out of him."

"Maybe he should consider hiring a minor-league hockey official to break up his family meetings. He'd charge a hell of a lot less an hour and he'd even bring his own whistle."

"Thank you. That makes me feel so much better." I stirred the soy sauce around on my plate with the end of my chopsticks. "This case depresses the shit out of me. And it's not just the dead people and the funerals. A week ago I thought I was a pretty competent lawyer. Now I realize that there's a big difference between the kind of technical knowledge that I have and the—I'm not sure what to call it—the kind of old-fashioned lawyerly wisdom that Daniel Babbage took to the grave with him."

"I'm sure that he didn't have it at your age either. In lawyer years, you're still a baby. You don't have gray hair or a potbelly or anything yet." Stephen helped himself to a piece of shrimp toast. It looked ridiculously small in his enormous hand. "I did something else this afternoon. I went looking at real estate," he said, taking a bite.

"What kind of real estate?" I demanded, chopsticks poised in midair. I knew that Stephen had long dreamed of moving his research facility from the south side out to Schaumberg, but I thought that the money for that was still a long way away.

"An apartment, actually." He ducked his chin and ran his fingers through the dark waves of his hair.

"Why would you think of moving?" I asked, taken aback. Stephen's apartment was spectacular: six enormous bedrooms with a view of the lake and a doorman named Randolph who made sure that his dry cleaning got delivered on time.

"I'm not sure that I am," he replied. "One of my bankers called me last week to tell me about an apartment that might be coming on the market. A big old place that used to belong to a little old lady who just died. Her family all live in California now and they're thinking of selling."

"So you went to look at it?"

Stephen lifted his bottle, signaling to the waiter for more beer. "Don't you ever think about leaving Hyde Park, Kate?"

"No," I replied. "I'm perfectly happy where I am." I was also so busy with work I didn't see where pointless speculation about places to live would fit into my schedule.

"What about after Claudia finishes her residency?"

"She won't be done until a year from June. I still can't get over the fact that you'd even think about moving. Your apartment's gorgeous and you just finished putting in an exercise room."

"Doesn't the grunge of Hyde Park ever just get to you? The winos on the street corners, the car alarms going off all night?"

"You didn't say you were thinking of moving to the suburbs," I protested, "because that's the only place you're going to get away from the winos and the car alarms. As for the grunge of Hyde Park, I can't imagine how much of it you actually see. Randolph brings your car around to the front door of the building every morning and you have everything delivered right to your apartment. . . ."

"I still think you should start thinking about what you're going to do when Claudia's gone. Two women living on Hyde Park Boulevard is bad enough, but I don't think it would be a very good idea for you to stay there by yourself."

"We've never had any trouble," I shot back, irritated by his Dutch-uncle routine. I felt like I was talking to my father, with whom I was constantly having to defend my choice of residence. The truth is I love Hyde Park. A truly integrated neighborhood, it is the melting pot in microcosm. Within its six-mile border you can find a little bit of everything that is right—and wrong—with America. Black people and white people, welfare mothers and millionaires, Nobel Prize winners and the illiterate, students and professors all stand in line for groceries at The Co-op and go out for breakfast at the Original House of Pancakes.

"The other night when I stayed at your place I got up to go to get a glass of water in the middle of the night and I saw two kids going through a woman's purse in the alley behind your building."

"That stuff happens everywhere. Even in the suburbs. My mother told me this afternoon that when Ann Stevens and her husband came back from Palm Springs, they found their housekeeper bound and gagged in the laundry room. A team of thieves had come through and cleaned out the house."

"It was just a suggestion," said Stephen, wisely choosing to drop the subject as our food arrived. I wondered what had gotten into him. As a rule, Stephen was better than most men about not offering unsolicited advice. When I was in law school I'd put my name on the squash ladder in order to get some exercise. I found myself playing mostly men. It never ceased to amaze me that even when I was clearly the better player, in the break between games my male opponent would invariably offer me tips on how to improve my game. It must be, I concluded, something to do with the Y chromosome.

CHAPTER

23

Monday morning began with a shrill summons to Superior Plating and Specialty Chemicals from Philip Cavanaugh. When I arrived at the plant I was immediately struck by the air of calamity that hung about the place. The reception desk was empty, the administrative wing deserted. Phones pealed unanswered. Finally, I located a single, beleaguered secretary in the tiny alcove outside of Jack Cavanaugh's vacant office—a heavyset woman with close-cropped gray hair and the studied calm of an air-raid warden during the blitz.

"Superior Plating and Specialty Chemicals, will you hold please?" was her measured refrain.

"Where is everyone?" I asked as she paused for breath.

"They quit when they heard about the cyanide," she replied grimly. "These young girls are so ignorant. You must be Miss Millholland. I'm Loretta, Mr. Cavanaugh's secretary. Mr. Jack Cavanaugh that is. Philip is waiting for you over in the specialty chemicals building."

"Will Jack be in today, do you know? I need to speak to him."

"He just got off the phone with Philip, but he won't be coming into the office until tomorrow. There's some sort of problem with one of our big customers, so he took the plane to Dallas this morning. I guess when it rains it pours."

The phones started ringing again and I waited until she'd answered them.

"I've never been to the specialty chemicals building," I told her. "Can you tell me how to get there?"

"Do you know how to get to receiving?"

"I think so."

"Then the best way is to just go out the loading dock and turn right. You'll see a long, white, one-story building. There's no sign or anything, but you can't miss it." She unclipped the ID card from the front of her jacket. "Here, you'll need this to work the lock. It's a swipe-card security system. You'll see the doohickey on the side of the door. I wish I could show you the way myself, but I'm the only one here. If you just drag the card through it, you'll hear the click when the door opens."

"What do you keep over there that you need such tight security?" I asked, accepting the card. I couldn't help thinking about the poisons that were kept behind a simple locked door in the equivalent of a hall closet.

"There's nothing valuable or anything, unless you count the lab equipment," she answered, punching the button on her ringing phone. "When it was so very cold this winter, Philip found out that the factory workers were sneaking into the specialty chemicals building to smoke. That's why he had the swipe-card system put in."

I FOUND THE SPECIALTY chemicals building without difficulty. Antiseptic and nondescript, it looked as if it had been built within the last five years. Like the rest of Superior Plating, function and the desire to avoid unnecessary expense seemed to have been the guiding principles in its construction. The swipe-card reader was mounted, just as Loretta had said, by the side of the door. I pulled the card through three different ways before finally hitting on the right one—yet another reminder that technology hates me.

Once inside, there was a spartan entry with vending machines on one wall and a vinyl couch on the other—no doubt a good spot for a smoke when it was thirty below outside. At the other end were two glass doors that opened onto a flight of linoleum-covered stairs. At the top was a large room laid out like every chemical lab I have ever been in, from Dr. Allen's sophomore chemistry class in high school to any of the research divisions at Stephen's company, Azor Pharmaceuticals.

Four rows of black-topped lab benches, all crowded with equipment, filled the room. Neon lights and a system of ventilation hoods hung from the ceiling. There were Gary Larson cartoons taped up every few feet and someone had hung one of those stuffed animals with suction cups on its feet upside down from the ceiling. White-coated technicians looked up from their work as I passed, obviously unaccustomed to seeing visitors.

I asked a woman with a pipette in one hand where I might find Philip Cavanaugh. She directed me to an office at the far end of the lab.

From the few words we had exchanged earlier that morning, I expected to find Philip in full rant mode. Instead, he was sitting calmly behind a cluttered desk, going over test results with another man, who excused himself as soon as I entered the room.

"You've never been over in this building before, have you?" Philip asked in a weary voice. His body was slumped in the chair, his hands flat on the desk in front of him, as if he found himself without the energy to move them.

"No. When I was here last week I never got this far."

"It's hard to believe it's only been a week since everything started happening." There was a catch in his voice when he said the word *everything*. Philip Cavanaugh was obviously a man strained to the breaking point. It was taking everything he had just to maintain his composure.

"I don't know whether you read the obituaries, but it was in the paper this morning," I said. "Daniel Babbage died on Saturday. The funeral is tomorrow."

"My father told me. Coming on top of everything else, this seems to have hit him especially hard. Did you know that our entire administrative staff quit this morning? They just walked out and left. Loretta, my dad's secretary, is the only one who stayed."

"I saw her a minute ago. That kind of loyalty is a rare thing," I said, thinking of Daniel's secretary, Madeline, weeping as she sorted through his papers the day after his death.

"Eugene's on the plant floor right now trying to convince the workers to stay. They're all afraid that there's some sort of poison in the air here. I can run a company without secretaries, but if the line workers walk out, we're out of business."

"Loretta told me that your father is in Dallas. When you talk to him next time, will you be sure to tell him that I need to speak with him right away?"

"After our last conversation, I don't know when that will be. We just had a big argument."

"What about?"

"This." He slid a single file across the desk toward me.

I picked it up and looked inside. There were two items: a single sheet of letterhead and an article that had been cut out of a magazine. A quick glance at the letterhead revealed it to be a bill from First Chicago, the investment banking firm that Lydia had hired to help her sell her shares. The total was for forty-seven thousand dollars. And people thought lawyers were stick-up artists, I thought to myself. I held up the magazine article.

"Do you want me to read this now?" I asked.

"Please."

It was taken from *Metal Plating Monthly* and it made for surprisingly interesting reading. The article was titled BREAKING AWAY: CAVANAUGH SHAREHOLDER AIMS FOR TOP BID. Beneath it was a half-page photo of Lydia scowling into the camera with her arms crossed on her chest. Arthur stood behind her, looking sinister with his dark beard. The picture had been taken in front of their house on Astor Place.

In the article, the reporter had painstakingly cataloged Lydia's list of grievances against her family, including the fact that her father had never been home while she was growing up; that Nursey, the black maid who had raised her, was the only real parent that she'd ever known, and that she felt that her father had always favored her brothers. She stated emphatically that she was "irrevocably committed" to selling her shares, citing "a complete lack of faith in my brother Philip's ability to do anything competently, particularly running a business." She went on to add, "Philip is one of the most ineffectual people I've ever met. It's been obvious since he was ten."

Lydia also announced that she was planning to use a portion of the money from the sale of her shares to start a foundation to support the work of women artists. She had already decided who was going to receive her first grant—an artist named Shirley Shegall, for a "public sculpture celebrating menstruation."

I put both items back into the file and handed it back wordlessly to Philip Cavanaugh. He might be a pompous, unmitigated putz, but for the first time since his sister's death I felt genuinely sorry for the guy.

"What did your father say?"

"He said to pay the bill."

"That's all?"

"That's all."

"Nothing about the article."

"Nothing at all."

"I assume that the magazine that ran this is widely read in the industry."

"If it wasn't before, it will be now," Philip replied ruefully. "It's bad enough that I've had to spend my whole life listening to people whispering behind my back, 'You know everything would have turned out differently if Jimmy hadn't died.' Or, 'You know that it's really Dagny who's the brains of the operation.' Now everyone is going to be laughing in my face! And my own father won't even say a word in my defense. Instead, he wants me to write a goddamned check for forty-seven thousand dollars so that I can make it easier for my little sister to stab me in the back!"

"So what do you want me to do?"

"Is the company obligated to pay Lydia's investment bankers?"

"Off the top of my head, I wouldn't think so," I replied. "Even though Lydia is a director of the corporation, she doesn't have the authority to contract with outsiders on the company's behalf without a majority vote of the board. I think it can be argued that Lydia's obligation to her bankers is a personal one. On the other hand, your father's chairman of the board and CEO, so no matter what Lydia's legal obligation may be, if he says pay it, I don't see that you have much choice."

"Isn't that the story of my goddamned life," spat Philip. I actually couldn't help agreeing with him.

"Maybe this is actually a step in the right direction," I ventured. "I mean, after he's finished shelling out the money for Lydia's investment bankers, it should be hard for him to delude himself about her not really wanting to sell her shares. Forty-seven thousand dollars is a whole lot of serious."

"That's not the way he sees it. He thinks once the bill is paid she's finished with it. He actually asked me this morning if Arthur had reported for work yet. I guess I have no choice but to face up to it," he said in a tone of bitter disbelief. "My father is a demented old fool and my life is turning into the final act of *King Lear.*"

IN THE CAB ON the way back to the office, I reflected that there was probably enough hatred in the Cavanaugh family to motivate a dozen murders. Who knows how Philip would have turned out if his older brother hadn't died tragically before his eyes? But it was clear that after decades of trying to earn his father's respect, he'd succeeded only in becoming his whipping boy—emotionally truncated and stripped of self-esteem. I felt sorry for him despite myself. Left hanging in the limbo of indifference by his father, publicly humiliated by his little sister; even his pathetic stab at extracurricular romance had found its conclusion not in the tearful recrimination of parting lovers, but in the tawdry inquisition of a police interrogation room.

I arrived back at my office with a headache only to find Cheryl in the midst of exasperated negotiations with two messengers about where to put a waist-high pile of dusty boxes, the kind the firm used for dead-document storage.

"What the hell is all of this?" I demanded, dropping my briefcase and shrugging off my coat.

"Back volumes of the Superior Plating file," Cheryl replied, brushing the dust from her hands.

"What are they doing here? Why aren't they in storage where they obviously belong?"

"Mr. Tillman's orders, miss," Mr. Jackson explained apologetically. He was the head of the mail room and had learned to deflect all manner of lawyerly abuse with the cheerful firmness of a kindergarten teacher. "All the files in storage that used to be Mr. Babbage's have to be hauled out and sent to the new lawyer who's assigned to the case."

"There's a memo that goes along with it," added Cheryl, searching on her desk for the copy. "You have to go through each box and inventory it before it's allowed to go back into storage."

I opened my mouth to protest.

My secretary cut me off. "I already called his secretary and she says he's serious."

I looked at the six-by-eight cubicle that composed Cheryl's work space. Every available inch of space was already filled. I motioned Mr. Jackson to follow me.

To a stranger, my office looked less like a place of professional employment than a cry for help. In terms of sheer volume of paper, my office alone probably accounted for the decimation of a small forest. One thing was certain: I needed either less work or a bigger office. I made a mental note to twist Skip Tillman's arm for more space.

In the meantime Cheryl and I succeeded in shifting some files around in order to accommodate the boxes. Unfortunately it meant that I had to climb over them every time I wanted to get up to go to the bathroom.

That accomplished, Cheryl disappeared to get me some coffee. She reappeared a few minutes later with a fresh cup and paper towels for wiping the outside of the boxes, some of which apparently dated back to the fifties.

"Anything urgent while I was out?" I asked, taking advantage of my first chance of the day to look at my calendar. "What's this at seven o'clock?" I demanded. "Dinner with Chelsea Winters. Who in God's name is Chelsea Winters and why am I having dinner with her at Ambria?"

"It's a recruiting dinner. She's an editor of the *Yale Law Review* who has also interviewed with Barker & West. Jim Swain is very hot to have her come to Callahan."

I sighed. Jim Swain was the head of the committee that hired new lawyers every spring and Barker & West was our chief rival in the legal-talent Olympics. No doubt because Chelsea was a woman, he'd set it up so that she'd be entertained by every female partner at the firm—all three of us—in the hopes that she'd somehow manage to draw the erroneous conclusion that Callahan Ross was by some stretch of the imagination a nurturing environment for female legal talent.

"You got two Federal Express envelopes," Cheryl reported. "They're by the phone on your desk."

I found them and opened the first one.

"I fucking can't believe it!" I exclaimed as I scanned the contents of the first envelope.

"Why? What is it?" Cheryl demanded.

"It's a letter from some lawyer in Zion, Illinois, who claims to represent Cecilia Dobson's estate. He wants me to call him to discuss a possible settlement so we can, as he so eloquently puts it, avoid the necessity of a wrongful-death suit against Superior Plating. Jesus, the world is full of shakedown artists."

"Funny how they all have the initials *J.D.* after their name, isn't it?" Cheryl piped in.

"That's awfully cynical for a woman who's only three semesters away from the bar exam."

"So do you want me to get this guy from Zion on the phone for you?"

"No. I'll dictate a buzz-off letter after I talk to Jack Cavanaugh—if I talk to Jack Cavanaugh. He hasn't called, has he? I need to talk to him about his crazy family."

"He's out of town today," came a soft voice from the doorway. Cheryl and I both looked up, startled.

It was Dagny's daughter, Claire, looking pale but composed in the doorway.

"Claire, come in," I exclaimed, jumping to my feet while Cheryl swept the stack of files off of the visitor's chair. "Can I offer you anything? Coffee, tea, a Coke?"

"A glass of water would be good, thank you," she said as Cheryl disappeared to get it.

"Have a seat. What can I do for you?"

"I can only stay a minute. Aunt Vy's waiting for me out front. I told her that I left my scarf and had to run back for it. I just had a meeting with Mr. Kurlander about my mom's will and stuff."

"How did it go?"

"That's what I wanted to talk to you about," she said, looking around my office uncertainly. "Wow," she exclaimed in a kind of hushed awe, "this is even worse than my room." Cheryl came back with the water and Claire took a sip before continuing. "It was pretty weird, I mean, hearing about the money and all. It *is* my money, isn't it? I mean, I know I've got to have an adult in charge of it until I turn eighteen, but after that it's mine no matter what, right?"

"It's yours no matter what right now," I told her. "Only you have to have your aunt and uncle's permission to spend it or invest it while you're still a minor. It's to keep you from blowing it all on motorcycles and trips to the Caribbean until you're old enough to supposedly know better."

"And then I can blow it all on trips and motorcycles?" she demanded, with a faint smile.

"When you're eighteen you can do whatever you want with it," I assured her. "Though I'm sure Mr. Kurlander will have all sorts of sensible advice about what you can do with your inheritance so that you'll have enough money for the things you want for a long time."

"Mr. Kurlander has plenty of sensible advice," she replied scornfully. "Whenever I asked him a question he basically told me not to worry my pretty little head about it. I might be young, but that doesn't make me stupid. And I don't understand how I'm going to learn enough to be ready to make decisions about my own money when I do turn eighteen if all he's going to do is patronize me."

"I guess Mr. Kurlander rubbed you the wrong way?" I asked. I wasn't surprised. Kurlander had the same effect on me. What I did find remarkable was Claire's intelligence and poise in the face of what most sixteen-year-old girls would find an intimidating situation.

"How can I even be sure he'll be alive when I turn eighteen? He looks like he's at least a hundred."

I laughed. "You don't have to use him as your attorney. If you'd like, I can help you find someone at the firm who you'll like who might be closer to your own age."

"Could you be my lawyer?"

"I already am," I replied, flattered by the question. "I'm the lawyer for Superior Plating and Specialty Chemicals, of which you are a significant shareholder. You need an attorney who's knowledgeable about how trusts work for the other stuff. Don't worry. I'll find you someone who won't patronize you. And you know you can always call me if you need advice about anything at all."

"Even if I just want to talk about my crazy relatives?" she asked with a sly smile.

"If you want to talk about the crazy Cavanaughs, I'm definitely the woman to call," I replied.

As I CLIMBED OVER the boxes of Superior Plating files in order to leave for the day, I reflected that I was now both physically and emotionally overwhelmed by the Cavanaughs—a situation that the prospect of dinner with Chelsea Winters did little to improve. No doubt the editor of the *Yale Law Review* was a very bright young woman setting out on a brilliant legal career, one that I would do my part to ensure included Callahan Ross. But I remembered the dewy-eyed idealism that I'd worn to dinner during the months that I was being recruited by law firms. Tonight I was feeling much too jaded and worn-out to enjoy being on the receiving end of Chelsea Winters's routine.

I had finished packing up my briefcase and was just getting ready to turn off the light when the phone rang. I picked it up. It was Elliott.

"You're not going to believe it," he exclaimed breathlessly. "Somebody kicked somebody who kicked somebody in the medical examiner's toxicology lab. They're almost finished testing the stuff they took out of Dagny Cavanaugh's office yesterday."

"I believe it," I said, smiling to myself.

"I bet you'll never guess what they found?"

"Cyanide?"

"In a bottle of perfume—enough to kill a horse."

"That's great! Now that we know how they got the poison, we have a place to start!"

"There's only one problem."

"What's that?"

"Think about it. They found the poison in a bottle of perfume."

"So?"

"So how did it get into their bodies? What did they do? Drink it?"

CHAPTER

24

As soon as I could, I ducked out of dinner pleading a crushing amount of work—probably not the most politically correct excuse, but what the hell. From dinner I could tell that Chelsea Winters was an intelligent and capable young woman with excellent table manners. I honestly hoped that she'd choose to come to the firm, but I wasn't about to lie in order to convince her. Besides, I was too preoccupied with poison to care one way or the other.

I called Elliott from the restaurant and again from my car. Both times I got his answering machine. I wondered if he was out working on the Cavanaugh case. I also admit that I wondered if he was just out. I detected a twinge of unease at the thought of him on a date and was disgusted with myself. I dialed Stephen's number, first at the office and then at home.

"Whatcha doing?" I asked after we'd exchanged hellos.

"I'm just playing around with our cash-flow projections for the next quarter, trying to figure out how the Swiss deal is going to affect us," he replied. I imagined him sitting at the big rolltop desk that he'd had rebuilt to accommodate his computer—his leonine profile illuminated by the glow of the screen. "Where are you? In the car?"

"I'm on my way home," I replied, swerving to avoid a pothole. Spring had finally come, revealing the winter's ravages on Chicago's crumbling streets and avenues. "I was wondering if I could stop by for a drink."

"Of course," Stephen replied, obviously pleased. Over the years our relationship had developed an elliptical vocabulary all its own. We never spoke directly about wanting to be together. This was probably as close as I'd ever come to telling him that I wanted to see him.

Stephen's apartment was right off Lake Shore Drive near the Museum of Science and Industry. I was there in ten minutes. I left my car with the doorman and took the elevator up.

Stephen was waiting for me at the door. He was wearing a pair of cotton shorts and an old Harvard T-shirt. His hair was ruffled and he was barefoot. The muscles of his legs stood out like steel cables.

"You okay?" he asked, taking my coat.

I opened my mouth, but for some reason Stephen's simple question unleashed a floodgate of answers, all of which tumbled over each other so fast in my brain that no words came out at all. No, I wasn't okay. I was exhausted, unsure of how to proceed with the Cavanaughs, and confused about my feelings for a private investigator for whom I had absolutely no business having feelings. On top of everything, I felt overcome by a sense of how far I'd traveled from being an idealistic third-year law student like Chelsea Winters to a preoccupied partner who could barely manage to feign interest in a recruiting dinner.

Stephen let my coat drop beside my briefcase on the floor. Perhaps we don't know how to talk to each other about how we feel because there are these moments when we just look at each other and understand perfectly what it is that we both want. Never, I thought, when we finished and lay panting on Stephen's still-made bed, never underestimate the distance truly great sex can take a relationship.

"TELL ME AGAIN HOW cyanide works," I demanded, absently stroking the hair on Stephen's chest.

"Cyanide, especially in high concentrations, is a powerful respiratory inhibitor. It's odorless, colorless, tasteless, and very powerful, even in small doses. It occurs naturally in a wide variety of seeds and pits. I remember reading about a case in medical school where a man ate a cupful of apple seeds and died. The coroner's ruling was poisoning by cyanide, which had been released when he chewed the seeds. Cyanide is commonly used in less concentrated amounts to kill insects and rats, and as you well know, its main industrial use is in the electroplating process."

"Yes, I know," I said, rolling back onto the pillows and staring up at Stephen's perfect crown moldings. "They have buckets of the stuff at Superior Plating. It looks just like laundry detergent. They also found cyanide in a bottle of perfume in the little bathroom in Dagny's office."

"Did both women use the bathroom?"

"Apparently."

"Was the cyanide mixed with something else, do you know?"

"I don't know."

"Because you realize cyanide is only lethal if it's released from its host compound by an acid. That's why it kills you if you eat it—the hydrochloric acid in the stomach releases the cyanide from the sodium."

"It's not absorbed by the skin?"

"Maybe if you took a bath in it," Stephen ventured dubiously, "or if you rubbed it in an open wound."

"According to the medical examiner, neither woman had any punctures or abrasions on her skin."

"Then the poison in perfume probably isn't the poison that killed them."

"Then what is it?"

"Maybe it's just a coincidence."

"A coincidence?" I demanded, sitting bolt upright in bed.

"You said yourself that they had buckets of the stuff. Maybe the poisoner wasn't much of a chemist. Maybe he or she put it in a lot of different things that he thought the person he was trying to kill would use. Then, after he'd succeeded in dispatching his victim, he poured them all down the sink."

"What about the perfume?"

"Maybe the poisoner forgot about it—or maybe it was in a busy place that he couldn't get back to without attracting notice."

"If that were the case, you'd have to assume that Dagny, not Cecilia, was the intended victim."

"Why's that?"

"Because the police didn't seal off Dagny's office until after her death. Assuming that the killer didn't forget about the poisoned perfume, he or she must have chosen to leave it in the bathroom after Cecilia died. What I don't understand is why the poisoner wasn't worried about other people accidentally taking the poison and dropping dead?"

"Maybe," said Stephen, reaching up to pull me back down into the circle of his arms, "maybe that's exactly what did happen."

BY NOW I WAS getting used to being sent for by the Cavanaughs. This time I was actually relieved. Whatever Jack Cavanaugh might have to say to me would be an improvement over the past two days' silence. However, I didn't view the fact that he asked me to come to his house as a good sign. By all accounts, Jack, like most CEOs, was so obsessed with work that he usually had to be dragged kicking and screaming from the office. The fact that he still hadn't returned there since Dagny's death was to me a sign that something was seriously wrong.

As I paid off the cabby I found myself contemplating Lydia's house, imagining her standing on her front lawn, staring at her father's house as the photographer took her picture for the article that was to appear in *Metal Plating* magazine. Arguably, it wasn't quite the same thing as trashing your family in the *Wall Street Journal*, but then again probably a higher proportion of her father's cronies read the former.

Climbing the steps to Jack's house, I was surprised to see Detective Blades coming out the front door with Elliott Abelman right behind him. A uniformed maid stood at the open front door, waiting to admit me.

"Good morning, Kate," said Blades cheerfully. "I believe Mr. Cavanaugh is expecting you." He looked better than he had on Sunday. He'd obviously managed to grab some sleep—either that or he'd gotten his second wind. Elliott gave me a smile that rivaled the sunshine and I felt my ears get hot. I told myself to get a grip.

"How are things going with you two gentlemen?" I asked.

"We're on our way to police headquarters to pick some things up, but then we're headed to Mariette's for some breakfast. Why don't you join us if you can spare half an hour?"

"I don't know how long I'll be here," I hedged, wondering whether this was just part of the homicide detective's ongoing campaign to fix me up with his friend or whether he had fresh information he was willing to share. "Where is the restaurant?"

"Corner of Monroe and Clinton," he said, beginning to move down the stairs. I could see where he'd doubled-parked the Cavalier. "We'll save you a seat," he tossed over his shoulder. Elliott passed me on the steps. I carried his smile in with me to my meeting.

THE PAST WEEK HAD turned Jack Cavanaugh into an old man. The fight had gone out of his eyes and he seemed shrunken into the dark folds of his suit. When he poured drinks for the two of us, there was a tremor in his hand. He was too preoccupied to notice that I didn't even bother to pretend to touch mine.

"I still can't believe it," he said after he had drained his glass. The bourbon seemed to have a steadying effect on him. "When they told us, poor Peaches had to go lie down."

"What happened?" I demanded.

"The police were just here. They found cyanide in a bottle of perfume that was in Dagny's bathroom at the office."

"I know," I said. "But I still think it's a little soon to be drawing any conclusions."

"You don't understand," Jack Cavanaugh said, his voice twisted in anguish. "That perfume wasn't Dagny's. That perfume was a present for Peaches."

25

"What do you mean, the perfume didn't belong to Dagny?" I demanded.

"It was sent to Peaches as a gift. Actually it was sent to me to give to Peaches," Jack replied, obviously still struggling with his own sense of disbelief. "That's what I've just been telling the police. It was a present for Peaches. It came in the mail to the office from one of our vendors—for our anniversary. When Dagny threw us that big party a lot of the guys who couldn't make it sent gifts.

"You can ask my secretary, Loretta, all about it. She was there, too. So was Philip. . . . We had just finished our weekly sales meeting when Loretta brought in the mail. There was a box on top. When I opened it there was some fancy kind of perfume inside. Dagny knew the brand right off. She said something about it, you know, I can't remember, something about it being really expensive, or smelling real good, so I said go ahead, you take it."

"But it was definitely sent as a present to Peaches?"

"That's right," Jack replied miserably. "At first Dagny didn't even want it, but I told her that Peaches already had enough of that kind of shit—pardon my French—to last a lifetime. I think she has a bottle of every goddamned perfume ever made; you should see the stuff in our bathroom."

"So tell me about the man who sent it."

"His name is Chip Polarski. He's a rep for one of the big chemical supply houses that we do business with. I've known him for years. I don't think he's even met Peaches."

"Just because the perfume was originally sent to Peaches doesn't mean that the poison was necessarily in it when it arrived," I assured him.

"But that's why this whole thing doesn't make any sense. Who would want to kill Dagny?" Jack asked in an anguished voice. "My daughter didn't have an enemy in the world."

"The bottle of perfume is the first solid lead that the police have gotten. Who knows? In a few days we may have all the answers," I replied helplessly.

"And what the hell am I supposed to do in the meantime?" Jack demanded. "I can't eat and I can't sleep. I can't work. I haven't been to the office in four days. All I do is sit at this damned window and look out at her house. I can't bear to look at Claire—she reminds me so much of the little girl that I lost. This is killing me. Just killing me."

I leaned forward in my chair. "The first time I met you, you told me that Dagny was the one person who loved Superior Plating as much as you do. Don't let its collapse be her legacy. I met with Philip yesterday. He needs your support if he's going to have any chance of guiding this company through the next generation. I think it's pretty clear from what Lydia said in that magazine article that she's determined, for whatever reason, to hurt you as much as possible."

Jack raised his hand in protest, but I cut him off. "I'm not saying that her reasons are good ones, I'm not even sure that they exist outside of her imagination. But I think the time has come, for the sake of the rest of the family and for the health of the company, to accept the fact that Lydia doesn't want to be a part of the business anymore. Jack," I implored him, "you've got to just let her go."

"No!" he said, his face turning an ugly shade of red. "This is my family, goddammit! This isn't some sales manager we're talking about who's not performing. This is my only daughter. I want you to go to her, talk to her . . . beg her if you have to. Find out what it is that she really wants."

Personally I suspected that Jack's pain was what Lydia really wanted, but I felt as though I'd already been as forthcoming as I dared. So I said nothing and instead let Jack Cavanaugh finish saying his piece.

"I've been thinking things over the last couple of days, reflecting on my life. Nothing can take the place of family," he announced solemnly. "Nothing. Life is so short and so precious." He looked me straight in the eye. Some of the old fire seemed to have returned. "I want you to go to my daughter and I want you to tell her that there is nothing more important to me than the love of my children. If it's the company that is keeping us apart, then I want the company to be sold. Go out if you have to and hire a team of investment bankers, get the paperwork started. I want them all to know that if I have to put Superior Plating on the block in order to keep my family together, then believe me, I'm going to sell."

MARIETTE'S WAS A TWENTY-FOUR-HOUR coffee shop on the ground floor of a seedy office building on the fringes of the loop, and was obviously a haunt of cabbies as well as cops, since my driver needed no directions to deliver me to its doors. I found Joe and Elliott comfortably ensconced in a corner booth, breakfasting handsomely on pancakes and bacon.

"I'm glad you're still here," I said as Elliott slid across the ancient vinyl to make room for me beside him.

"Are you kidding?" said Blades. "Of course we waited. Elliott told me you were picking up the check."

Elliott grinned hugely and motioned to the waitress that I needed coffee.

"Breakfast is a small price if you tell me what's going on with this bottle of perfume. Jack Cavanaugh is busy beating himself up over the fact that it was originally sent to Peaches and he decided to give it to Dagny. But what I want to know is whether there's any evidence that the cyanide was already in the perfume bottle when it arrived?"

A waitress appeared and filled my cup with coffee. I took a sip. It was surprisingly good.

"Here's the lowdown," said Blades, laying down his fork and knife and briefly applying his napkin to his lips. "The lab turned up cyanide in a one-ounce bottle of perfume taken from the medicine cabinet of the bathroom in Dagny Cavanaugh's office at Superior Plating and Specialty Chemicals. The brand of the perfume is Forever, and according to Jack Cavanaugh, it was sent to him at the office by a sales rep named Chip Polarski as a present for his wife, Peaches. When we dusted the bottle for prints we came up with a partial that might belong to Jack Cavanaugh, but it's such a small fragment the lab says they can't be sure. But they lifted clear prints from both of the dead women.

"According to Jack Cavanaugh's secretary, the perfume arrived in a cardboard box. I've got a couple of uniforms over there right now turning the place upside down in case by some miracle the box wasn't thrown out. Not that I'd hold out much hope of it being of much use as evidence after it's been kicked around the plant for a couple of weeks."

"Fortunately," interjected Elliott, offering me a piece of his pecan roll, "the secretary kept the card that arrived with the perfume. It was just this guy Polarski's business card with 'best wishes' scribbled on the back."

"No signature?" I asked.

"Nope," Blades replied, "and no prints on the card. Not that you'd expect any. Paper is a shitty surface for lifting prints."

"But you're leaving out the best part," Elliott complained.

"I was going to let you tell her."

"That's okay—you tell her."

"Are you sure?"

"Would one of you just spit it out already," I demanded. The two of them together were no better than a couple of little kids.

"We just stopped and paid a call on Mr. Polarski, the chemical rep who supposedly sent the perfume in the first place," Elliott replied.

"And?" I prodded.

"And he denies sending it."

"I don't know what that proves," I replied, disappointed. "If you had sent someone poisoned perfume, wouldn't you deny it when the cops came calling?"

"In the first place, I believe him."

"And in the second place?" I asked. I couldn't believe it—this was like pulling teeth.

"In the second place Jack Cavanaugh remembers receiving the perfume a few days after the anniversary party that Dagny threw for them on the tenth of February. Not only that, but we checked with his secretary and Jack dictated a thank-you note to this guy Polarski on the sixteenth. Well, according to Polarski, he was in the hospital having hip-replacement surgery from February sixth through the twenty-fourth. According to his wife and his doctor, there is no way he could even go to the bathroom without help during the entire month—not to mention go out, buy, and mail a bottle of perfume. Of course we'll follow it up, but I'm inclined to believe him."

A beeper went off and both men instinctively went for their belts. The page was for the homicide detective. While he excused himself to use the phone Elliott cut me off another piece of pecan roll.

"I don't know if I told you," he said, "but a check of personnel records at Superior Plating turned up diddly. No litigation, no likely cause for a grudge, and no obvious psychopaths. Also, Joe and I both did a thorough background check on both women—Cecilia and Dagny. Dagny checks out completely. As far as I can make out, she was exactly what everyone thought she was. Did you know that she was pulling down two hundred and ten thousand dollars a year in salary? Joe got her financials. She was a sharp investor, too."

"I got a letter from the lawyer Cecilia Dobson's family hired," I said, mentally kicking myself. I had wanted to mention the possibility of a lawsuit to Jack Cavanaugh, but in the face of his distress, I'd forgotten. "They're threatening a wrongful-death action."

"What did you expect?"

"I guess I just didn't expect it quite so soon."

"There's nothing like the promise of big bucks to spur people to action."

Detective Blades came back to the table.

"Guess what, boys and girls?" he inquired genially. I couldn't help but notice that there was a spring in his step and mischief in his eyes.

"What?" Elliott and I chorused.

"They found the box. Cavanaugh's secretary put it away in a closet in case she ever had to mail something small. According to the uniform, she hasn't touched it since."

"Now what?" I demanded excitedly.

"Now the uniforms wait for the guys from the crime lab to get off their coffee breaks and get their asses over to Superior Plating to dust it for prints," Blades reported, calmly helping himself to a piece of toast and starting to butter it. "Then they'll bag it and tag it and dump it on my desk. Haven't you ever heard the phrase 'the wheels of justice grind slow, but . . . ' hey, Elliott, how does the rest of it go?"

"Stop giving the lady a hard time," said Elliott with mock severity, "especially since she's paying for your damned breakfast."

"Before we get too excited over this whole perfume thing," I said, cutting into the little Laurel and Hardy routine they were getting going, "would someone kindly tell me how we can even be sure that the poison in the perfume is the same poison that ended up killing the two women? I was talking this over with someone I know who is a chemist." I felt Elliott stiffen beside me at this reference to Stephen. "He says that it wouldn't be fatal if it was absorbed through the skin. Since it strikes me as unlikely that the two of them were drinking it, where does all of this evidence about who did or did not send the perfume get us?"

"Maybe nowhere. But right now it's all we've got. I talked to Dr. Gordon at the medical examiner's office about it. She wants to send the perfume to the FBI lab in Quantico for testing, see if maybe there's something else in it in addition to the cyanide."

"How long will that take?" I demanded.

"Three to six weeks, but she says she'll sit on them and see if she can get them to turn it around faster."

"I don't believe it," I groaned, my frustration mounting. "What the hell are they going to do with it that takes three weeks?"

"From what Dr. Gordon tells me, the test only takes a couple of minutes, but it's done on a very expensive, high-tech piece of equipment called a G-mass spectrometer that the FBI has only one of. It's the waiting list to use the machine that runs the three to six weeks."

"If I can find you one somewhere else—in a research lab somewhere—could you release a sample to be tested?"

"It would be up to Dr. Gordon. She's the one who's responsible for maintaining evidentiary integrity at this stage of the game."

"But if I could make arrangements for the perfume to be tested privately and could get Dr. Gordon's permission, the police department would have no objections."

"Again," Blades replied, "I can't speak for the department. If it's okay with Dr. G, it's okay with me. Between the two of us, the sooner we know what else—if anything—was in that bottle, the better."

WHEN I GOT TO the office Cheryl informed me that Ken Kurlander had spent the better part of the morning in Skip Tillman's office screaming bloody murder, claiming that I had encouraged Dagny's daughter, Claire, to change attorneys.

"For God's sake, Cheryl," I moaned. "This is the absolute last thing I need to deal with today. Can't Kurlander think of anything better to do—like retire?"

"Mr. Tillman said he wants to see you in his office as soon as you get in. Also, there's a pile of stuff on your desk chair that Daniel Babbage's secretary, Madeline, says goes with the Superior Plating file."

"Wonderful. Why don't you put it on the pile with the rest of the Superior Plating stuff I have no intention of reading. And while I'm tap-dancing in Tillman's office, will you get Bob Halloran at Goodman Peabody over here today? Jack Cavanaugh's finally given permission to get a valuation started on Superior Plating, so I'll need you to pull a copy of their incorporation papers and any financials we have as well. And make sure that I call Stephen when I get back. I have to ask him for a favor on the Superior Plating file."

"When you're through with your trip to the woodshed," my secretary continued as she followed me down the hall, "Wesley Jacobs wants you to call him on Cragar Industries and Adam Beeson says he needs your opinion before three o'clock on that securities offering he sent you the memo on."

"What securities memo?" I asked, rounding the corner toward the managing partner's office. Cheryl rolled her eyes heavenward and struck a dramatic pose of martyred secretarydom.

"I'll put it on the top of the pile." She sighed.

HAVING ALREADY FRITTERED ONE hour away that morning in cop talk with Joe Blades and Elliott Abelman, I found the time wasted in Skip Tillman's office unruffling Ken Kurlander's feathers especially painful. The truly sickening part of the whole thing was that all three of us, including Tillman, who reportedly billed three hundred and eighty dollars an hour, would undoubtedly bill the time spent reinflating Ken Kurlander's ego to the Superior Plating file. It was a perpetual mystery to me how the clients put up with it.

PRODDED BY CHERYL, I managed to get Stephen Azorini on the phone about the G-mass spec test and the problem we were having getting the cyanide-laced bottle of perfume tested. It turned out that Azor Pharmaceuticals possessed no fewer than three G-mass spectrometers, any one of which Stephen was more than willing to put at our disposal. When I brought up the possible objections of the medical examiner's office, Stephen merely took Dr. Gordon's phone number and said, "Leave her to me."

The rest of the afternoon flew by. Bob Halloran at Goodman Peabody and I played at least six rounds of phone tag before actually speaking to each other. When we finally made contact I set up a meeting for six o'clock at my office. I also spent a couple of hours on Frostman Refrigeration, a deal I'd mentally filed as completely sewn up that suddenly showed alarming signs of coming unraveled. Between phone calls, I also sat down with a highly regarded third-year associate named Nora Masterson, who agreed to take on the matter of Claire's estate.

Elliott Abelman called at some point to report that the box that the perfume had been delivered in was made of plain brown corrugated cardboard. Furthermore, the package had arrived regular U.S. mail and was postmarked on February 12. While the exterior of the box was covered with the fingerprints of half of the U.S. postal service, the interior was negative for prints. The only item of any possible significance was that neither the address nor the return address had been written on the box by hand. Instead, one of Chip Polarski's business cards, identical to the one that had been included with the perfume, had been taped to the upper-left-hand corner while one of Jack Cavanaugh's business cards had served as the address of the intended recipient.

I had no time to either absorb or contemplate the implications of any of this. I had less than two hours before the meeting with the investment bankers from Goodman Peabody. In desperation, I took the memo on the proposed securities offering that Adam Beeson had sent me more than a week before and read it in the ladies' room on the couch usually reserved for typists with the vapors. By the time I flipped the cassette onto which I'd dictated what I hoped was a coherent legal opinion, Cheryl came to tell me that Stephen was on the phone, saying that it was urgent.

"What is it?" I demanded, once I'd gotten to the phone and had Stephen on the line.

"I need to see you for a few minutes," Stephen said.

"When?" I demanded.

"Now."

I looked at my watch. The investment bankers from Goodman Peabody were due in just about an hour.

"Has something happened with the Swiss," I demanded, "or can it wait? I've got a meeting at six."

"It can't wait, but it will only take ten minutes," he replied cryptically.

"What is it?" I demanded again.

"I can't tell you," he replied. "You have to see it for yourself."

CHAPTER

26

It was raining, so naturally, every available taxi in the city of Chicago had vanished from the face of the earth. The address where Stephen had asked me to meet him was on the north end of the Magnificent Mile. From the number I figured it was either the Drake or the Mayfair Regent. As I made my way miserably up LaSalle Street, waving frantically at every yellow cab that passed, I wondered who or what it was that I had to see in person and not be told about over the phone.

Finally, a cab pulled to the curb. There was already someone in it, an associate at the firm whose name I had once known but could no longer remember. He was on his way to a Bar Association function and had spotted me slogging through the rain. Out of either charity or an unwillingness to pass by an opportunity to suck up, he decided to stop and offer me a lift.

By the time we got out of the loop, we were in the thick of rush hour and traffic on Michigan Avenue had coagulated to its usual near standstill in front of the Water Tower, so I thanked him and bailed out, deciding that I'd cover the last four blocks faster on foot. I dodged through the crowds of aggressively fashionable shoppers on Michigan Avenue like a running back.

Stopping under the awning of the Drake, I scrabbled through my pocket for the scrap of paper on which I'd jotted the address that Stephen had given me. He wasn't at the Drake. Sodden and out of breath, I continued walking toward the Mayfair Regent, reassuring myself that the numbers increased as I proceeded toward the lake. I stopped in front of the Mayfair Regent to check the number and was surprised to see that I still had a couple of buildings to go. Everything west of the Mayfair was residential— beautiful old buildings that had been built at the turn of the century, a quiet pocket of real grandeur set between Michigan Avenue and the lake.

Fifty feet ahead of me I spotted Stephen standing beneath a dark blue awning. There was a woman at his side with whom he chatted amiably. No doubt expecting me to arrive by car, their eyes were fixed on the street.

I was in a snappish mood, my feet were soaked, and I was feeling damp and overheated from running in my raincoat. Moreover, I was anxious about getting back to the office in rush hour in time for my six o'clock with the investment bankers.

"Stephen, what is it?" I asked breathlessly, once I'd gotten close enough to speak. He held his hands out to pull me into the circle of their conversation.

"Patty, this is Kate Millholland. Kate, Patty Malloy."

"Are we ready?" Patty inquired, pertly.

"If it's okay with you, I'd like to take her up alone," he said.

"Of course." Patty smiled knowingly and handed Stephen a set of keys as I looked on, bewildered. "I'll just wait for you downstairs."

"What is it?" I demanded. "Where are we going?"

"You'll see," said Stephen, taking me by the arm and steering me into the building. The doorman snapped to attention and swung the door open for us, putting his gray-gloved hand to the bill of his cap and wishing us a good evening.

After the wet dusk outside, the lobby of the building seemed bathed in a golden light. The walls were covered with butter-colored damask. A crystal chandelier glittered above an enormous arrangement of yellow roses and calla lilies set on an antique pedestal table of carved rosewood. Very little had changed since I was a little girl.

The elevator doors slid open silently and Stephen and I stepped in. My heart turned over when he pushed the button for twelve, but I did not say a word. My heart was beating absurdly fast and suddenly the air seemed thin—I knew exactly where I was going.

When the doors opened I stepped out into the apartment that had been my home until just before my sixth birthday. Stephen turned the key in the door and I brushed past him to get inside. The place was completely empty and smelled vaguely of Murphy's oil soap and old lady. I ran from room to room like a little girl, my high heels clattering on the parquet.

It was an enormous apartment—eight bedrooms, if I remembered, with a formal double drawing room and a separate ballroom— in what was arguably the city's most opulent address. Fourteen-foot ceilings and a wall of windows in the living room that seemed to actually own the lake. Every apartment took up an entire floor of the building, but my grandparents, who had once occupied the apartment upstairs, had given their apartment to my parents so that Mother could combine the two. They hired an architect and broke through the ceiling in the living room to accommodate a grand staircase and an upstairs portrait gallery.

Whoever had lived there after us had done little to alter my mother's decorating. There were so many things I remembered:

the yellow chintz in the sunroom, the enormous six-burner restaurant range in the kitchen, the black-and-white checkerboard of linoleum on the floor. There was a dumbwaiter that still worked in the butler's pantry, as did the bell system that was connected to the servants' quarters, which were located in the basement of the building.

I climbed the kitchen stairs that led to the second floor, taking them two at a time. I hurried past the rooms once occupied by my parents, the nanny, and my older brother, Teddy. The door to my old bedroom was closed. I turned the handle and stepped inside. The wallpaper was still the same—Regency stripes of Wedgwood blue on a white background; Mother believed that anything that smacked of the nursery was in poor taste. I walked into the closet and turned on the light. There on the inside of the doorjamb were the tiny penciled marks that set out my growth through the years.

I went to the cathedral window and stood looking out at the traffic snaking northward on Lake Shore Drive, the headlights forming a luminous necklace against the edge of black water beyond. Stephen came up behind me and put his arms around my shoulders.

"So what do you think?" he asked softly.

"It's so strange," I said, turning to face him and taking a step away. In the best of times just the size of him makes me feel like a little girl. Standing in the bedroom of my childhood, the feeling was overwhelming. "I haven't been here since I was five years old. I cried so much the day we moved I gave myself a fever. You know, from the day Mother bought the house in Lake Forest, she's been redecorating it. Nothing stays the way it is long enough to get attached to it. But this place hasn't changed at all. I know I lived in the house in Lake Forest for more years, but when I close my eyes and think of home, this is the place I always remember."

"That's good," said Stephen, "because I just bought it this afternoon."

I took another step back and felt my face stretch into a cartoon of surprise.

"Remember the other night at dinner when I told you that my banker tipped me off about an apartment that was coming on the market? When your parents bought their house in Lake Forest, they sold this apartment to Lucille West and her husband. He died four years later, but she stayed here, living alone until she had a stroke six months ago. I made her son an offer this afternoon and he accepted it."

I just stood there, gaping at him like an idiot.

"I was hoping you'd come and live here with me," Stephen continued quietly.

"So it's done?" I finally managed to stammer. "You made him an offer and he took it? The deal is done?"

"Subject to inspection and the approval of the co-op board, naturally."

I think I opened and closed my mouth, but I knew that no words would come out. Stephen took a step closer and laid his hand against my cheek.

"Tell me that you love it," he said.

"I love it," I replied, still hollow with surprise.

"Tell me you can't wait to move in."

I turned to look him in the face, but my eye caught the watch at his wrist.

"Christ!" I exclaimed, the time hitting me like cold water. "You told me ten minutes! I have to be back at the office by six. I have to go!"

"You can't!" he exclaimed, taken aback. "Not until you tell me."

"Stephen," I replied, suddenly in motion, "I've got three lawyers, five investment bankers, and two secretaries who are being paid overtime waiting for me back at the office. We can talk about this later."

Then I stood up on tiptoe, kissed the end of his chin, and was out the door.

I BEGAN THE MEETING with the bankers from Goodman Peabody in a preoccupied state of mind. A part of me was still intoxicated by the apartment. Besides being a true architectural gem, it was like being offered the best piece of my childhood back as a present. But try as I might to beat them back, there were other voices in my head, voices that wondered about a man who tells you that he wants to live with you but can't scrape up the words to tell you why. Voices that questioned what a man who felt easy making a unilateral decision about buying a multimillion-dollar co-op knew about equality in a relationship between a man and a woman. And a terrible little voice, an echo of Mother at her worst, who whispered that he only wanted my name on the mailbox to grease the way with the co-op board, who might not hesitate to blackball the son of an Italian businessman whose father was rumored to have ties to organized crime.

Fortunately, before too long, the investment bankers launched a fusillade of technical issues with regard to a sale of all or part of Superior Plating that forced me to turn my mind to the matter at hand. By the time we had sorted them out and had developed a plan of action to carry us over the next few days, it was after nine o'clock.

When I got back to my office I found a note from the switchboard. Stephen had called to say that he was taking a night flight to Geneva and did not expect to return until late Friday night. That explained his insistence that I see the apartment before he left. Relief flooded through me. More than anything else, I needed time and space to think.

I was wired from the meeting with the bankers and still reeling from Stephen's little surprise. I knew that if I went home, sleep would be next to impossible. I called home hoping that Claudia wasn't working and I would find her there. I wanted to hear what she had to say about Stephen and the apartment, but it was the answering machine, not my roommate, that picked up after four rings.

Rather than going home to the empty apartment, I took my shoes off, clipped my Walkman to my belt, slipped an old U-2 CD into the machine, and set to work on the small monument of Superior Plating files. The oldest ones were the most interesting, just for their glimpse back into time: typewritten pages blotched with Wite-Out reminding me that there had been a time without computers or even self-correcting typewriters; carbon copies smudged and faded; handwritten notes from Jack's father, who was as uneducated as he was tough. I flipped through the oldest boxes just to say, if challenged, that I'd done it. The nitty-gritty of actually inventorying the contents I'd leave to Cheryl. Once she was done with this term's exams, I'd have her come in over the weekend. I knew she'd be grateful for the overtime.

It wasn't until I came to the pile of things that Madeline had turned up in Daniel's office that my task got interesting. The material fell into two categories: private documents that fit into no neat category in a corporate file, and memorabilia. In the former category were the records that made up the kind of client's dirty laundry that every lawyer accumulates over the years: personal-loan documents between Jack Cavanaugh and his children—Dagny seemed to have been the only one who'd never had to go to her dad for money; a document setting up something called the Zebediah Hooker trust to the sum of one hundred thousand dollars, signed by Jack Cavanaugh and witnessed by Daniel Babbage more than twenty-five years ago; even a copy of Jack and Peaches's prenuptial agreement, surprising in that it had obviously been drafted to protect her assets from Jack and his children, not the other way around. I also came across a file jammed with bank records, including a set that appeared to pertain to the payment of some sort of ongoing annuity through a Georgia bank. I put it with the old trust agreement with a note to ask Madeline about them later.

The cardboard box that held memorabilia was the most interesting of the lot. There were old photographs, some of them black-and-white and crumbling with age. They were all of Daniel Babbage with various members of the Cavanaugh clan. There was a young Jack Cavanaugh, his hair a sandy brown and his brow less wrinkled, but with the same bulldog expression, his arm flung around Daniel's much-younger shoulders. There was Daniel in hunting attire, shouldering a six-gauge shotgun and surrounded by teenaged Cavanaugh boys. I recognized the barn at Tall Pines in the background and the un-formed features of Philip and Eugene. Eugene was gazing adoringly at a tall youngster with broad shoulders and a winning smile who I assumed was Jimmy Cavanaugh, the older brother who'd died trying to rescue Grace Swinton from drowning. I tried to guess from the picture how old they all were and decided that Jimmy couldn't have been more than fifteen, which would have meant the photo was taken about a year before the tragedy.

There were more recent photos as well. Snapshots of Daniel shaking hands with Eugene in military uniform. Yellowing thank-you notes written in a child's shaking hand, speaking of gratitude for a birthday gift and signed by Mary Beth, Eugene's oldest. More recently there was a copy of an article about Peaches clipped from the newspaper, under the headline TV REPORTER STALKED BY DERANGED FAN, and another follow-up piece detailing the arrest of a west-side food-service worker who'd broken into Peaches's north-side apartment claiming to be her estranged husband. I read it with interest, but it seemed like tabloid stuff.

I found a photograph of Dagny and Claire, both still in climbing harness, standing arm in arm in jubilation at the summit of some mountain, and a copy of an engraved invitation to the party celebrating Jack and Peaches's first wedding anniversary. No doubt to help

Daniel overcome his well-known aversion to parties, Dagny had written on the front of the invitation in her bold hand: *It just won't be the same without you!*

I sat looking at the invitation for a long time, seeing a kind of epitaph in her words. Finally, I set the card upright against the base of my desk lamp, propped the photograph of Dagny and Claire beside it, and forced myself to move on to another file.

27

Lydia refused to come to my office, so I had to go to hers. The new offices of the Illinois Foundation for Women were in a building on Wacker Drive where the Chicago River bends south just opposite the Merchandise Mart. They were still in the process of moving into their new space, so our conversation was punctuated by painters walking through with ladders and telephone installers asking questions about where Lydia wanted the lines put in. But I suspected that Lydia could not wait to show off her new digs—currently in the process of being painted an alarming shade of salmon, in order, she explained, to counterbalance the bright tones of the aquamarine carpeting currently rolled up in the hallway. I thought the whole thing was going to end up looking like the waiting room of a color-blind gynecologist, but I didn't say so. This was, I reflected, my final peacemaking attempt with Jack's wayward daughter and I wanted at least to get started on the right foot.

Lydia was in her element, parading from empty office to empty office, explaining which artists she planned on funding and laying out her grandiose plans for herself in her new role as feminist patroness of the arts. She'd changed her looks completely from the time I'd last seen her, which was at her sister's funeral. Today she wore a black jumper over a black T-shirt, black tights, and a pair of brand-new black Doc Martens. Her hair hung straight and didn't look like it had been brushed recently. She'd changed from the elaborate makeup she'd worn to emulate Peaches to plain white powder and generously applied lipstick in a particularly dramatic shade of dark red. I wondered how Peter felt about the fact that his mother suddenly looked as though she'd just raided one of his girlfriends' closets. He was probably used to it. His whole life had no doubt been spent watching his mother's attempts to reinvent herself.

Lydia was clearly enjoying herself. From behind an enormous desk of polished teak in an otherwise vacant office, she sat posed as if for an audience of reporters. She had already hired a woman from Los Angeles, she explained in the voice of announcement, to edit a woman's alternative-healing newsletter. Its focus would be on ways to rechannel negative energy and the use of herbal cures for stress-related disorders like migraines and cancer. As I tried to keep my face under control and stifle an almost overpowering desire to laugh, I reminded myself that I was temperamentally unfit for this kind of law practice. Daniel had been wrong about me. I was not a sympathetic listener and I certainly wasn't very forgiving—especially when it came to fools like Lydia.

"How are you going to get your funding?" I broke in, cutting her short on the subject of domestic violence. From her rambling discourse, it was impossible to tell if she believed that it was caused by a kind of mental illness that afflicted only the male of the species or was a symptom of men's financial oppression of women. Personally, I couldn't imagine what Lydia knew about either.

"Naturally, the Republicans are cutting off funds for any kind of meaningful programs for social change," she replied bitterly, "so we're going to have to raise the money privately. I am personally funding the initial phase of the foundation's work, but if we are to institute the kinds of sweeping programs that are so necessary, we're going to have to raise substantial amounts of money. Right now we're still evaluating our fund-raising alternatives."

"I confess I'm curious about the evolution of your feminist conscience," I said, trying hard to sound earnest. "What exactly is it that made you decide to launch the foundation at this point in time?"

"I came to be under the care of the most wonderful therapist. She's the one who really helped me to understand the issues of my life, especially how they relate to my family in terms of the feminist class struggle. She suggested that as part of my therapy I do volunteer work at a battered women's shelter. Unfortunately, because of the twins, I was only able to work there one afternoon, but I'm telling you, that afternoon completely changed my life. I can't begin to express how strongly I related to those poor, abused women. I knew instantly that we were sisters under the skin."

I had no doubt that if Lydia succeeded in selling her shares, she would soon be parted from the money. And it didn't bother me that Jack would end up footing the bill one way or another. But it seemed too bad that the proceeds were going to be frittered away on sculptures about menstruation and a crackpot newsletter instead of her "sisters under the skin" at the shelter.

"I admire your ambition," I said, I hoped sincerely. "But as you've probably guessed, I've come to talk to you about your family's business. Your father asked me to speak to you today. He is desperate to make peace with you. I'm sure you realize how much he loves you. He sent me to find out what it will take to mend this rift between you."

"Ten million dollars," Lydia answered in a hard voice without a moment's hesitation. "I've been through the numbers with my bankers and that's the price I want for my shares. Once my business is concluded, we can go back to being family as family. But until I get my ten million, there is no way that I can separate the two."

"I'm sure you know that the company hasn't concluded its own independent valuation," I protested, "but I'll tell you right now I think it's unlikely that they'll come anywhere close to ten million as a fair market price for your shares."

"That's your problem."

"I understand that you want the money for a good cause," I said, giving diplomacy my best shot for Daniel's sake, "so naturally you want to get top dollar. But you have to be realistic. There just aren't that many people out there who are interested in a minority stake in a family-owned company."

"My bankers ran the numbers based on two different scenarios," she reported. I found it disconcerting to be talking about a multimillion-dollar deal for shares in an industrial concern with a woman who looked like an aging groupie for some sort of grunge band—especially since she'd looked like a Nancy Reagan wannabe the week before. "They said that it would not be inconceivable to net ten million dollars for my shares if the entire company were sold."

"But no one has said anything about selling the company," I protested. I was confident that Jack Cavanaugh's talk of a sale the day before was the desperate rambling of a grieving man. I certainly didn't want to give it any more credibility by repeating it in front of Lydia.

"I don't care if people think I'm being unreasonable," Lydia replied, haughtily. "I want my money out of the company and I want ten million dollars for my shares. I might be willing to consider a lower offer from an outsider, but as far as my family is concerned, the price is ten million dollars or nothing."

I got to my feet and reached for my briefcase, thanking Lydia Cavanaugh for her time. I'd seen enough of Jack's youngest daughter not to be completely taken aback, but I was still surprised. I'd come to discuss a fair price for her shares, not blackmail.

WHEN I GOT BACK to the office there was a stack of phone messages and twelve yellow roses arrayed in a crystal vase. The card was from Stephen. All it said was *Thinking of you*. The messages were less remarkable, but I was pleased that they included one from Nora Masterson asking me to join her and Claire for their first meeting over dinner the next day. According to Cheryl, Nora hoped that the presence of someone Claire already knew would put the teenager more at ease. When Cheryl added that we'd be dining at the Hard Rock Café, I knew that I'd picked the right lawyer for the job. I told Cheryl to check my calendar and tell her that I'd be there. Also I needed to see Daniel Babbage's secretary for fifteen minutes later that afternoon if there was some time that Cheryl could squeeze her in. I continued flipping through the pink phone slips, dealing them into piles— urgent, must call, leave until tomorrow, delegate—like cards at solitaire. When I came to the message from a Dr. Roger Dorskey, I put the rest of them down and reached for the phone. I didn't know anyone by that name, but I recognized the number as being from Azor Pharmaceuticals and the message said he'd called about test results.

I got the good doctor on the phone and introduced myself. He sounded young and eager to please. Better still, he got right to the point.

"Dr. Azorini asked me to test the two samples that I got yesterday from Dr. Julia Gordon. I'm sure you know that all they're set up for at the medical examiner's office is gas chromatography, which is pretty basic stuff. Here we can use something called a spray mass spec, which is what I used on the two samples."

"And what did you find?"

"Lots of things, actually. I hadn't realized how chemically complex perfume is. There were more than twenty compounds in the control sample that we ran. But I'm assuming you're interested in the differences we turned up between the two samples, not the composition of the control."

"Exactly."

"It turns out that the other sample is pretty scary. In addition to the cyanide—and there was enough in the two-cc sample that we tested to take out an elephant—there was another compound called FC-170C. That's its generic chemical name. It's sold commercially as Fluorad. Ever heard of it?"

"No," I replied, beginning to take notes. "What is it?"

"Fluorad is a halogenated hydrocarbon, which is just a generic term for fluorinated hydrocarbon, which is related to chlorinated hydrocarbons. Those are the agents that environmentalists are currently going apeshit about—you know, things like PCBs which are supposed to harm the ozone layer, but I don't think that Fluorad is one of the 'bad' fluorinated hydrocarbons—"

"You're losing me with all of this. Tell me, what exactly is Fluorad used for?"

"I had to make some calls to find out exactly," he confessed. "As far as I can tell, it's a kind of surfactant."

"What's that?"

"You can think of a surfactant as a penetrating agent; it works kind of like a very powerful water softener that's used to decrease surface tension. Most often Fluorad is added to embalming fluid. I'm sure you realize that embalming fluid is injected into arteries and veins to preserve a dead body. Well, in this case the Fluorad lowers the surface tension of the body fluids as well as the body surface linings—like the lining of the arteries—which allows for better penetration of the embalming fluid out to the capillary beds."

"So what would be the point of putting it in the perfume?"

"No point, unless you also happened to mix it up with cyanide first."

"I still don't get it."

"Think of Fluorad as a messenger, a carrier molecule that picks up another molecule and carries it through a barrier—like skin."

"Are you telling me that someone mixed Fluorad with cyanide so that when it was put in with the perfume, the Fluorad molecules would carry the cyanide molecules through a person's skin? Is that possible?"

"Oh, it's possible all right," Dr. Dorskey replied. "And it wouldn't take too much Fluorad either. It's very powerful stuff."

"How powerful?"

"Let's put it this way: If you put a drop of Fluorad in a martini and then stuck your finger in the glass, you'd get drunk."

CHAPTER

28

I met Elliott Abelman and Detective Blades at Flannagan's, a corner tavern three blocks from police headquarters. It was a cop bar and well patronized despite the fact that it was only three in the afternoon. I'd immediately phoned Joe Blades after I'd hung up with Dr. Dorskey and told him of the chemist's findings. I offered to bring him the copy of the doctor's preliminary report, which I'd asked him to fax to my office. Blades was just coming off of his shift and on his way to meet Elliott for a drink.

The entire way to Flannagan's, all I could see was the bottle of perfume laced with Fluorad and cyanide. All I could think of was the level of hate or pathology that must have possessed whoever was behind the crime. I was haunted by images of Cecilia Dobson sneaking a dab of her boss's expensive new perfume and paying for it with her life. Of Dagny brushing her hair and putting on fresh perfume to go to the funeral and ending up in agony, collapsed on her own floor, as she crawled toward the phone for help.

I found the two men at a table in the back. Both had bottles of Old Style in front of them, but neither was drinking. I took a seat and laid copies of the spray-mass-spec tests and the material safety sheets on Fluorad on the table.

"I don't see how the ME's office will be able to do anything except rule both deaths homicides," announced Blades once he'd finished reading, "especially since you said that they make the stuff at the plant where both women worked."

"They make it in the specialty chemicals division. It's a new product that Philip unveiled at the last board meeting. He even did a little show-and-tell to demonstrate the compound's properties. I remember reading about it in the minutes."

"So what's the big deal?" Elliott asked. "I thought you said this was some sort of additive for embalming fluid."

"According to Philip Cavanaugh, embalming chemicals are a four-hundred-million-dollar market that's growing all the time."

"No shortage of customers, that's for sure," remarked Elliott.

"According to the material safety sheet, up until now there's only one company that's made this Fluorad stuff and that's 3M. It's odorless, colorless, and very expensive."

"How expensive?" I asked.

"Two hundred and fifty dollars a gallon."

Elliott whistled softly.

"The reason that Philip was so eager to show it off to the board is that his people have come up with a cheaper way to make the stuff. I'm sure he figures the company can make a lot of money breaking up 3M's monopoly," I said.

"I wonder how he'll react when you tell him that it was used to kill his mistress and his sister?" Elliott demanded in a hard voice.

"I'm going to see him, now," Blades replied, "but it wouldn't hurt if you put one of your guys on him, Elliott, once I'm done with him, just to see if he does anything stupid."

"You meeting him at his office, you said?" Elliott asked. Blades nodded. "Then let me go and make a call."

The homicide detective and I faced each other across the sticky top of the bar table.

"You're right," I said, "this isn't turning out at all like I expected."

"Well, it sure surprised the hell out of me. I thought I'd seen it all, but someone dying from a drop of perfume is a new one. It's also going to be a bitch to prove, even if we figure out who did it."

"Why's that?"

"Let me tell you how cops solve murders—not Columbo, mind you, real cops: physical evidence, witnesses, and confessions." He raised a long finger as he counted each one off. "First the physical evidence. So far the physical evidence in this case is slim, to say the least. The first death was originally thought to be accidental, so there was no attempt made to preserve or analyze the crime scene, and even after the second murder the scene yielded shit. All we've got so far is the bottle of perfume. The only solid fingerprints on the bottle are of the two dead women. We also have the box that it was mailed in. It's got only the fingerprints of people we already know handled it. It was postmarked on the twelfth of February, which is not exactly a breakthrough since it was supposedly sent as an anniversary present. You never know, we may get lucky with the business cards that were used to address the box, but according to the sales rep whose name is on them, he's been handing them out twenty times a day for about the last ten years. Likewise, we may get a break on the Fluorad. I've got the crime lab scheduled to dust at Specialty Chemicals for prints once Philip shows me where it's kept. I'm also sending some uniforms to see if anybody noticed anything unusual. But again, I'm not holding my breath. So far our killer hasn't made any mistakes, and I'd be surprised if we started finding finger-prints now. So that's your physical evidence." He held up a second finger.

"As far as witnesses, that's pretty easy. You're the only one and you saw diddly. And third"—he put up another finger—"confessions. I guess there's a chance that someone will come in beating their breast and confess. Not likely, but always possible."

Elliott returned to the table. "I sent a man over to Superior Plating. He'll stick to Philip Cavanaugh like glue," he reported.

"What about the perfume?" I demanded. "Surely there's a chance you'd be able to trace the sale of the bottle. You said it was expensive."

"That's the angle we're working on now," Blades replied, taking his bottle of beer in his hand. He took a swallow and made a face. "Elliott's got four people on it, too. But I'm telling you, it's like looking for a needle in a haystack. The perfume could have been bought any-where—Chicago, the suburbs, the duty-free shop at a dozen airports. At this point there's no way of knowing whether the perfume was doctored before or after it arrived in the mail. We can't even be sure who the intended victim or victims were. Did someone help them-selves to cyanide and Fluorad from Superior Plating, lace the per-fume with it, and send it to Peaches? Or did someone slip into Dagny's bathroom to put the poison in?"

"It sounds like you've ruled out Cecilia Dobson as the intended victim either way," I observed.

"So far we've got no possible motive."

"What about Philip Cavanaugh? I think we can all agree that he might have had a reason for wanting her out of the picture," Elliott suggested.

"But then why leave the perfume in the bathroom, where his sister was likely to use it?" Blades countered. "Surely, in the days fol-lowing Cecilia Dobson's murder, he had more than enough opportunity to get rid of it. Even if for some reason he wasn't afraid of his sister using it, why leave it lying around? It's the one piece of physical evidence that might link him to the murder."

"Did anyone benefit financially from any of the deaths?" Elliott asked.

"As far as I can see, no one. Except for Dagny's daughter, Claire, of course, but so far we have no reason to treat her as a suspect."

"What about malice?" I suggested. "It seems to me that Lydia Cavanaugh hates every member of her family enough to want to poison them. By all accounts, she was pathologically jealous of her sister, Dagny, and her mother-in-law. For a while she changed her hair and started dressing like Peaches. They even traced crank phone calls they were getting last year to her."

"I know. And we're running a check on the phone records for the entire family for the last three months. Believe me, we're not ruling out anybody at this stage. Especially since Peaches was the victim of a felonious stalker two years ago."

"Surely that can't be tied in to all of this?" I demanded, remembering the newspaper clippings Babbage had saved.

"The Fluorad points to it being someone inside the company," said Elliott. "But from what Joe tells me about the guy who was stalking Peaches, I don't think we can rule him out."

"How could he have found out about the Fluorad," I demanded, "much less have gotten his hands on it?"

"The guy's a real piece of work—not smart, but cunning. He managed to get a job as a janitor at the station where Peaches worked so that he could steal her keys and have copies made. He broke into her house on a number of occasions. When we finally went in to arrest him, his room was plastered with pictures of Peaches."

"So what happened to him?" I asked.

"We sent him to jail for eighteen months with three years' probation."

"So where is he now?"

"He got out of jail on February first of this year," said Blades, his voice heavy with resignation. "According to his parole officer, he's living in an SRO on Halsted—about two miles from Peaches and Jack Cavanaugh's house."

CHAPTER

29

D aniel Babbage, a man who'd spent his whole life in the city, was laid to rest in Naperville, Illinois, a suburb he would have visited only at gunpoint while he was alive. The day was sunny but it was cold, and the wind blew so sharply that it ripped the petals off the flowers that had been mounded on top of the casket. In the wind, the lawyers who had come to see him buried seemed to flap around the graveside in their black coats like a flock of crows.

Skip Tillman, the firm's managing partner, spoke movingly at the internment—as ever, the consummate public man. His remarks were anecdotal. He recalled Daniel's early years at the firm, his determination to serve family-owned businesses over the objections of his partners, his service, his loyalty, and above all his love for his clients. He talked from the heart about the bravery with which he faced his final illness.

I look back at the morning of Daniel's funeral as one of the low points of my life. Emotionally exhausted by the blitzkrieg of crisis surrounding the Cavanaughs and at sea about my personal life, I was tormented by the unsolved murders of Dagny Cavanaugh and Cecilia Dobson as by open sores. I had also quite simply been to too many funerals in too short a time. The fact that they had been for people I had really cared about just darkened the water at the bottom of the well.

I had spotted Jack Cavanaugh across the crowd during the service and sought him out after the final benediction. Eugene, ever dutiful, was at his side. Father and son both seemed beaten down by the events of the past few weeks.

"It was a beautiful service," I said, falling into step beside them as we began to walk back to our cars.

"Philip should have been here," Jack complained.

"Sally called this morning and said that he was in bed with the flu," Eugene explained. Judging from his tone of voice it was clear he'd been defending his brother all morning.

"That's no excuse," snapped Jack. "He could have at least pulled himself together for an hour. Daniel was like a member of the family. It's wrong that he wasn't here."

We walked several yards in silence, neither Eugene nor I willing to break into Jack's angry reverie.

"The police came to the house again this morning to talk to Peaches," Jack said finally. "They seem to think it's that psycho that she had all that trouble with who's behind everything. As soon as he got out of jail, we started getting those calls again. I told that judge at the parole hearing he should never be released. He's a nut. But he didn't have the balls to keep him behind bars, which is where he belongs. Now two innocent women had to pay with their lives. I suppose now they'll give him the electric chair. So what? It won't bring my Dagny back. I ask you, what's wrong with this world?"

"If it was him, how did he get access to the plant? Not only would he have to get into Dagny's office, but he'd have had to get into the specialty chemicals building as well, and that has a security system," I remarked.

"The swipe cards get lost all the time," answered Eugene. "Dad's secretary just came to me to get hers replaced. She told me she lent it to you and you never gave it back.

"And another thing," Eugene continued, "the cops said they picked the guy up for vagrancy the night of Dad's anniversary party. He was hanging around the neighborhood."

"I'm still surprised," I replied. "I'd always imagined that there was a big leap between mooning around someone's house and sending them poison in the mail, but I don't have much experience with these things."

"You sure as hell don't." Eugene was suddenly angry. "Don't you think my family has been through enough without you making small talk about it like it was some kind of guessing game?"

"I'm sorry," I said quickly. "I want to find out the truth as much as you do." If the police didn't find the killer soon, I reflected, everyone in the Cavanaugh family was going to have a breakdown. As it was, everyone's nerves were frayed. "How is Peaches handling all of this?" I inquired of Jack.

"Naturally she's upset," he said. We had come to a stop beside his shiny black Lincoln. "Have you spoken to Lydia yet?"

"I went to see her yesterday at her new office. She's already rented space for the foundation she plans on funding with the proceeds from the sale of her stock."

"What did she say?"

"She's determined to sell. Not only that, but she's named her price. She says she wants ten million dollars from the family for her shares or she's selling to an outsider."

"She's only doing this for attention," Jack announced gruffly, lowering himself into his car.

"It doesn't matter why she's doing it," I insisted through the open window. "She's doing it."

Jack Cavanaugh didn't bother to respond. His face was set like stone as he drove away.

WHEN I GOT BACK to the office I found a copy of a letter from Philip Cavanaugh on my desk. It was from his new attorneys and it had arrived by messenger while I was at the funeral. It said that unless Lydia resigned from the board of directors of Superior Plating and Specialty Chemicals and signed the original buyback agreement within seven days, Philip was going to put his shares of the company's stock up for sale. No doubt the original of the letter was waiting on Jack Cavanaugh's desk at his office. Suddenly Philip's bout with the flu made perfect sense. If I'd sent that letter to Jack Cavanaugh, I'd be at home hiding in bed, too.

I waited for the rest of the morning for an angry phone call from Jack and was surprised when none came. By lunchtime I wondered whether he had still not returned to his office, or perhaps it was just that his powers of denial were so strong that he was treating Philip's threat with the same lack of seriousness as he had Lydia's.

I was busy deciding if I should do anything about it when Cheryl came in to say that Elliott Abelman was in reception asking whether I had the time to see him. Grateful for an excuse to put off a call to Jack, I told her to bring him back to my office.

Elliott slouched in wearing a nondescript navy-blue parka, a pair of jeans, and sneakers. Against the backdrop of Callahan Ross, he looked like a kid, a partner's son home from college for the weekend. He didn't sit down, choosing instead to lounge in my doorway.

"I was just on my way to pay a call on Leon Walczak."

"Who's that?"

"Peaches's not-so-secret admirer. It turns out he works about a block from here washing dishes at a coffee shop on Quincy. I figured you might want to have a look at him."

I took a look at my watch. "What the hell," I said, getting up to grab my coat.

LEON WALCZAK WORKED IN the filthy kitchen of the coffee shop in the Liberty Building. It was still the tail end of the lunch hour, so Elliott was careful to slip twenty dollars to the Greek behind the cash register who owned the place. He accepted the bill with a cynical shrug and pointed the way to the back of the restaurant.

We found Walczak hunched over a basin of dishwater, dipping greasy plates into the suds and then loading them into a plastic rack. He was a big man turned to fat, with greasy hair escaping from under a paper cap, a pasty face splattered with acne, and a grimy T-shirt showing beneath his dingy apron. His jaw was slack as he worked, his small eyes squinting through the steam. I felt sorry for Peaches. Walczak was a low-life creep. I couldn't imagine anything worse than being the focus of his obsession.

When Elliott introduced himself Leon's face was so flooded with fear that for a moment I half expected him to bolt and run. But Elliott, speaking firmly, managed to steer him out the back door into the alley behind the restaurant. Even so, it took several minutes for Leon to calm down. The police, it seems, had come to see him earlier in the day and his panic at all the sudden interest in him was palpable.

Still, he was eager to convince us of his innocence, at least of trying to harm Peaches.

"I would never hurt my Peaches! Never!" he insisted in a juvenile whine. "She's my wife, you know. A man never does nothin' to hurt his wife!"

"She's not married to you, Leon," Elliott said in the tone of someone breaking bad news. "She's married to some guy named Jack Cavanaugh who owns a big factory in Bridgeport."

"She just says that on account of the aliens," Leon explained. "They're trying to confuse her, sending those beams through the TV. They're tricking her into thinking she's married to somebody else." He moved a step closer. "She doesn't really love him," he confided. "Her heart belongs to me. To me. She told me that at our wedding. She was a beautiful, beautiful bride."

"I heard the cops caught you hanging around her house a couple weeks back," Elliott scolded him. "I thought the judge told you what would happen if he caught you near her again. You don't want to go back to jail, do you, Leon?"

"She never came to see me in jail," Leon whined. "Not once. Other guys, their wives came. Wrote letters. Not Peaches. I used to be able to see her at least, see her on the news. But now that man made her stop. He made her quit to keep her from me. He's very jealous. I know that about him."

"What were you doing near her house, Leon?" Elliott demanded.

"I didn't do nothin'," Leon protested sullenly.

"The police think that someone might have sent her poison in the mail, someone who might want to hurt her."

"I'd never hurt her! Never!" Leon shrieked.

"What were you doing at her house, Leon? You know what the police think? They think it was you!"

"No, no, no!" Leon shrieked, clamping his hands over his ears as if to blot out the horror of Elliott's words. "I would never hurt her. I was just watching. Just w-w-w-watching over her."

I BOUGHT ELLIOTT A cappuccino at the Starbucks on the corner of Monroe and LaSalle. We sat side by side on a low brick wall surrounding a tiny patch of public grass at the foot of the El station.

"So what do you think of Leon?" he asked, carefully prying the white plastic lid from his cup.

"Nothing in my background has given me any insights into evaluating psychopaths," I confessed, taking a sip of coffee. "But I'll say one thing, aside from being seriously nuts, he doesn't strike me as being particularly bright."

"Joe went back to the files and pulled the original arrest jacket and let me read the psychiatric evaluation last night. According to the shrink who wrote the report on him, Leon is a paranoid schizophrenic suffering from delusional psychosis in the form of the belief that Peaches Parkenhurst is his wife and that space aliens are interfering with her memory. According to Leon, he and Peaches are pawns in a secret war being waged between the aliens and NASA."

"He mustn't be as dumb as he looks. That sounds like a pretty sophisticated delusion."

"Don't be impressed. It's actually the plot of an old episode of the *Twilight Zone*."

"He seemed very upset that we'd think he would hurt her."

"Who knows what someone with bat shit for brains thinks? Maybe he thinks that if he kills her, he'll be saving her from the aliens. Maybe he got jealous and decided the only way he could keep her from Jack would be to kill her. You never know. Joe pulled copies of the phone records for all of the Cavanaughs. There's no denying that Leon started calling her the day he got out of prison. Maybe he turned violent in jail. It's been known to happen."

"Again, I'm no expert, but I could see Leon breaking into her house and killing her in a jealous rage, even lying in wait for her. But putting together something as sophisticated as mixing cyanide with Fluorad? And what about the package? How would he have gotten his hands on the business cards? All those things would be hard for him to get. Even if he could have thought of it—and how the hell would he know about the Fluorad and what it can do?—I can't imagine that he'd be able to think clearly enough to pull it off. The space aliens would always be getting in the way."

"Joe showed his picture around the Superior Plating plant this morning."

"And?"

"Nobody's seen him."

"So where does that leave us?"

Elliott stared thoughtfully into his coffee. "It leaves us exactly nowhere," he said.

BACK AT THE OFFICE there were still no messages from Jack Cavanaugh. Just to be on the safe side, I had Cheryl call his office to make sure that he had indeed received Philip's letter. Loretta, his secretary, assured her that he had, but when Cheryl asked if he was available to speak to me, his secretary said that he wasn't taking calls.

Fine, I thought to myself, when Cheryl came in to tell me about it. Be that way.

"Did you still need to see Madeline?" asked my ever-efficient secretary as she turned to go back to her desk.

"Is she in today? I'd have thought she'd at least take the afternoon off after the funeral."

"No. She's here. I just bumped into her in the ladies' room, that's what made me think of it. I'll ring her extension and see if she's free. And while I'm thinking about it, don't forget you're going to dinner at Hard Rock at five-thirty."

I DUG THROUGH THE papers on my desk for the things I'd set aside to ask Daniel's secretary about.

"I see you've put that picture of Dagny out," Madeline observed. "It was a favorite of Mr. Babbage's, too. I guess he must have been right about the two of you hitting it off. He was a good judge of people, you know. That's one of the things that made him so good at what he did."

I reflected that in the short time I'd had the Superior Plating file, I'd managed to piss off practically every member of the Cavanaugh family. And with Jack Cavanaugh I'd done such a good job that he wasn't even taking my calls. But I didn't say anything about it to Madeline.

"Here's what I'm looking for," I announced, finally pulling the documents out from underneath the Frostman Refrigeration file and passing them to her. "There were just a couple of things with no explanation. I didn't want to bother Jack Cavanaugh unnecessarily, so I thought I'd check with you to see if you knew what they were about."

She took a quick look at the bank statements and handed them back to me.

"This one's easy. It's a retirement fund that Mr. Cavanaugh asked Mr. Babbage to set up when their old housekeeper retired. Her name's Henrietta Roosevelt, but they always called her Nursey. I'm not exactly sure how it's set up, but I think the money came from Superior Plating. Dagny transferred it into an account with a bank in Chicago every quarter and they paid it out to her bank in Georgia."

I wrote a note to Cheryl and clipped it to the statements. She would need to figure out the mechanics of the transfer. I didn't want old retired Nursey to miss out on one of her checks.

"What about this?" I asked, handing her the yellowing trust agreement pertaining to Zebediah Hooker. "It looks like some sort of trust was set up and I was curious what it was all about."

"I couldn't tell you anything about that," Madeline said tersely. I could tell immediately that she knew more than she was willing to tell.

"I just thought you might remember something about it," I said, flipping to the last page where the originator of the document and typist's initials were noted. "See, Daniel dictated this and you typed it."

"I typed a lot of things for Mr. Babbage. I never remembered from one day to the next what they were about," she snapped defensively.

"It doesn't matter." I tried to sound casual. "I'll just ask Jack Cavanaugh next time I see him." I looked at Madeline sitting rigidly in my visitor's chair. She looked miserable. "That's all I wanted to talk to you about," I continued, obviously dismissing her. Still she made no move to go.

"I think it's something that Jack Cavanaugh doesn't want to talk about," she said finally, every word like pulling teeth.

"If you'll tell me what it's about I promise, I won't mention it," I coaxed. Still it took her a moment to make up her mind to speak.

"Mr. Babbage never told me the details. I don't think he ever told anybody. But I know it had something to do with his son. The money in the trust was to compensate someone who'd been hurt because of his son."

"Which son?" I asked.

"Jimmy. The one who died."

30

I finally heard from Jack Cavanaugh just as I was leaving to meet Claire and Nora Masterson, the attorney from trusts and estates, for dinner.

"I've decided to take matters into my own hands," he bellowed over the phone. I wondered what that meant. "Without Daniel, I've let myself be talked into all sorts of pussyfooting nonsense. By God, I didn't get where I am today by listening to a bunch of lawyers—and I didn't get here by asking nicely or asking for favors from my own goddamn children!"

"So what have you decided to do?" I inquired, bracing myself for the answer.

"I put them on the plane down to Tall Pines, that's what. Just the three of them; no wives, no husbands, no outside influences. They're all staying in my house—in the same rooms they had when they were kids. I've had Tom change the locks on their houses. I don't want them hiding from each other."

"Do you really think that locking them out of their own houses is a good idea?" I ventured.

"They're my goddamn houses!" roared Jack. I wondered how many bourbons he'd put away before coming up with this hare-brained idea. "I own the land, I own the buildings, and every stick of furniture was bought and paid for by my money. It's all my money, and from now on it's all my way. What's more, they're not leaving until they've figured out a way to get along together. Period."

"Jack, they're adults," I reasoned. "I don't know whether treating them like little children is going to help."

"If they act like little children, then that's how they're going to be treated. They *are* children, *my* children. And you're my lawyer, so from now on stick to writing letters and checking contracts and leave my children to me!"

I HAD ONLY BEEN to the Hard Rock once before and I hated it. Stephen and I had taken a group of Japanese lipid chemists there when it first opened. All I remembered was loud music, indifferent service, and mediocre food. The appeal of a restaurant with a thirty-foot neon sign in the shape of an electric guitar out front, rock memorabilia hanging from the ceiling, and a souvenir stand by the front door eluded me completely.

But one look at Claire's face as she and Nora bent over their menus and I knew that they'd hit it off. By the time I sat down, they were already tasting each other's milkshakes and had agreed to share an order of onion rings.

Claire was looking better. The color had come back to her face, and when she spoke some of her usual animation had returned. I couldn't help but admire her resilience.

"How are things at your aunt and uncle's house?" I asked. "Are you settling in?"

"I guess. It's hard being so close to my old house. I try not to look at it, but it's sort of impossible since it's on the same street and all. Still, it helps that I can be with Mary Beth all the time and I like having all the little kids around. It's hard to be depressed with so much going on. All the church stuff takes some getting used to, though. Did you know that Aunt Vy and Uncle Eugene kneel down and say the entire rosary every night before they go to bed?"

"I heard your uncle Eugene's down in Georgia," I said.

"That's right. Aunt Vy says that Grandpa's laid down some sort of ultimatum. The whole thing's made Vy really unhappy and I'm not sure it's such a good idea either. Uncle Eugene's been so strange since Mom died—angry and withdrawn. You heard that he sort of went crazy when my uncle Jimmy died. I think Vy's worried having him down in Georgia. She doesn't come out and say so, but I think she's afraid he'll crack up without her."

"I'm afraid they'll all crack up," I said, with more honesty than tact.

"No they won't, they'll just tear each other's hair out! You should have heard the fight they had the night of Mom's party. Mary Beth and I were over at Peter's house watching a movie and the yelling was so loud we couldn't hear the TV."

"What were they fighting about?" Nora inquired.

"According to what Mom told me afterward, it all started over a piece of jewelry that used to belong to my grandma. I guess Grandpa gave it to Peaches as a present and Aunt Lydia was really mad about it."

"That's not that unusual," Nora counseled. "Families fight all the time about who gets what. The thing to remember is that the jewelry, or the house, or whatever it is they're arguing over, is not what the fight's really about. Those arguments are always really about love and different people's place in the family."

"Well, by the time they got back to Peter's house, they were fighting about a lot more than that," continued Claire. "I never realized how much Aunt Lydia hates Grandpa—I mean *really* hates him. She was screaming that he didn't really love any of them, that he just wanted to control them—stuff like that. Lydia just went on and on, with Uncle Philip trying to calm her down. In a way it was neat to listen to, because Aunt Lydia dragged out all the dirty laundry and the three of us heard about a bunch of stuff the grown-ups never told us about—like that Grandma's sisters wanted to take Philip and Mom and the rest of Grandpa's kids away from him after Grandma died and all the stuff about how Uncle Jimmy really died."

"What about your uncle Jimmy?" I asked, thinking about the old documents that Madeline had unearthed from Daniel's personal files.

"I don't know. By that time they'd stopped shouting and it got kind of hard to hear, but it sounded like Lydia was accusing Philip of knowing something that he wouldn't tell—you know, some big secret that he was keeping for Grandpa."

BACK AT THE OFFICE I pulled out the copy of the trust agreement that had been among the documents that Daniel had kept about the Cavanaughs. I read it through carefully. It was a straightforward document that set up a trust to pay for the care and maintenance of one Zebediah Hooker until the time of his death. Nowhere was there any mention of who Mr. Hooker might be, what he was being paid for, or where he might be found. From the notary's seal I learned that it had been signed and witnessed in Thomas County, Georgia—a fact I didn't find particularly enlightening.

I still had it in my hand when Elliott Abelman appeared in my doorway. "I brought you a present," he said. He set a small box wrapped in gold paper on the desk in front of me. "Pretty flowers," he said, bending to smell the roses on my desk. "I guess they're from him."

I didn't say anything. Instead I went to work unwrapping the box. Inside, I found a small bottle of perfume in a red velvet box lined with white satin like a small coffin. The stopper of the bottle was made of frosted glass and shaped like a perfect rosebud. The name of the perfume was Forever.

"Can I smell it," I asked Elliott, "or will it kill me?"

"There's no poison in this one."

"But am I correct in assuming that this was the kind?" I asked, pulling the stopper from the bottle and giving it a sniff. Normally, I think it must have been a heavenly perfume, but for me there were too many associations. I remembered the scent distinctly and for me it would forever be linked with death.

"This is the one."

Self-consciously I put my finger over the top of the bottle and turned it over to get some on my finger. I dabbed some quickly behind my ears—the same innocent gesture that had killed Cecilia Dobson and Dagny Cavanaugh.

"What's the occasion?" I asked lightly. "You've never come bearing gifts before."

"Jack Cavanaugh just called me up and fired me," Elliott replied, stretching his legs out in front of him. "Under the circumstances, I thought I should do something to mark the occasion."

31

"You're kidding!" I exclaimed. "Why on earth would Jack Cavanaugh fire you?"

"He told me the police were about to make an arrest and my services were no longer needed."

"Are they? The cops, I mean."

"I talked to Joe this afternoon. He didn't mention any big breakthrough."

"So what's Jack Cavanaugh talking about?"

"I think he assumes that because Joe has his boys following up the Leon Walczak thing pretty hard that Leon's the bad guy. But let's get serious. You've seen the guy. Do you honestly think he could walk up to the perfume counter at Neiman Marcus or Saks—and believe me this junk's only sold at the most expensive stores—plunk down two hundred plus dollars for a bottle of perfume, and not have anyone remember him?"

"Maybe Joe's right. It could have come from anywhere. The duty-free shop at some airport."

"And what would Leon Walczak be doing in the duty-free shop?"

"Maybe he stole the stuff."

"Not the perfume. They keep testers on the counter for the cologne, but the perfume is kept under lock and key. I won't bore you with all the fascinating information I've managed to absorb recently on the subject of perfume, but believe me, they guard the expensive stuff like it was diamonds. Come to think of it, they have a hell of a lot tighter security at the perfume counter than they do for the cyanide at Superior Plating."

"So if you came up empty on the perfume, what makes Cavanaugh think that the police are about to make an arrest?"

"I wouldn't say we came up empty. Joe and I went through the interview sheets together on the perfume and we came up with a few things."

"For example?"

"Well, for one thing, this particular brand of perfume is brand-new. They just started selling it—*launched,* I believe, is the correct cosmetics terminology. It was launched on February first of this year, which means they didn't sell it in stores before that date. They also sell a ton of the cologne and the toilet water and all the inexpensive parts of the line, but they barely move any of the perfume. This particular brand is only sold in Chicago at Saks Fifth Avenue, Neiman Marcus, and a store called Barneys that I didn't even know existed until I went there yesterday. Joe got them to open up their books, which is not that big a deal now that they all have computerized inventory systems. It turns out that among the three of them they only sold twenty-six bottles of the perfume between February first and fourteenth—which is the date the box it was mailed in was postmarked. In addition, more than half of those bottles were sold to people who put their purchases on their store charge account. I've got somebody checking them out, but so far they're all well-dressed women who drive Mercedes. I've also been able to check on the people who paid with other kinds of plastic—a lot of them are from out of town, so again we haven't turned up anybody likely. Not that I'd expect the killer to have actually gone to the store and charged it, but you never know, dumber things have been done in the name of crime."

"How many bottles were sold for cash?" I demanded, agreeing with Elliott that this would have been by far the likeliest method of payment.

"Six. Three at Neiman Marcus, two at Saks, and one at Barneys."

"Anybody who sticks in memory?"

"It's harder than you'd think. For one thing, it's not that unusual for a guy to come in and drop a chunk of cash on an expensive gift— lots of times guys buy stuff for their girlfriends and they don't want their wives stumbling over the receipts."

"I hadn't thought of that."

"That's because you're not a P.I. Lawyers usually deal with cheating on a bigger scale. P.I.'s get stuck with the petty stuff."

"So nobody remembers anyone buying the perfume—or at least nobody who would help us."

"Well, there was one salesclerk we interviewed who was pretty sharp. She didn't actually make the sale, but she remembers a man who came in asking questions about perfume. He was looking for a gift for a woman who had every kind. He wanted to surprise her with something new. He smelled them all and thanked her for her time but left without making a purchase."

"So he did his research in one store and did his buying in another. Clever. I assume you showed her Leon's picture?"

"We showed her everybody's picture. The only one who she thought it might be was Jack Cavanaugh, but she was a long way from sure."

"Jack Cavanaugh!"

"Don't get so excited. We showed Jack's picture at the other stores and nobody remembered having seen him."

"Do you think maybe that's why he fired you? He found out that you were showing his picture around and he decided that wasn't what he wanted to be paying you for?"

"Maybe. Or maybe he's got something to hide and all of a sudden he feels like I'm getting too close."

"You can't think it was Jack. He had no reason I can think of to have wanted to kill his own daughter. He's been just crushed by her death—just crushed. Your scenario would fly a little better if the perfume really had gone to Peaches, but it was Jack who turned around and gave it to Dagny. The more I think about it, that's where the killer's whole plan went wrong—if we assume that Peaches was the intended victim. He or she had no way of predicting that Jack wouldn't take it home and give it to her."

"That's what makes me think that the perfume was meant for Peaches. Nobody raised a whimper after Cecilia died. I don't think the killer realized she'd been poisoned; he was too busy waiting for Peaches to drop dead."

"Nobody realized she was poisoned." Neither of us said anything for a minute. I sat at my desk, thinking. Suddenly the picture of Dagny and the invitation to the party for Jack and Peaches caught my eye.

"What day did the saleswoman who remembers talking to the man about the perfume say he came in to the store? Does she remember?"

"She only works on the weekends. She said she wasn't sure, but she thinks it was a Sunday."

In an instant, I was shifting files on the crowded surface of my desk, clearing things off to find my calendar that was buried in the rubble. As soon as I found it, I began frantically turning back the pages to the second week in February.

"Shit, will you look at this!" I exclaimed. "There was only one Sunday in February that it could possibly have been. You said yourself that they didn't sell the stuff before February first. Well, there's only one Sunday between the first and the day the package was mailed to Jack's office—Sunday the eleventh."

"Why didn't I think of that?" Elliott demanded, starting to flip through his notes. "If that's the case, then he had to buy the stuff either on that Sunday or on the Monday it was sent. Let me see what happened at the other stores. There was only one bottle sold on the eleventh—at Saks Fifth Avenue—for cash."

"That's pinning an awful lot on that one clerk's story," I cautioned, frightened by my own enthusiasm. "What if it wasn't him? What if it was just some guy from Dubuque who was shopping for a birthday present for his wife and decided that the perfume was too much money?"

"You're right. I don't want to jump to conclusions."

"And still, the dates—the dates can't be a coincidence."

"What do you mean?"

"Everything keeps on coming back to that party for Jack and Peaches that Dagny threw."

"I don't get it. What's so special about the party?"

"Everything. For one thing, the board met that afternoon—it was the meeting where Philip did his little show-and-tell about the properties of Fluorad. I remember Dagny telling me they'd had to reschedule the meeting at the last minute. She was furious. Lydia was down in Georgia grilling her old nanny about her past and didn't get back until the morning of the party. It infuriated Dagny because the party was at her house and she needed to be there while they set up, but because of Lydia they had to have the board meeting that afternoon. And after all of that, Lydia didn't even pay attention; she sat there and wrote out the checks for her bills. But that wasn't the only time that day that one of the Cavanaughs lost their temper. That night at the party Lydia caused a huge scene because Jack had given

Peaches a necklace that had belonged to her mother. Daniel told me that he'd never seen anything like it—that by the time her brothers managed to hustle her out of there, she was literally foaming at the mouth. And after that, when they took her back to her house, she got into another fight—this time with her brothers."

"About what?"

"Claire—that's Dagny's daughter—was listening with her cousins from upstairs, so I only know what she overheard, but she said that Lydia and Philip were going back and forth about Philip covering something up for their father—something that happened around the time their oldest brother died."

"What brother is that?"

"His name was Jimmy. He drowned more than thirty years ago trying to rescue a girl who was trying to kill herself. The whole thing happened down in Georgia, where the Cavanaughs have a place. I don't think it's got anything to do with this; Lydia was just dragging out everything she could think of. But don't you see? From the very beginning, these murders haven't made any sense because nobody seems to have gained anything from them. We've always been thinking that because it was poison, it was a rational act, a planned crime, not a crime of passion. But think about it—the day of the party emotions in the Cavanaugh family went off the Richter scale. Dagny was furious at Lydia for forcing her to postpone the board meeting until she came back from Georgia and then didn't even bother to pay attention to what was going on. Lydia was rabid about the necklace, and Peaches, no doubt, was horrified by the scene her stepdaughter had caused at what should have been a lovely party. Lydia then turned around and savagely attacked her brother. The whole day was filled with nothing but hatred. It can't be coincidence that the very next day someone bought a bottle of expensive perfume, laced it with poison, and sent it off to Peaches. It just can't be!"

"But what about the poison?"

"They all had access. They were all there when Philip showed them what the Fluorad could do. Really the only one who would have had even the smallest problem would have been Lydia, who didn't as a rule come into the plant. But she could have stopped by and asked to borrow someone's keys—she could have come up with some kind of excuse—and no one would have given it a second thought."

"But what was her motive?"

"Malice. Hatred. According to Dagny's daughter, Claire, Lydia went on and on that night about how much she hated her father. She'd just come back from Georgia, where she'd been trying to unearth evidence that she'd been assaulted as a child. Who knows? Maybe she had been. It would explain her desire to strike back at her father. Maybe she just decided that the best way to hurt him would be to kill Peaches—take away his last happiness as an old man. She also went through a real sick period right after Jack and Peaches were married; they caught her making nuisance calls to her father's house in the middle of the night. Also she changed her appearance to look like Peaches. Maybe this is all part of the same thing?"

"And you said Lydia had just come back from Georgia?"

"Yes. The day of the party."

"May I use your phone?"

"Sure. Why?"

"Your mentioning Georgia just made me think of something."

"What?"

"You know that Joe got the phone records for the Cavanaughs for the three months before the murders. He pulled records on all five houses on Astor—Jack's and all four of his kids."

"And?"

"And the night of the party there was a fifty-two-minute call from Lydia's house to a rural exchange in Thomas County, Georgia."

CHAPTER

32

Driving like a maniac, I managed to get Elliott to the airport just in time to catch the last plane to Tallahassee. He would rent a car at the airport and drive to Bainbridge first thing in the morning. That was the name of the little town where the woman the Cavanaughs called Nursey lived.

I was certain that whatever happened the day of Dagny's party for her father and Peaches was central to understanding why and by whose hand two women lost their lives. No one calls an old woman who lives in the country at nearly midnight to chat, and yet the phone records showed that Lydia had placed a call that lasted close to an hour to Nursey's number on the night of the party. Elliott had sternly warned me not to get my hopes up, but I was convinced that Nursey held the key.

Pulling up to the curb in front of the Delta terminal, I handed Elliott copies of the bank records for the annuity that Jack Cavanaugh still paid to his old housekeeper. I figured that questions about the account would be enough to get him through the door. From there he'd have to improvise. I thought it shouldn't be too hard to get a lonely old woman to talk about the people she'd worked for all those years.

As an afterthought, I dug into my briefcase for a copy of the Zebediah Hooker trust. I figured it might be worth looking into as long as Elliott was poking around Thomas County—especially since it was me and not Jack Cavanaugh who was paying for the trip. As I handed him the document Elliott surprised me by leaning over toward me in the front seat as I said good-bye. I thought he meant to kiss me and I drew back in confusion. But he stopped just short and gently smelled the perfume on my neck.

"Very nice," he said quietly. Before I could reply he was gone.

I WENT HOME TO an empty apartment. I was too nervous to sleep and too anxious to settle down to work. My mind kept on straying to Elliott Abelman and what it was that he might find in Georgia. Finally, I forced myself to go to bed and spent the night restlessly sorting and resorting the little I knew about the circumstances leading up to the deaths of Cecilia Dobson and Dagny Cavanaugh. At some point I must have fallen asleep, because I woke up at half past nine, numb and exhausted. Feeling horrible, I dragged myself into the office.

It wasn't until I arrived at Callahan that I realized that it was Friday—the day Stephen would be returning from Geneva and expecting an answer about the apartment. Cursing myself for cowardice—I had neither the stomach for hurting him by saying no nor the conviction to say yes—I took refuge in petty anger at him for having put me in the position of having to make any decision at all.

Arriving at my desk, I peevishly picked up the vase of roses that Stephen had sent me, marched them down the hall, and gave them to Madeline to brighten up her day. What depths I've sunk to, I remembered thinking to myself, that I was feeling pressured by a bouquet of flowers.

This exorcism complete, I was able to turn my attention to the last few odds and ends on the Frostman Refrigeration file. I also had several long conversations with the investment bankers at Goodman Peabody about the correct depreciation of Superior Plating's equipment as it related to the valuation of the company. When Cheryl buzzed to say that Philip Cavanaugh was on the phone, I was surprised. He was the last person I expected to hear from.

"I thought you were at Tall Pines," I said, picking up the phone.

"We are," he replied. "Dad sent us down here the same way he used to send us to our rooms."

"So what can I do for you?" I asked, worried that Nursey had called Philip to complain about the private detective snooping around her.

"The company plane is fueled up and waiting for you at Meig's Field. I want you to fly down."

"Why?"

"We need a lawyer."

DARLENE MET ME AT the door of Jack Cavanaugh's house at Tall Pines in a ruffled apron, a wooden spoon in one hand. She looked disgusted.

"They're waiting for you in there," she said. I didn't need to ask where. I just followed the sound of angry voices into the living room.

It was obvious that Philip, Eugene, and Lydia had been arguing for hours. From their rumpled clothes and red-rimmed eyes, I wouldn't have been surprised if they'd been at it all night. They were surly and sick of each other, clearly having reached the point in their debate where the sight of a new face, even mine, was a relief.

"Oh look, if it isn't the fucking cavalry," announced Lydia.

She was still dressed in her arty, person-in-black wardrobe, which looked even more incongruous in Georgia than my plane-rumpled navy suit.

"So what's going on?" I asked, sitting down on the couch and laying my briefcase on the coffee table in front of me in the manner of lawyers the world over. "Have you reached some kind of agreement?"

"We have," Eugene announced.

"We may have," hedged Philip.

"You know what your problem is, Eugene?" Lydia demanded, as if addressing a child. "You think everything in the world is black and white. This is a very complicated financial transaction we're talking about. I don't expect you to understand it completely, but I do think you have to accept that there are subtleties to be considered." There was no mistaking the put-down in her voice. I couldn't help thinking that whoever killed Dagny Cavanaugh had murdered the wrong sister.

"What financial transaction are we talking about?" I prompted.

"We've agreed—" Philip began, but Lydia immediately cut him off.

"In theory!" she snapped. "We've agreed in theory. I don't know about you, but I'm still a long way from signing anything."

"Well, surprise, surprise. You're always willing to be flexible and accommodating just as long as it doesn't mean anything. As soon as it comes time to put it down on paper, you come up with a million objections. You forget we've seen you pull this shit before."

"Oh, have you?" his sister inquired sarcastically.

"Stop it!" I half shouted. "I've just flown two thousand miles. Was there something you wanted me for or did you just need an audience?"

"We've agreed that there is no way that we can continue to work together in the family business," said Eugene. His face had the same bulldog set to it as his father's.

"Our goals for personal self-fulfillment are just too different," Lydia piped in a "shrinky" voice.

"Would you just let me finish?" Eugene snapped. "We all agree that we have no choice but to sell our shares. The question is, are we bound to give Dad first crack at buying them?"

"Arthur says that we are under absolutely no obligation to Daddy," Lydia declared.

"The next time I need brokerage advice, I'll call Arthur," Philip announced pompously. "In the meantime I'll just consult the company's attorney on the legal issues. That is, if you have no objections."

"In the absence of a signed buyback agreement, no one is under any legal obligation to offer the shares to your father before putting them on the market. But as your attorney, I'll tell you right now, it's probably in your best interest to at least try to structure a deal with your father."

"We'd never have gotten into this predicament if you'd just signed the goddamned buyback in the first place," Philip accused his sister.

I couldn't believe it. Two thousand miles away from my next change of clothes and they were starting in again on the damned buyback agreement. The Cavanaughs, as a family, seemed to have a tremendous amount of trouble moving on from old issues. I was about to tell them so when Darlene came to tell me that I had a phone call.

I went into the kitchen and picked up the phone expecting to hear Cheryl's voice, but was surprised instead to discover that it was Elliott on the line.

"Your secretary told me where to find you," he said by way of greeting. From his voice I could tell he was excited. "You'll never guess where I am."

"Where?"

"The Laurel Acres Convalescent Home."

"Is that where Nursey lives? I thought she had her own house."

"She does. I'm heading there now. I couldn't see her this morning because she had to go into Lawson for her clinic appointments."

"So who are you visiting at Laurel Acres?" I demanded. The Cavanaugh children's contentiousness must have been contagious. I was in a terrible mood.

"I've been to see Zebediah Hooker."

"So who is he?"

"He's the redneck drunk who Eugene Cavanaugh beat to within an inch of his life when they were both sixteen years old."

"Whatever made him do that?"

"Eugene caught him in a bar one night telling anyone who would listen that Jimmy Cavanaugh killed Grace Swinton because she was carrying his child."

IN THE END, I left the three remaining Cavanaugh children to duke it out while I went with Elliott to visit Nursey. In light of what he'd found out by visiting Zebediah Hooker, I figured it was going to be much more enlightening than listening to Philip, Lydia, and Eugene cover the same ground over and over again. As we drove Elliott told me how he'd found him.

"I just went to the feed store and asked. The feed store's the center of the universe in a place like this. All I had to do was mention the name and three guys in John Deere caps were falling all over each other to tell me the story. In a small town like this, you can't go to the bathroom without people knowing what color it is. And Eugene Cavanaugh savagely beating a good old boy like Zebediah certainly caught everyone's attention. I didn't even really need to go out to Laurel Acres, but it was close and I had time to kill."

"So what did he have to say to you?"

"Who? Zebediah? Not only did Eugene break just about every bone in Zebediah's body, but he cracked his skull in so many places that he left him a vegetable. Zebediah doesn't say anything. He hasn't said anything since the night he shot his mouth off in front of Eugene in that bar."

NURSEY WAS A SHRIVELED-UP crone with a tight perm of snow-white hair that stood out in stark contrast to the wrinkled ebony of her skin. She must have already been an old lady the day she came to Chicago to work for the Cavanaughs. Under a crisply ironed red dress, she was all skin and bones, but aside from being a little deaf, she seemed both intelligent and alert.

Her sister, who looked every bit as old and frail as Nursey, served us sweet iced tea with lemon in plastic tumblers and then left us on the porch to chat. By city standards, the home of the two elderly sisters was little more than a shack with a bare wood floor and a tar-paper roof. But from what I could glimpse of it through the dark screen of the door, it seemed tidy and comfortably furnished.

"Don't know what's wrong with Lydia," Nursey said sadly, after she'd finished telling Elliott about the nice banker who handled her monthly check from Mr. Cavanaugh and what the doctor had to say about the trouble she'd been having with her back. "Lydia's always been a mean-spirited child, always wantin' to believe that life's done her wrong. Never could understand it. I know it's hard losin' your mama when you's a baby. But you'd think from talkin' to her that he's the only person in the whole wide world has ever lost their mama, if you get what I'm sayin'. I told Mr. Cavanaugh, I told him time and time again he should have let me take the hairbrush to her. I'd have smacked the wickedness right out of her, but he would never hear of it. She looked too much like his dead wife, she did. Every time he looked at her, he saw his Eleanor lookin' back at him. That's why he never could raise a hand to her. He spoiled her something rotten."

"I understand she came down to see you in February," I said.

"Dagny told me that her sister came down to talk to you about some things that happened to her when she was little—"

"Phantasms!" Nursey exclaimed, with a disgusted wave of her hand. "Phantasms and made-up stories. One of those crazy psychiatrists got her believing that her father'd molested her. Now, I won't say to you that kind of wickedness don't happen, but I can tell you just like I told Lydia; nothin' like that happened in that house, not while I was there. I watched those children like a hawk. I'd have know if there was anything like that going on."

"She called you, though, the day she got back to Chicago," said Elliott. "She called you late at night and talked for almost an hour. Would you mind telling us what you two talked about?"

"Oh honey, it wasn't Lydia that called me at eleven o'clock and woke me up out of a sound sleep. Scared me half to death. I thought it was one of my grandbabies who lives in Atlanta killed in a car accident, I swear to God. No, no. It wasn't Lydia that called me. It was Eugene. All in a lather about Lydia telling him the truth about what happened to poor Grace Swinton."

CHAPTER

33

Philip, Lydia, and Eugene sat miserably on their father's couch all in a row. They reminded me of the three little monkeys in that old proverb—see no evil, hear no evil, and speak no evil. I wanted to strangle each of them. Elliott was standing by in the kitchen to be sure I didn't do just that.

"So which one of you is going to tell me the truth about Grace Swinton?" I demanded.

"It's none of your business," Philip protested, rising to his feet.

"Sit down," I commanded. The whole ride back to Tall Pines, I'd been so furious I was ranting. I was in absolutely no mood for games. As far as I was concerned, Dagny Cavanaugh and Cecilia Dobson were both victims of the Cavanaughs' inability to be straight with one another. From here on in, there was only one thing I wanted from them and that was the truth. "Philip, you were there, why don't you start the story?"

"She was a slut, a nothing, a piece of no-good white trash. I don't see why you want to drag it all back up."

"Tell me what happened," I growled, suddenly wishing I had a gun. I fervently hoped that Elliott did.

"From the sound of it, you know already," said Eugene.

"I want to hear it from you." There was no disguising the contempt in my voice.

"Goddammit!" Philip burst in. "She was already dead when we threw her in the water. There! Are you satisfied? She went to Doc Prisser to get rid of the baby and something went wrong. I don't know what. Things were different back then. By the time she got to the pond, she was just gushing blood. We didn't know what to do. We were just kids, for Christ sake. She died in Jimmy's arms."

"And so you filled her pockets with rocks and decided on the suicide story."

"We had to get rid of the body. We thought Dad would kill us. It was Jimmy's idea to take her out in the rowboat and dump her. He knew how screwed up she was. It was his idea to say she'd killed herself."

"So what went wrong?"

"It was the buttons on his shirt," Philip replied. He sounded eager to be done with it. "They must have gotten caught in her hair. That's how he got pulled under."

"Why wasn't there an investigation?"

"Dad took care of the police. That's when I found out that he'd known all along. He was the one who'd paid for Doc Prisser."

"And he made you promise not to tell."

"He made me swear it," Philip said miserably.

"It was just going to be your dirty little secret," hissed Lydia. "But it's hard to keep people from talking in a place like this. Daddy couldn't buy everyone. The police dropped it, but there was no way he could stop people from talking."

"So you knew, too," I said to Lydia.

"Not at first, not everything. But I always knew that there was something funny about it, something that people weren't telling. It wasn't until my therapist helped me understand the real impact these childhood tragedies had on my psyche that I was motivated to find out the truth about what happened."

"So you came down to Tall Pines in February to find out the whole story from Nursey."

"Do you know what the funny thing is?" Lydia asked. "Everyone down here knew it already. Our big hush-hush family secret was common knowledge in this little hick town. Everyone knew that Jimmy was sleeping with Grace. Everyone knew about the botched abortion. Everyone knew that Daddy'd paid for it. Everyone knew that Daddy'd paid to have it covered up. The only people he was keeping secrets from were his own family. Everyone else knew."

"But not Eugene," I said slowly, the anger rising up inside of me. "No one ever told Eugene. Your father and Philip were terrified of what it might do to him if he learned the whole story. So Eugene didn't know until the night of the party. I bet you just couldn't wait to tell him, could you?"

"I was still very angry about it," Lydia replied defensively. "When I'm angry I get emotional—it's just the way I am."

"So emotional that you never stopped to consider the impact it would have on Eugene. He's never been able to handle things, has he? The trauma of your mother's death left him unable to speak for nearly a year when he was a child. After Jimmy died, he got into all sorts of trouble—drinking and drugs. And then there was that unfortunate business about Zebediah Hooker. Poor man. A friend of mine paid a call on him today. What a sad story. All those years and he's still a vegetable." I turned to face Eugene. "I wonder how it made you feel when you realized that you'd done that to him just because he repeated what everyone else had been saying—when he repeated the truth about Grace Swinton. What I don't understand is why you didn't kill your father. Or Philip. Why didn't you kill them right then?"

"It wasn't like that!" Eugene protested in a voice that was close to a scream. "I put it in the Lord's hands. I prayed for guidance."

"And the Lord didn't tell you to forgive them?" I demanded.

"An eye for an eye," answered Eugene. "The Lord exacts a price. Jimmy was the most important person in the world to me. He told me to take Peaches from my father the way my father took Jimmy from me!"

"Oh God! Eugene!" Lydia gasped, horrified.

Eugene leaped to his feet. I braced myself for impact, but he rushed past me and ran from the room.

"Elliott!" I screamed, turning to race after him, but I wasn't fast enough. He made a mad dash for the bathroom and slammed the door in my face.

I heard the sound of running water.

"Eugene!" I shouted. "Come out of there now!" I beat my fists against the door as Elliott came running. We heard the sound of something heavy falling—the crash of bone against porcelain. Elliott pushed me out of the way and kicked down the door.

We found him on the floor. He was writhing in pain, his body rocked by a seizure, his head banging sickeningly against the base of the sink.

"Help me get him out of here!" commanded Elliott, bending to grip his shoulders.

I grabbed his legs and staggered backward under the impact of their disjointed kicking. Together we dragged him out into the hall. Lydia and Philip stood by like terrified children. Elliott ordered them to phone for an ambulance, but we both knew that it would never come in time. We had both seen the container of white powder on the sink in the bathroom—the odorless, tasteless powder that looked as harmless as laundry detergent.

I'm sure that Elliott had seen worse in Vietnam. He bent to the task without hesitation. Unflinching, he stuck his fingers down Eugene's throat to make him vomit. That done, he cleared his airway, stuck a washcloth in his mouth to keep him from biting through his own tongue while he seized. Together we tried to hold him down to keep him from hurting himself as he lay thrashing on the floor.

Philip came back to report that the ambulance was on its way from Bainbridge, nearly thirty miles away. From the other room we could hear the ragged sound of Lydia's hysterical sobbing.

It was all over in a few minutes.

Wordless, Elliott helped me to my feet. I don't remember what I felt; a lot of things I suppose: anger, pity, grief. . . . But mostly what I remember is the overpowering relief that the killing would be over.

WE STAYED ONLY LONG enough to make our statements to the police. I'd had a bellyful of the Cavanaughs. All I wanted was to get as far away from them as I could. I practically threw myself into Elliott's rental car, shivering despite the heat, desperate to get away.

We made the drive to Bainbridge in silence; neither of us felt much like talking. After all, what was there to say? Eugene had sent perfume laced with poison to his father's wife. He meant to wound him with her loss the way he'd been wounded by Jimmy's. An eye for an eye. I had no idea how he'd managed to live with himself once he realized he'd poisoned Dagny instead. Perhaps, seeing his father in his grief, he figured he'd come close enough. I really didn't care. I had no interest in analyzing the finer points of tragedy.

When we got back to Elliott's hotel we went back to his room so that he could call Joe Blades. I stood mutely by the door and listened as he explained what Eugene had done. That finished, he came to where I stood.

Without a word, he took me into his arms. I feared that I was lost. My own need completely overwhelmed me. In a world that had recently seemed so scrambled, tainted by tragedy and loss, Elliott's mouth, his strong hands against my skin, seemed to feed a deep and insistent hunger.

I forced myself to be free of him, to put my hand against his cheek and tell him I must go. In his embrace I knew I'd stepped up to a line that, once crossed, could only lead down a tangled path. Looking back, I realize that I ran from him the same way I'd wanted to run from the Cavanaughs.

From the pay phone in the lobby, I telephoned Stephen to tell him that I loved the apartment and couldn't wait to move in.

GINI HARTZMARK attended the law and business schools of the University of Chicago and was a business and economics writer for textbooks. She has written articles on a variety of topics for the *Chicago Sun-Times*, the *Chicago Tribune*, and a number of national magazines. She is the author of two other Kate Millholland novels: *Principal Defense* and *Final Option*.

Ms. Hartzmark and her husband live in Arizona with their three children.